Hazard at the 19th

April Hardy

T0349955

ACCENT

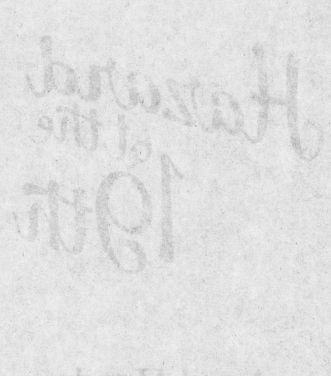

First published in Great Britain in 2017 by Accent Press

This paperback edition published in 2020 by Headline Accent
An imprint of HEADLINE PUBLISHING GROUP

1

Cataloguing in Publication Data is available from the British Library

ISBN 978 1 7861 5578 8

Printed and bound in Great Britain by Clays Ltd, Elcograf S.p.A.

Headline's policy is to use papers that are natural, renewable and recyclable
products and made from wood grown in well-managed forests and other
controlled sources. The logging and manufacturing processes are expected
to conform to the environmental regulations of the country of origin.

HEADLINE PUBLISHING GROUP
An Hachette UK Company
Carmelite House
50 Victoria Embankment
London EC4Y 0DZ

www.headline.co.uk
www.hachette.co.uk

About the Author

April Hardy grew up on the outskirts of the New Forest. After leaving drama school, her varied career has included touring pantomimes, children's theatre and a summer season in Llandudno as a Butlins red coat. All interspersed with much waitressing and working in hotel kitchens.

After moving to Greece, she spent many years as a dancer, then choreographer, and did a 7-month stint on a Greek cruise ship before working for a cake designer and training as a pastry chef in a Swiss hotel school in Athens. Whilst living there, she helped out at a local animal sanctuary.

Relocating to the UAE with her husband and their deaf, arthritic cat, she has lived in both Abu Dhabi and Dubai, where she is delighted to have found herself so unemployable that she's had plenty of time to devote to writing her romantic comedies!

At the 2014 Emirates Lit Fest she won the inaugural Literary Idol competition with the opening page of *Hazard at The Nineteenth*. Encouraged by this, she went on to finish writing the book.

In 2015, she signed a 3-book deal with Accent Press. *Sitting Pretty*, her début New Forest rom-com, was short-listed for the Joan Hessayon Award. *Kind Hearts & Coriander* was a runner up in the Exeter Novel Prize.

Other books by April Hardy:

Sitting Pretty
Kind Hearts and Corriander

Chapter One

Stella

I didn't realise just how much my future mother-in-law hated me until the day she tried to kill me. It was something of a shocker, I can tell you. Ma Hazard is the last person you would associate with criminal behaviour.

In her Pringle jumpers, pressed polo shirt collars framing their ladylike little V-necks, and those tartan, three quarter trousers that always make the song *Rupert, Rupert the Bear* pop into my head, she is the very picture of respectability. Add the jolly hockey sticks voice and you've got a sporty, sixty-something cross between Joyce Grenfell and Margaret Thatcher. No. She definitely does *not* look like a murderer.

Nobody else could see it. Jonathon, my fiancé, never believed me when I repeated any of the double-edged comments that she'd make to me when no one else was within earshot.

'You're imagining it, Stella,' he would say. 'You must have misheard her,' or, 'she must have been distracted or in a hurry and just picked up the wrong size,' when she bought me a pair of size twenty Spanx for my last birthday.

Well, I didn't imagine the look on her face when,

after the Sunday roast beef and Yorkshire pudding, she *accidentally* gave me a slice of the wrong homemade carrot cake – the one with the ground walnuts in it. I didn't imagine seeing her rummaging about in my handbag *looking for paracetamol*, just moments earlier, even though she has half a pharmacy in the cupboard over the microwave. And I certainly didn't imagine the untimely disappearance from the little zipped pocket of my handbag of my life-saving Epipen. If Jonathon hadn't sprinted to the car, grabbed the spare from the glove compartment and jabbed it into my thigh, I could have been having tea with St Peter right now. At least I hope that's the direction I would have taken.

I don't know what I ever did to make her dislike me so much – well, apart from not being Cordelia. The silken, honey-haired goddess that is Cordelia Page is the girl next door. A talented horsewoman, with her own stud and riding stables, she is slender and smart, can parallel park, and *always* says the right thing. I, on the other hand, am a mousey-haired, size-sixteen bookworm, who knocks things over, trips on the stairs (cleverly I can do it going both up or down), have scraped more cars than I care to remember, and always, *always* manage to say the wrong thing. Cordelia and Jonathon used to play in the sand pit together while they were growing up. She could, if she wanted to, eat nuts morning noon and night without her head swelling up and making her look like something out of a science fiction film. And she's the girl Jonathon's mother has always wanted him to marry.

Ma, or Joyce as I have to call her to her face, just can't, for the life of her, fathom why Jonathon picked me. And frankly, after each fresh glimpse of Cordelia's perfect little jodhpur-clad bottom, I can sort of see where she's coming from. And it's really annoying.

'Poor Mum, she'll be mortified,' Jonathon said, as he drove me home from the hospital. 'You know how careful she is around you, with anything with nuts in it.'

'Hm,' I mumbled, unable to hurt his feelings by saying what I really thought. What is it about fully grown men and their mothers?

There was a message on my answer phone from her when we got back to my place.

'Stella! It's Joyce here. I do hope you're alright, my dear. What a silly thing to have happened. I hope you're feeling better.' *Yeah, I'll bet you do.*

You'd think the fact that Jonathon and I are happy together would count for something, wouldn't you? Well, I would, but apparently I'd be wrong, if murder by anaphylactic shock seemed like a good idea to her. What would she try next? I certainly wouldn't be eating anything with mushrooms in it at her house, just in case she thought the old switcheroo trick with a toadstool might be worth a try.

Jonathon stayed the night, as he never liked to leave me

3

alone after an allergic episode. It was comforting having him there. It would have been more comforting if he was snuggling up to me, rather than snoring for England, but you can't have everything. I tossed and turned, wondering how I was so awful that Joyce would go to such lengths to get rid of me.

Sure, Cordelia is successful and ambitious. I'd be willing to bet she's quick and resourceful in an emergency. I can just imagine her, sliding her slender, capable arm up a distressed mummy horse's rear end and gently easing out a slippery foal, before dashing off for a quick shower, effortlessly zipping up a size eight party frock and wafting fragrantly to the local hunt ball.

But Jonathon and I share the same daft sense of humour, and we both care about the same things. That was how we met in the first place, doing a charity fun run, him looking all toned and trained in his running shorts and t shirt, and me, along with the other girls from the book shop I had been working in at the time, dressed up as a character from a children's story. In my case, *The Cat in the* stupid *Hat* – for my sins – which must have been big, if karma had anything to do with the discomfort of the straining – and in one embarrassing area, split – seams on the ridiculously mis-sized costume.

Being a village librarian might not be a high flying career – it won't be a career at all if the library closes, but Jonathon's the biggest supporter of my campaign against that happening. He even marched to the town hall with me and my army of ladies, waving soggy placards in the drizzle, when they tried to computerise the local libraries, replacing us librarians with barcode reading scanners. Joyce's face was a picture when she saw us in the local paper. I thought her head might actually explode.

Anyway, she would just have to get used to the idea of being stuck with me – unless, of course, she was thinking of dragging me out onto the golf course and bashing my head in with her nine iron when no one was looking. But I was sure she wouldn't go that far. Or would she...?

At work the next morning, I closed my eyes and inhaled the scent of camomile tea and well-thumbed books. What a blissful way to start the day. Five minutes until opening time – I savoured the silence. Not that the library is ever noisy. Well, apart from on Friday afternoons, when the shrieks and giggles from the children's section as I attempt all the different voices for *Story & Rhyme Time* can probably be heard from the other side of the village. It's just a different kind of quiet when I'm there alone.

The peace was disturbed by a loud rap at the big double door, under the clock that now said three minutes to go. Who on earth was trying to get into the library before it was even open? Had some desperate drinker mistaken it for The Badger's Inn across the village green? Unlikely, but you never know.

'Hello?' I called out, sliding the heavy bolt at the

5

bottom of the door.

'Hello? Stella?' Oh no! What was *she* doing here? Hadn't trying to poison me yesterday been enough? Now here she was at my place of work, first thing Monday morning. I forced a smile on my face before opening the door.

'Joyce. Hello. This is a surprise.'

'Hello, my dear.' Joyce was looking around her – was she searching for a heavy encyclopaedia to bash me over the head with? That would explain her presence here – although I couldn't really imagine her doing anything quite that messy.

Joyce hasn't ever been a regular at the library, which was really annoying me lately. With the now constant threat of closure, those in the village who used the library were coming in as much as possible to keep the numbers up. Especially the elderly ladies, whose pensions didn't run to buying large print copies of their favourite books, and who would probably struggle to download them as e-books. One lady whose son had bought her a kindle for Christmas had, in January, wound around it all the wool from a favourite old cardigan she had unravelled and, all these months later it was still there. Unused and unread. They were borrowing extra books they would never even read to keep me in my job. But not Ma Hazard. Apparently she doesn't like the thought of handling books other people have had their dirty hands on. Sheer snobbery if you ask me, as I have never noticed any other germaphobic tendencies. She belongs to one of those book-buying clubs. They all sit, unopened, on the Harrods bookcase in the hall, with their posh logo on show to anyone who comes round.

'Good morning, Joyce, I don't usually see you here.' I wondered if I could get away without the usual, obligatory kiss on the powdery cheek. With Jonathon not here, I decided I could give it a miss. 'Is there a particular new release that you're in a hurry to get your hands on?'

'No, my dear, you know how I like my books,' Joyce said, completely missing my attempt at humour. 'I just wanted to see how you were, you know, after yesterday's little mishap.'

Would that be the mishap where she tried to kill me and didn't quite manage it? I was itching to ask. Had she come to finish the job off?

Joyce reached into her enormous handbag – the sort of accessory that could floor a mugger with just one swing. What on earth had she got in there? Was I about to get bumped on the back of the head with a frozen leg of lamb, before she took it home and cooked it to get rid of the evidence? I've read *Tales of the Unexpected*. She would never get away with that now – It's 2015, and forensic science has advanced light years since that story was written.

'I'm fine, thank you,' I said, keeping a very firm eye on the arm delving into the bag. If she thought I would be turning my back on her while she pulled out her

7

weapon and finished me off, she could think again.

'Oh, that's such a relief,' Joyce said, pulling out a wedge shaped, tin foil wrapped parcel. I brought you this, as you didn't get to eat any of it yesterday. I know how much you enjoy my homemade carrot cake. Don't worry, dear, it is the right one, I have made sure.' She thrust it into my hands.

'That is very kind of you, Joyce. Thank you.' Was it my imagination, or could I hear ticking?

'That's fine, my dear, I was on my way into town anyway,' she said. 'Raffle prizes to sort out for the golf club dinner dance. I don't know what the matter is with people now – they all keep coming up with excuses for not doing it any more. I don't understand them – it is wonderful publicity for their companies, after all.'

I bit my tongue. Had she really forgotten that there'd been a recession going on? Did she not realise that even if things had picked up again for some businesses, others were still struggling? I imagined her bustling past the food bank in Wintertown with no idea what its existence meant to those who needed it.

'Well, good luck with that,' I said, hoping I didn't sound sarcastic. Not that she would notice. She never really listened to me anyway. Luckily, I was saved from more awkward conversation by two of the library's regular elderly ladies turning up.

'Good morning, Stella,' they chorused, bustling in with their matching wicker baskets and their hand knitted cardigans.

'Good morning, ladies.' I hoped my relief at the interruption wasn't too obvious. 'Did you have a good weekend?'

'Ooh, yes!' Mrs Jenkins, who always had a couple of murder mysteries on the go, clapped her hands. 'We went to London to see *Warhorse*. It was lovely. The puppetry was out of this world, Stella. You must take your Jonathon to see it. You forget that it isn't a real horse on stage!'

'Oh yes, you do,' Mrs Poole, who favoured books on knitting and needlecraft, and was responsible for most of the cardigans in the village, agreed. 'It was lovely, Stella. You *must* go.'

'Well, I'd better be toddling off now.' Joyce gave the ladies a polite smile and me a creepy one that put me in mind of the child catcher in *Chitty Chitty Bang Bang*. How did she do that?

I watched her get into her car, before closing the door and holding the cake to my ear – well you can't be too careful, can you.

'How was your weekend, Stella?' Mrs Jenkins enquired, placing this week's top choices, and two Ruth Rendell's I knew for a fact she had already read, on the counter.

'Oh, fine thanks,' I hedged. She would never believe me if I told her.

Not quite knowing what to do with the wedge of

9

cake, I shoved it in the direction of the shelf where I kept my handbag. Then I turned back to stamp Mrs J's books.

I didn't pay much attention to the sound of the door opening as, out of the corner of my eye, I saw the cake move. The narrow end had made it onto the flat shelf, but where the heavy end hadn't quite made the edge, its weight was pulling it floor-wards.

Time seemed to stand still as the parcel slipped down, hitting the side of the waste paper basket. It teetered, undecided for a split second, before opting for freedom, tipping the fortunately empty basket over with it.

'Stella, I forgot ...' I heard Joyce's voice as I lunged to retrieve the cake, hoping she hadn't seen it. Carefully replacing it on the shelf, I turned back round. She'd gone.

Chapter Two

Jonathon

Yawning, I pulled into my parking space behind the office. It had been an eventful weekend.

My heart still raced at the thought of what might happen if there was ever a time Stella needed her Epipen and couldn't get hold of it. We kept spares just about everywhere we could think of, just to be on the safe side. And thank God! Though how she had managed to lose the one from her handbag, we hadn't been able to work out. Of course, she didn't really believe what she had been saying on the way to the hospital, about Mum giving her the cake with the nuts in it on purpose – that had been the shock and adrenalin talking. She was much calmer on the way home.

Grabbing my briefcase from the passenger seat, I got out of the car. When Dad had decided to ease himself into the world of retirement, he had started taking Saturdays off. Then, a year later, Fridays too. Now, delegating Saturdays when possible, I was in charge at Hazard Estate Agents on Mondays and Fridays while he played golf and pottered about in the garden. I suspected it would be another year before his three day weeks turned into two day ones.

'Good morning, Jonathon.' Linda, our secretary and office manager greeted me with her usual warm smile before I was halfway through the door. 'I hope you had a good weekend. You have a nine thirty meeting with Mr and Mrs Sitwell.' Her raised eyebrow agreed with what I was already thinking.

The Sitwells. My jaws clenched as I carried on into the office, feeling like a coward for wishing the nightmare couple were coming tomorrow when Dad would be at the helm. It had become their habit, however, to come down to Hampshire most Friday mornings and make a long weekend of it. They would probably only head back to London once they had ruined my Monday. And anyone else's they came into contact with. I had no idea what either of them did for a living, but whatever it was, unless their entire business was conducted by smart phone, they only spent three days a week doing it. And they were way too young to be easing themselves into retirement.

The problem with the Sitwells was that they knew exactly what they wanted. Until they were shown it. Then they wanted something else. Until they were shown that. And so it went on. What fanciful demands would they come up with today?

'I thought you could do with a nice cup of coffee before you get started.' Linda put Dad's china cup and saucer down on the desk and left, quietly shutting the door behind her. It usually tickled me that she made my coffee in Dad's china on Mondays and Fridays – it felt a bit like being allowed to wear his shoes for the day – but nine thirty was fast approaching and I could already feel my shoulders tensing up.

Picking up the cup, I stared out of the window at the village green, but my last meeting with the Sitwells ran, like badly edited footage, through my head. It was like a cross between a *Hammer House of Horror* and a *Carry On* film. He was a cocky character, a bit like the used car salesman in *Only Fools and Horses* – he just needed a fat cigar to complete the picture. She looked like that dreadful model – what was her name? The one who was supposed to write books, except someone else wrote them for her – all inflated boobs, tarantula eyelashes and orange skin. Her vicious pink trout-pout made her look like a pantomime dame who had got made up in the dark, and as for her clothes ... If Widow Twanky had shared her unlit dressing room with a lap dancer and put the wrong costume on, she wouldn't have looked out of place next to Alana Sitwell, the trophy wife half of the couple.

Last week they had grumbled on and on about the lack of houses with swimming pools in the area. Then they'd given me a hard time because the house they had seen and fallen in love with whilst out for a Sunday drive wasn't even for sale. They just couldn't seem to understand that the owners of a property which had been in their family for a couple of centuries were not going to move out just because they clicked their over-manicured fingers. They obviously thought if they came down to

13

bumpkin-land and started bandying Mickey Mouse figures about, then the carrot crunchers should fall over themselves to give them what they wanted. As far as they were concerned, everything was *my* fault and I wasn't doing my job properly. They probably described me to their London friends as the village idiot.

It was my job to sell homes, but whenever I thought about the Sitwells buying a second home in our quiet triangle of the New Forest, I felt my hackles rise. And I'd never even known I had hackles until that fateful week when firstly, the Sitwells first came into our lives, and secondly, Stella was notified that the library was scheduled for closure.

I realised I was still holding my coffee and took a gulp. What was happening in the Netley villages? This was our home. This was where I grew up. That tree on the other side of the green was the first one I ever climbed – the first one I fell out of, too. Stella and I wanted to settle down and raise our own family here, and suddenly huge spanners were being hurled into the works. Spanners like the Sitwells who, given the chance, would buy something charming and characterful, then rip the heart out of it and turn it into something ghastly. Then they would arrive on Fridays with their Harvey Nicks hampers, and have Ocado vans turning up to deliver their more mundane groceries from Winchester or Southampton. They wouldn't care about supporting local businesses, or fitting in. They would turn whatever they bought into an extension of their London life, speeding round the country lanes in their flash four by fours, terrorising the ponies and deer.

Lush lawns would be dug up to give way for enormous hot tubs full of half-naked orange people getting drunk and raucous. I must have put my cup down more forcefully than I meant to. The loud chink brought Linda to the door.

'Is everything alright, Jonathon?'

'Sorry.' I forced a smile. 'Just ruminating on second homers buying up the area.'

'I know what you mean,' she nodded. Before she had a chance to say any more, the old fashioned bell on the front door jangled. The vultures had landed.

'You'd better go and see to them,' I fought to unclench my jaw, 'before they make themselves welcome and wander through anyway.'

I could feel myself choking on heavy, musky perfume and too much aftershave before they even entered the office. It was like being whacked round the head with two expensive, clashing air fresheners. Getting up, I quickly opened the window and took a deep breath. I wondered what Stella was up to right now – my lovely Stella who always smelled of orange blossom, and looked sexy without looking like she should be wrapped around a long pole. Whatever she was doing, I hoped she was having a much better morning than I was.

Chapter Three

Stella

From: astrid@thainet.com

To: stellamoon@librarymail.co.uk

Subject: **Greetings from Mum and Dad!**

Monday ...

Hello Stella darling,

You'll never guess what happened to your father today – he was on the beach helping Thaksin (you remember him – my friend Tasanee's husband) put some new slats in a couple of the sun loungers and a coconut fell on his head! It bounced right off into the sea (the coconut, not your father's head). Such a shame! You know how I just adore fresh coconut – and I've got some Malibu I could have poured into it – it would have been delicious! I'll just have to send your father out to buy one. It was so funny though, and it gave me an idea for a wedding present for you and Jonathon. How do you think a coconut tree would fare in Hampshire? We could bring a baby one back with us. That would be something different, wouldn't it? Anyway, think about it and let me know.

Hope all the wedding prep is going well. You will let us know if there is anything we can do, won't you?

Give our love to Jonathon.

Bye for now,

Love from Mum and Dad xx

Another gem of a missive from my mother. Only my parents could decide to turn an early, voluntary retirement into a middle-age gap year and then, three years later, still be in Thailand, doing odd jobs in return for a tiny apartment upstairs from a beach-side restaurant. Mostly I was glad for them, doing their own thing, enjoying their adventure. Sometimes though, mostly when I'd had to spend any longer than five minutes with Joyce, I would think how much nicer and easier it would be, having my mum here in the run up to the wedding. We might not have had to have our reception in a stuffy old golf club. And though I didn't really fancy the idea of a flower-decked yurt either, I would pay good money to see Joyce in one.

Jonathon was next to me on the sofa. He had come

to my place straight from the office, humming the Boom Town Rats' *I Don't like Mondays,* that my dad used to like so much. Now, half a large glass of Sauvignon Blanc later, he was watching a repeat of *The Big Bang Theory.* I nudged him in the thigh with the corner of my laptop so he would read it.

'A baby coconut tree?' He looked back at me in horrified amusement.

'Yep, a baby coconut tree,' I grinned back. 'Could be worse, could be a baby elephant.'

'Don't tempt fate,' he groaned. This was only the latest in a long list of unsuitable things my mother had suggested we might like as a wedding present, which included a refurbished, bright yellow tuk tuk, complete with flashing disco lights, that she had fallen in love with. Although sponsorship of a baby gibbon at the Gibbon Rehabilitation Project had actually appealed to both of us. That was the one suggestion we would have liked her to go with. 'And I take it she means that it's a shame the coconut bounced away before your dad could retrieve it, not that it was the coconut rather than your dad's head?' He chuckled. 'I hope to God your mother is never called on to give evidence in a murder trial – she would have the jury so confused they'd end up thinking the victim had done it.'

'You can laugh now,' I took the laptop back and put it on the arm of the sofa, laughing myself. 'Can you imagine how parents' evenings at my school went? I used to get the strangest looks from the teachers afterwards. Especially after the time she spent the whole of their allotted ten minutes trying to get them to let me off wearing school uniform because she insisted it would stifle my individuality.'

Jonathon rolled his eyes heavenwards and looked at me, mock-serious, nodding towards my laptop. 'I shouldn't laugh at all really. This is what I've got to look forward to in our twilight years isn't it – you turning into your mother?'

'*Twilight years?* They're not that old! And to be fair to Mum, she has always been a bit of a free spirit ...'

'Yes,' my fiancé raised an eyebrow ever so slightly, 'I have seen her Greenham Common photos from the 80's.'

'Well, be thankful she's too far away right now to join in the fracking protests,' I teased him. 'What would your mother say?!'

'Probably something about the library protests, and apples not falling far from their trees ...'

'Oh! So I'm a Cox's Orange Pippin now, am I?' I dug him in the ribs and he put his glass down and grabbed my hands.

'No, I would say more of a Golden Delicious,' he said, pulling me closer.

'At least you didn't say a Granny Smith.' I nuzzled into his neck before turning my face to his kiss. His lips tasted of wine. Mine tingled at their touch, and my insides

19

started to melt like a bowl of chocolates by a roaring fireside.

'No, definitely delicious,' he murmured, his fingers scrunching up my hair while he pressed his body even closer to mine.

'Mmm, that makes two of us,' I sighed, as those slender, artistic fingers moved down towards the buttons on my shirt.

'Stella ...' he breathed in my ear, as I arched my back slightly to make it easier for him.

'Mmm ...' I ran a finger down his cheek, a little shiver of anticipation running through me as his hands brushed against my skin.

'Stella ...'

'Mmm ...'

'Stella ... The laptop ...'

'Mmm ... What?' I opened my eyes and saw we were about to send it toppling to the floor. Reluctantly breaking away from Jonathon for a moment, I grabbed it and shoved it on to the coffee table. A vision of Joyce's cake falling off the shelf earlier flitted across my mind. She must be feeling even more murderous about me than usual. I opened my mouth to tell him about it and stopped. I was not going to let her spoil this moment for us. 'Now then,' I smiled, shutting her out of my mind and pulling my fiancé back to me. 'Where were we ...'

Chapter Four

Stella

The following evening, Jonathon's mother had commanded – I mean invited – me for dinner after our appointed wedding chat with the vicar. Netley Mallow didn't have its own vicar. It had its own Norman church – all three of the villages did – and, as in *Goldilocks and the Three Bears*, Netley Magna had the daddy bear sized one, we in Netley Mallow had the mummy bear sized one, and Netley Parva had the baby bear sized one. The unusually glamorous vicar of Netley shared her time between these three churches, along with the bigger, more modern church in Wintertown, and the pastoral care of all their dwindling congregations.

The Reverend Marianne's pillar-box-red motorbike was parked at a jaunty angle outside the new vicarage when we arrived. It looked like some boy racer had sped along the road and parked it in haste before running off and leaving it there.

'Looks like you parked it – you've not been borrowing the vicar's bike have you?' Jonathon winked at me and I tried my best to look indignant, before stepping round it and ringing the doorbell.

'Good evening, good evening,' the tiny flame-haired vicar greeted us, flinging the front door wide open and ushering us inside. 'How lovely to see you both. Tea? Coffee? A cold drink?' She waved us through to the tiny kitchen with the invitingly frosted bottle of pear cider she had in her hand, and we found ourselves sitting at the scrubbed pine table, that took up most of the room, before either of us had even said a word. This new, smaller vicarage was a cottage, built in the corner of the grounds of the old vicarage, which had been sold to a family much more suited to its numerous and enormous rooms. How many church fêtes, Brownie jamborees, Girl Guide and Boy Scout camps must have taken place over the years, in the huge gardens. It was like a little model of the original, about a quarter of the size.

Without waiting for any answer, the Reverend Marianne opened the cider and poured three chunky tumblers of the pear-scented, pale amber liquid.

'Right then, Jonathon and Stella,' she smiled, reaching for her notebook from the top of the leaning tower of paperwork at the other end of the table. 'A quick prayer and down to business.' We both bowed our heads as she uttered the familiar prayer, 'Dear Lord, as Stella and Jonathon head towards marriage, please bless them, their families, and their preparations for their forthcoming union ...' Jonathon's hand brushed against mine at the word 'union', an expression which always made us both smile. 'Amen. Now then, have you come up with your final hymn selection yet?'

Jonathon and I grimaced at each other. Was the matter of choosing hymns a minefield for all brides and grooms, or was it just us? Marianne had suggested we each pick one and have each of our sets of parents pick one. Apparently she had found this solved a lot of arguments and although a lot of weddings had only two or three hymns, the fourth one could always be sung by the congregation while we signed the register. This was one of the times when I blessed my parents' lack of convention; they had said it was up to us. Joyce, however, had wanted her input and then some. She had suggested her own favourite – *Jerusalem* – and that of Jonathon's grandmother –*The Lord's My Shepherd* – but played to the old Crimond tune, claiming that as this would most probably be the last wedding the old lady would ever attend, it would be nice for her to hear her favourite hymn. Which it would, but as the old lady in question was completely gaga and wouldn't know her favourite hymn from a bag of sugar, we both suspected it was a ploy to get to choose half of the hymns herself. James had given his input by suggesting *Lord of All Hopefulness*, but without sounding particularly hopeful of getting it. Joyce, on hearing of my parents' laid back attitude, decided that she should choose for them, which left nothing for Jonathon or I to choose. Jonathon wasn't too bothered and to be honest, neither would I have been really, if it wasn't for the fact that it smacked of Joyce taking over in yet another area of our wedding. That made me want to dig in my heels and insist on choosing something myself. Joyce seemed to think I was just being silly, and poor Jonathon felt like the piggy in the middle.

We gave Marianne the edited highlights of the battle of wills that had been taking place. She rolled her eyes and took an un-lady-vicar-like swig from her glass.

'Well, there's no immediate rush, the order of service sheets don't take that long to print up. But don't leave it to the last minute – or there won't be time to reprint if there are any little mistakes or printing errors. Now, if you will allow me to give you some advice,' she looked at both of us, 'it would be best to pick your battles. You have already found out that weddings involve a lot of compromise. As your parents, Stella, are happy with whatever is chosen, and neither of you have any strong leanings towards any particular hymn, I think it would be a good idea to let Jonathon's parents have the three hymns they have selected. But I would suggest that the fourth one definitely be of your choosing. You don't want any feelings of resentment building up.'

I wondered what she would make of my feelings of resentment at being nearly killed at the weekend by the woman who was having so much say in our wedding. It would be so tempting, if Jonathon weren't with me, to confide in her. I could imagine kicking back with another bottle of cider, sharing my fears with this unlikely pocket rocket of a vicar who always made me feel there was nothing that could not be overcome. She would know just what to do, but now wasn't the time to bring that up. Joyce would have dinner ready for us and, much as I was in no hurry to return to the scene of the attempted crime, I doubted even she would try anything again quite so soon.

Leaving the vicarage, a flash of purple in the corner of the garden caught my eye. Foxgloves. Snatches of Agatha Christie plots flashed through my mind – foxglove leaves mixed in with sage? Or was it with spring greens? My heart skipped a few beats until I remembered we were having lamb chops and peas. It had just about regained its regular rhythm by the time we reached Joyce's kitchen door.

***

'That *Vicar of Dibley* has a lot to answer for,' Joyce announced to no one in particular, as she turned over the chops we were having for dinner, shook some salt over them and slid them back under the grill. The aroma of cooking lamb was still a joyous thing to someone who had grown up in a vegetarian household. If only I didn't feel the need to grit my teeth as soon as I walked through her door, I would be able to really enjoy it.

'*The Vicar of Dibley*, Mum? Still?' Jonathon chuckled.

We had all given up trying to make sense of Joyce's weird perception that Dawn French's 90's sitcom was in any way responsible for instigating the ordination of women vicars. Especially as, when Jonathon googled it, we found out that the change in church law had actually happened about two years before the first episode even aired, and would have been the inspiration for the series itself, rather than the other way round.

Of course, it was typical of Joyce to be a bit of a fuddy-duddy about female vicars. She also thought all those outdated rules about women in golf clubs were perfectly acceptable and, if she were ever to use public transport, woe betide the man who didn't jump up at once and offer her his seat. But whatever Joyce thought, the Reverend Marianne was a vast improvement on her doddery predecessor, who had dropped the last baby he had been allowed to christen in the font – there had been a hastily hushed-up rumour that he had given the poor little thing concussion.

'The Reverend Maurice was a *wonderful* man. He married us, and he christened Jonathon,' she carried on, regardless of Jonathon, myself and even James, raising our eyebrows at each other. 'It would have been lovely to have had him perform your wedding service. And maybe,' she looked from Jonathon to me and back to Jonathon again, 'in a year or so, christening our grandchildren.'

'A year or so?' The mint sauce, made from freshly chopped garden mint, that I was stirring to dissolve the sugar, nearly ended up splashed all over the table cloth. Was she now giving us a timetable for when we she wanted us to start a family?

'Wasn't he getting the names mixed up on the

marriage certificates?' Jonathon quickly changed the subject and scuttled down to my end of the table we were laying for dinner. 'Didn't one of the grooms end up married, on paper, to one of the witnesses, or something?' He shook his head gently at me as I mouthed *grandchildren?*

'I heard,' James added, *sotto voce*, 'that he made a whole Sunday school class cry, by telling them that the Easter Bunny wasn't real ...'

'Don't be silly, dear.' Joyce turned round from prodding the potatoes, the knife still in one hand, the saucepan lid in the other, brooking no argument from any of us. 'Now, Stella,' she said, waving the knife pointedly in my direction. 'What did this *Marianne* have to say about the wedding hymns?

Chapter Five

Jonathon

After walking Stella back to her place, I'd come home and spent ages online, trying to work out when would be the best time to go and see this *Warhorse* show that she'd said she would like to go and see. We would have to go for a Saturday performance and, of course, they were the shows that were the most booked up in advance. I had wanted to get really good seats, but the only seats still available for any Saturday performance before the wedding apparently had a restricted view of the stage. Not being a theatre-goer myself, I didn't really know how restricted a restricted view of the stage would be and I didn't want to promise Stella a lovely evening at the theatre if she was only going to be able to see half the stage. In the end I emailed the theatre box office to ask their advice.

I then spent most of the night staring at the ceiling, trying to decide what she would like best as a wedding present. This was a much bigger problem and one which had been bugging me for ages. I really should have had something sorted out by now. Mum was clearly itching to help as much as we would let her with plans for the wedding day itself, even though Stella wasn't too keen, but I had a cunning plan of my own for afterwards. I knew that with the wedding less than a month away I'd left it late, but trying to think of a perfect wedding gift for my beautiful bride to be had been so hard. She wasn't an accumulator of things. She wasn't interested in jewellery, except, of course for meaningful things like wedding rings. So I had been thinking about surprising her with a little extra trip, tagged on to the end of our honeymoon in Thailand – a week somewhere without any of our parents around – like newlyweds were supposed to have. After all, as easy going as Astrid and Francis were, we could hardly spend all day in bed with them on the other side of the wall.

It wasn't that I was ungrateful. It was very kind of them to arrange a fortnight for us on the little island where they'd made their current home. Phuket wasn't really my cup of tea though – it seemed more of a week-long stag party kind of place. But their little village on the west coast was quite sweet and they had made good friends with the locals there. And, where they were, you could go out in the evenings without being accosted by persistent touts trying to sell you tickets to watch poorly paid girls pretending to enjoy doing uncomfortable looking things with ping pong balls. Or, as I heard recently, budgerigars – budgerigars! The mind boggles – they clearly don't have a Thai version of the RSPCA. Although, on second thoughts, that might have just been somebody winding me up.

The obvious thing would be to stop off somewhere on our way back from Thailand, rather than go further east. Dubai was roughly half way, and I quite fancied finishing off the trip with a week in a five star hotel. It wasn't really Stella's kind of place though, although after a couple of weeks of lounging about on a beach, counting coconuts ... I still thought Stella would prefer something more low key, maybe somewhere in Europe – seeing the historical sites in Athens, eating moules frîtes in Paris, or cycling round Amsterdam.

The trouble was, thinking about it was as far as I'd got. I wanted it to be perfect, but nothing I came up with was. And the more time I spent thinking about something perfect, the less time there was going to be to actually book it. At this rate I would be giving it to her as a second honeymoon.

It was a shame Alli, her maid of honour, was so busy at the moment. Between us we could have come up with something Stella would love, I was sure of it. Maybe I'd give her a ring, anyway. She could ask Stella some surreptitious questions and give me some ideas – that way Stella wouldn't guess I was up to something. She might even have some ideas anyway – they had known each other since they were kids. Yes. That was what I'd do. I would get Alli to help me organise something amazing for Stella.

I didn't know why I hadn't thought of it before.

Chapter Six

Joyce

I just could not understand why Jonathon and Stella wouldn't let me go along with them to these meetings with this new vicar. It all seemed very odd to me, my son being married by a female vicar, and a female vicar who didn't even know him, to boot.

They thought I hadn't noticed them all laughing at me, even James, insisting I've got something against *The Vicar of Dibley*. I actually used to admire Dawn French very much, although not since she started doing those silly adverts with that talking dog. Julie Walters was always very good too, and that nice Victoria Wood, so clever and witty. They were a far cry from the comediennes and comedy actresses who were popular now, with all their swearing and unladylike behaviour and talking about things they should only be discussing with their gynaecologists. I shuddered to think how their parents must feel when they read about them in the papers or watched their shows on television.

But it seemed to be the way some young women behaved nowadays, celebrities or not, all that staggering out of nightclubs drunk and falling out of taxis with no underwear on. I wouldn't have put up with it from *any* daughter of mine. Although it seemed there were no limits to the sort of behaviour I was expected to put up with from a prospective daughter-in-law.

I was furious about the incident with the cake in the library. All the effort I had gone to and that was how Stella had treated it, just dumped it in the bin, and she hadn't even bothered to do that properly and it had ended up on the floor. There was gratitude for you! I always knew Stella was a thoughtless girl.

And she was practically feral, which was hardly surprising, considering those hippy dippy parents of hers. Francis wasn't too bad, but that Astrid? What a silly name! What was the obsession with stars in that family? I prayed that Jonathon's first born, if he married Stella, would be a boy. There were far too many names that meant star for them to choose from for a girl, and I couldn't bear the thought of any granddaughter of mine being christened Asteria or Hester, or some other ridiculous name. Although Estelle Hazard had quite a nice ring to it. If it looked like they were going to go for something like that, I would have to make sure they chose Estelle.

It was just typical of that family that Astrid didn't think it was important to be here. If I had a daughter who was getting married, everything would have been organised and arranged with precision. But here we were with the wedding less than four weeks away and the only thing to have been sorted out properly was the reception.

And that was only because James and I were giving it to them as their wedding gift, and so it was the one thing I had been able to make sure was organised properly. If I had been allowed to speak to this vicar woman, I would have had the service all sorted out by now too. But at least I had managed to make sure we were going to have a proper selection of hymns. It didn't bear thinking about, the sort of happy clappy songs the congregation would be expected to sing, otherwise. I would have been a laughing stock in my own church.

I still needed to do something about Stella though. But what?

Chapter Seven

Stella

From: stellamoon@librarymail.co.uk

To: astrid@thainet.com

Subject: **Re: Greetings from Mum and Dad!**

Wednesday ...

Hi Mum,

Hope Dad's head is alright. Maybe you should insist he wears a crash helmet when he's working under the coconut trees!

Jonathon reckons the climate in Hampshire wouldn't really suit a coconut tree, but thanks for the thought anyway. And honestly, you and Dad organising our honeymoon is a big enough present already, we really don't need anything else.

We had lunch with his mum and dad on Sunday and dinner with them last night after our meeting with the vicar. You'll love the Reverend Marianne, - there's not much that's reverent about her – she's almost as laid back as you. Anyway, she came up with what sounds like a solution about the wedding hymns ...

More soon.

xxxx

Sending the email, I logged off the library computer. It was officially two minutes to closing time, which meant thirty two minutes until I met my best friend, Alli, for a drink in town. The hands on the clock always seemed to go round more slowly during the last few minutes of a really quiet afternoon, but you could bet if I closed up now someone would suddenly appear at the door, desperate to change their books, and then spend ages looking for new ones to take out.

I had decided there was no point in telling Mum and Dad about the carrot cake incident – it would only worry them. I always got the impression they thought Joyce was a bit *Hyacinth Bucket*, but essentially harmless, although mum would be beside herself if she knew the amount of dead animal flesh that got roasted, grilled, stewed and served up in her kitchen. Dad would just get himself invited for dinner and never leave. But then, as he wasn't about to marry her precious son, I couldn't think of any reason she could have to dish him up anything that would bump him off.

Actually that wouldn't be such a bad idea between

now and the wedding. If I could prise him away from Mum, he could come and be my bodyguard, protecting me from toadstools in my mixed grill, or foxglove leaves mixed with my portion of spring greens. And I am sure I've read somewhere that apple seeds contain something that produces cyanide – probably in an Agatha Christie. It would probably take a lot of them to kill you, but then, Joyce's spare room always has a hell of a lot of apples from their garden stored in it.

Chapter Eight

Stella

'Two glasses of Pinot Grigio please.' Alli, head of music at Wintertown technical college and my very best friend since junior school, was saying to one of the slicked-back-haired, long black apron wearing barmen, as I walked through the door. Nettles was the least trendy and therefore the quietest and most up my street of the three wine bars in Wintertown, and we came here whenever one of us needed to unload. Which more often than not was me. She was rummaging, Mary Poppins-style, in her handbag, presumably for her purse, but it could just as easily have been for a pot plant or a lamp stand. I'd seen the inside of that bag and it wouldn't be beyond the realms of possibility for Lord Lucan and the crew of the *Marie Celeste* to be enjoying a game of Hide & Seek in it.

'Cancel that,' I zoomed over to her side, 'and make it a bottle.'

'That bad a day?' She stopped rummaging, slipped her arm through mine and pulled me over to a table by the window.

'That bad a week.' I hooked my bag over the back of my chair, slumped myself onto the seat and mimed banging my head rhythmically against the table.

'Uh oh, what's she done now?' Alli settled into her chair and into listening mode, neat little elbows on the table, dainty chin propped on the bridge of her elegantly folded hands. She already knew about both the cake incidents, nearly wetting herself laughing when I'd described the wedge of cake falling off the shelf towards the bin at the exact moment Joyce had come back into the library. She already knew about the wedding hymn battle and had suggested I demand *Fight the Good Fight,* with actions. I was still considering it.

'She's only started dropping sledgehammer hints about Jonathon and I starting a family and giving her grandchildren almost straight away.'

'You're kidding ...' Alli couldn't say any more for the moment as the barman arrived, putting two glasses and an ice bucket down on our table. He then whipped out a bottle with a flourish and waved it under our noses, before making a meal of opening it and deciding which of us to give a thimbleful to try.

While I watched him, last night's dinner replayed itself through my mind – Joyce smugly filling the two men's plates with a couple of large, meaty lamb chops each and four perfectly cooked potatoes, inviting them to help themselves to the sliced carrots and baby peas, while her plate and mine received two tiddly little chops and two miniscule potatoes, all of which were overcooked because they were so much smaller than the men's. While I had scooped up as many peas as I dared and waited for one of her little digs about my weight, Jonathon had kept a flurry of conversation going and I wondered if I was the only one who realised how desperately he was trying to keep the women at the table distracted from the subject of grandchildren. He hadn't allowed for his mother's 1950's ideas on washing up though, because as soon as the stewed apples – last year's crop from the four trees at the bottom of the garden, carefully stored, wrapped in newspaper in the spare room – and custard had been eaten, she was shooing him and his father into the living room so that she and I could take our right and proper places at the kitchen sink. I tried not to think about how many pips I had inadvertently chewed on – I would have to look up later, how many of them someone would have to swallow to produce enough cyanide to be deadly.

Biting the bullet before I chickened out, I had plunged in with, 'You were saying something about grandchildren, Joyce? In a year or so? Don't you think Jonathon and I should spend a bit more time than that settling in to life as a married couple first?'

'Oh! Well, my dear, you know I don't like to interfere ...' she'd frowned slightly, as I coughed to cover the squeak of disbelief that had escaped me, 'but Jonathon has always wanted a large family, and ...'

'Has he?' That was news to me.

'Of course he has. Being an only child ... Well ... You must know what that's like. And anyway, Stella, as soon as the library closes and your little job there finishes, it will give you something to do, a sense of purpose …'

Luckily Jonathon had walked back through the kitchen door right at that moment, otherwise my sense of purpose might have wanted me to fulfil it by whacking her over the head with the grill pan …

'Go on then,' Alli leaned forwards again, now the waiter had gone, clinking her glass against mine.

I picked mine up and took a good sized mouthful, savouring the taste. 'Well, first of all she tried to tell me that Jonathon had always wanted a big family. I don't know if she thinks we don't ever actually talk to each other, but whenever we have discussed children we have both agreed that a couple of kids would be nice and that there's no hurry. He was mortified when I told him afterwards. He said that she's been on at him, telling him that I want to have lots of children and that I want to start having them straight away …'

'So it's pretty bloody clear who is desperate to hear the patter of little Hazard feet.' Alli shook her head.

'It's also pretty bloody clear that she just can't wait for the library to close and take my "little job",' my fingers did angry quotation marks in the air, 'with it …'

'She said that?' Alli's voice went up an octave, indignant on my behalf.

'The bit about the little job, yes, and how starting a family straight away will give me something to do, and a "sense of purpose". My fingers waggled in the air again.

'Oh my God! What did you say?'

'I didn't. Luckily we were saved by Jonathon coming back in.'

'Jonathon saves the day!' Alli clinked her glass against mine again. 'You know, Stella, this harping on about grandchildren ...'

'Yes?' I knew exactly where she was going with this. She didn't believe Ma Hazard was trying to kill me either.

'Well, if she wanted you out of Jonathon's life, then she'd hardly be encouraging the pair of you to start a family together, would she?'

'She might be saying it to put me off the scent,' I reasoned. 'Or she might just be desperate for a grandchild. That would make her want me to get pregnant quickly so Jonathon would have a baby son or daughter and she'd have her grandchild and then ... well, then I'd be expendable ...'

'Expendable?' Alli's lips twitched. 'Honestly, Stella! You've been reading far too many crime novels, you know.'

'You'll remember you said that and eat your words when I meet with a sudden and fatal accident on the way home from the maternity hospital.' Ok, that sounded a bit far-fetched, even to my own ears, but I still knew I was on to something. 'Anyway, that is more than enough talk about Ma Hazardous,' I said, feeling guilty for hogging the conversation since I'd got here. Poor Alli had been working eighteen hour days getting her A-level music students ready for their practical exams and her pre-A-level students ready for their various turns in the end of year concert. 'How has your week been, then?'

'Hectic,' she grimaced. 'Histrionics with a hyperactive harpist, despair with a deeply depressed drummer. And I don't even want to think about the cat fight between two clarinet players over a cellist who's so chilled out he doesn't even know they're there, let alone that they're almost tearing each other's hair out over him!' She took the bottle out of the ice bucket and poured generously into both our glasses.

'That doesn't sound very harmonious,' I teased, unable to help myself.

'Don't,' she groaned. 'But at least I can forget about them at the end of the working day. Cheers!' She waved her glass at me before about a third of its contents disappeared down her throat. 'Here's to the future Mrs Hazard not killing, or getting killed by, the present Mrs Hazard!'

'Hey! I'll drink to that,' I took a sip and put my glass back down. 'But I can't make you any promises. Just in case I have to break one of them.'

Chapter Nine

Stella

From: francis@thainet.com

To: stellamoon@librarymail.co.uk

Subject: **Sawadee Krub – Greetings from Thailand!**

Thursday ...

Dear Stella,

Dad here. Hope all is well with you. Your mother is at the vet's. Some brainless idiots left a load of beer bottles on the beach after their barbeque last night, and one of those stray mutts that she insists on feeding got a piece of broken glass stuck in its paw. I swear if it had been my foot, she would have just made me bathe it in the sea and wrap a hankie round it, but you know your mother!

Anyway, while she is out I just thought I would send you a quick email and warn you about this shell necklace thing she has started making for you. I know you were just humouring her, saying you thought it would be lovely, but it really has grown completely out of hand, Stella. It has now turned into a wind chime, or at least I think that is what it is, and she still goes out wandering the beach every morning looking for more shells to add to it. Fingers crossed that it might end up too big and heavy to bring!

A bit of local gossip for you – do you remember that time you were here and you came with us and looked at some little one bedroom apartments in a condotel, that were being sold off? And your mother and I were thinking of buying one and staying in it while we were here and then renting it out when we moved on to somewhere else? Well, it seems there has been some kind of problem with them. I haven't been able to find out what yet, and Thaksin and Tasanee don't know anything about it, but it looks like it was a good job we decided not to buy one. We probably dodged a bullet there.

Well my lovely girl, we hope you and Jonathon are both well. Give him our best.

And please don't forget to let us know if there is anything at all that we can do towards the wedding, won't you? I do feel guilty that we're not there for you right now. So if you need us to come back early, you only have to say and I can change our flights.

Lots of love, my lovely girl,

Dad xxx

Poor Dad! If I knew my mother, she would have that dog moved in with them the moment she got it back there and they would both be waiting on it hand and foot while it made itself at home on their bed. He had the patience of a saint, my father – he still always laughed about the time Mum brought home an injured cat that she'd found by the side of the road. Its convalescence had included it being fed freshly cooked, organic, free range chicken, bought specially for it, while we munched our chickpea burgers and alfalfa sprouts and pretended we weren't thinking about wrestling the feckless feline for a bit of cooked meat protein.

With a bit of luck, the dog would mistake the wind chime for his own personal toy and then dad wouldn't need to worry about bringing it anymore. And it wouldn't have to become one of those hideous gifts that Jonathon and I would hide in the loft and hopefully remember to bring out every time my parents came to stay. I could but hope ...

Chapter Ten

Jonathon

Isn't it amazing the number of people you cross paths with when you're trying to do something in secret. Two of Stella's favourite old ladies from the library, the bossy one and the dotty one, came out of the tea rooms in the high street just as I was driving past. I found myself shuffling my shoulders down in my seat, as the last thing I wanted was them gossiping to Stella that they'd seen me at this end of town. Then I thought I saw Mum's car just before turning into the car park at Wintertown technical college but, even if it was her, I didn't think she saw me, which was just as well, as she would only insist on helping, and I wanted to do this on my own – well, with a little bit of help from Alli. All I needed now was for the Sitwells to pop out of a doorway and demand to know what I was doing here, instead of sorting out their far more important needs.

Alli had suggested I come and meet her in her little office on the top floor of the college's music and drama block. I had been to the little performance studio on the ground floor there once before, when Alli had just taken over from her predecessor and Stella had persuaded me along to support her very first end of term concert. Poor

Alli had been thrown in at the deep end with no time to reorganise the unrehearsed shambles she'd been left to deal with. It hadn't sold very well, and it hadn't taken long to work out why, or to start wondering where the tom cats that were being tortured were being held, but of course, we didn't tell Alli that. The smell of the building, as I walked up the stairs, still took me back to doing my own A-levels there, although this particular space had been part of a sports field, and this block wasn't built until years later.

She was busy scribbling on a large green *post it* note and sticking it to the top sheet of one of half a dozen piles of manuscript paper, stacked all over her desk, when I looked through the window in the door. She was frowning in concentration and there was some kind of concerto playing on the CD player, wedged between a spiky pot plant – the sort that looked as if it didn't mind too much if you forgot to water it for ages – and a metronome, on top of the filing cabinet. I didn't like disturbing her, but she had told me to come, so I tapped gently on the door.

'Oh! Hi Jonathon,' Alli tucked her pencil behind her ear, rummaged for the remote control, nudging a pink *post it* topped pile nearer the edge of the desk, and silenced the music. 'Come on in. How about a cup of tea? Sorry I can't offer you anything stronger.'

'No, tea's fine,' I told her, taking a step towards the nearest chair. There was a pair of cymbals on it.

'Sit down then, you're making the place look untidy,' she grinned, switching the kettle on and pulling a couple of teabags out of a tin next to the CD player.

I went for the chair on the other side of the desk from Alli's. That had a cardboard box on it. It was full of sheet music for show classics, if the top one was anything to go by, the edges of yet more multi coloured *post its* sticking out from between their pages. I wondered just how much untidier the place could look without a bull wandering in, and thinking it was in a china shop that it must have already been in earlier. How did Alli ever manage to find anything? I hadn't ever given it much thought, but wouldn't teachers be expected to have tidy and organised desks in tidy and organised rooms, as a reflection of their tidy and organised minds? I'd have to watch those *post it* notes. They were sneaky little beggars. They never stuck to the things you wanted them to and always ended up stuck where you didn't want them. I was going round to Stella's after this. The last thing I wanted was a random piece of sticky paper with Alli's spidery handwriting on it to give the game away and tell her exactly where I'd been.

'Here you are,' She handed me a mug with *Keep Calm And Pretend It's On The Lesson Plan* printed on it. 'Cheers!'

'Cheers!' I took a sip, remembering the time she had once, absent-mindedly, given me a cup of tea that she had also put a spoonful of instant coffee in, and then a more appreciative one of what was actually a very good brew. 'Just what the doctor ordered.'

'Don't sound so surprised,' she feigned indignation. 'I am a very good tea maker, I'll have you know!' She took a less than ladylike slurp from her own *Keep Calm And Carry on Teaching* mug.

'I wouldn't dream of suggesting otherwise.'

'So, you want to pick my brains about a surprise romantic honeymoon add-on for Stella?' She peered at me over the top of her mug. 'I've been having a think about it, Jonathon. Does it have to actually be an add-on to the honeymoon?'

'What do you mean?' I had a feeling I was about to look foolish.

'Well, just bear with me while I run some ideas by you.'

I took a mouthful of my tea and wondered what crazy scheme she was going to come up with.

'My first thought was *Murder on the Orient Express,*' she announced. 'She's always said how she'd love to take a trip on the most romantic train in the world ...'

'Of course,' I almost slapped my forehead, it was so obvious. Stella loved her Agatha Christies. And all the old fashioned romance of steam trains. Was the current Orient Express a steam train? I'd have to look into it. But ... 'Hang on though. That will be well booked up months in advance, won't it? We wouldn't have a hope of getting

49

tickets at this late stage.' I felt my shoulders slump a bit.

'True. And then there's that lovely hotel in Devon,'

Alli was getting into her stride now, 'Burgh Island, where Agatha Christie used to stay. It's just off the coast of Devon, you know, the one that's an island when the tide is in and they transport you to the hotel itself by sea tractor, if I've remembered it right. Anyway, it's all Art Deco and there's even an Agatha Christie room, although that probably gets booked up furthest in advance of all of them ...'

What was Alli playing at? Both these ideas would have been perfect, if they'd been thought of about a year ago, maybe even as little as six months. But now? Now she was just teasing me.

'And of course,' Alli carried on, 'you would have to pack a whole separate wardrobe each if you did take her there – I mean, what looks good for lounging about with a cold beer on a Thai beach would be a definite no-no for sipping cocktails in such a stylish environment.'

'Right. Except that's not going to be a problem is it, as we won't be able to get in there.' I tried not to sound impatient, but I was back to square one. I would have to go straight home, get online and find something to book that I hadn't left it too late for. I'd ring Stella with some little white lie to get out of going to her place tonight, but it would be worth it in the end. Well ... as long as I could find something that she would like. 'Well, thanks for trying to help anyway, Alli,' I took a huge gulp of my tea and stood up.

'Where are you going?'

'I've got to go and get started,' I told her. 'Time's running out ...'

'Why?'

'What do you mean, why? The wedding's in just over three weeks!'

'I know when the wedding is, you dope, but why does this trip that you want to be so special and memorable have to be tacked on to the end of your honeymoon?' Alli asked slowly, hands on her hips, as if trying to explain why there are eight notes in an octave to someone a bit slow. 'Why can't this special trip be a trip in its own right?'

'Because I wanted to give it to Stella as a wedding present.' It was my turn to do the octave thing. For such a well-educated woman, she really was missing the point.

'So give it to Stella as a wedding present.'

'What? But ...'

'Book it for when you *can* go, pay for it, print up the tickets and put them in a fancy envelope. Hell, you can even tie a pink ribbon round them, or put them in a shiny box. Then give them to Stella on your wedding day. That way she can have all the pleasure of looking forward to it and shopping and packing for it, as well as the pleasure of actually going.' Alli stood still and waited, a bit like she had at the end of that awful concert when she'd been waiting for the kind hearted applause to start.

Except that this time, I suddenly realised, this extremely clever woman had just orchestrated what was bound to be a resounding success.

Chapter Eleven

Stella

From: stellamoon@librarymail.co.uk

To: francis@thainet.com

Re: Sawadee Krub – Greetings from Thailand!

Friday ...

Hi Dad,

Thanks for the warning about the shell thing. Sounds like mum is keeping busy, as usual. How is your head after the coconut incident?

I expect she has got that dog moved in with you by now – it will be in your bed while you are consigned to sleeping on a mat on the floor, before you know it!

It sounds like it's a good job you held off on buying one of those apartments, though I know Mum really liked the thought of your very own little place in the sun. If you both still want to do that, then something better will turn up. Mum always says that things happen for a reason, doesn't she!

> All is well with the wedding prep, thanks. We
> are both really looking forward to relaxing on
> our honeymoon in the sun ...

At least I hoped Jonathon was looking forward to our honeymoon as much as he said he was. I knew that a beach holiday wouldn't have been his first choice and that a city break, somewhere with museums, historical sites and more upmarket restaurants would be more his cup of tea. But there was the tin mining museum, up in Kathu I think – I'd have to check that – which I thought would be interesting. We could incorporate it with a trip to the Kathu waterfall – this was supposed to be the best time of the year to visit that. Maybe we could also spend one night at the Indigo Pearl, a lovely hotel in the area. It was just a good job we were not going to be there in October, as there was supposed to be some sort of vegetarian festival in Kathu and I could see my mother having a field day and making us all go along.

I really hoped that Jonathon wasn't just going along with the Thai plans to keep me happy. It was easy to see the pattern both our sets of parents had followed. James would clearly do anything for a quiet life and Joyce pretty much ruled the roost, with her ladies' groups and her strong opinions on floral prints, Royal Worcester and what constitutes an ideal daughter-in-law – which was pretty much anything other than me. My meat-loving dad would let my mum get away with the vegetarian equivalent of murder as long as she was happy. Were he and James happy in their own rights, though? Or were they happy because their wives told them they were?

And was that going to be us in thirty years' time? What a scary thought. I would have to do something about that, but there wasn't time to think about it right then because the library was about to be over-run with little people. There was however, just time for a quick energy boost, courtesy of the fun size Mars Bar in my handbag, and half a mug of instant coffee to wash it down.

It was just five minutes from closing time, and Jonathon was on his way to pick me up, when Joyce came bustling through the door. I did my best to look pleased to see her, but her timing could have been better – I had been about to slap on a bit of fresh lipstick and run a brush through my hair. I hadn't wanted to look quite so much like someone who had spent the afternoon trying to get a group of hyperactive three and four year olds to calm down and listen to *Story & Rhyme Time,* when my lovely man arrived. But no such luck.

'Hello, Stella dear,' she glanced around – I don't know what she was expecting to find in an about-to-close-for-the-day village library – evidence of cock fighting? Gun running? A weekend crack cocaine factory being hurriedly assembled? 'Have all your eager readers gone for the day?'

I was about to answer when Jonathon came through

the door. 'Hello, you two!' He kissed my cheek and then his mother's. 'I thought that was you, Mum. What are you doing here?'

'I just wanted to have a little chat with Stella, dear. I've got a surprise for her – a treat for tomorrow.'

'Have you?' Jonathon asked, as he and I exchanged curious glances. Well, he looked curious. I felt as if I'd just been invited to put on my most Christian outfit and go and pet the lions at the Coliseum.

'Yes, dear. Why? You don't have anything important planned for tomorrow morning, do you?' She clearly took our silence as acquiescence to her plan. 'Ten thirty. Sharp,' she added for my benefit. I'd once had the temerity to be a couple of minutes late, meeting her back at the car park after a shopping trip in Southampton, and now I clearly couldn't be trusted to be anywhere on time ever again. Any arrangement that involved being somewhere at a certain time always ended up with an extra instruction, just for me, to be there on time and not keep everyone waiting. As if I were a naughty five year old. 'Oh, and do wear something nice, Stella.' Of course, because God forbid I should turn up looking like a sack of King Edwards, as I obviously normally did. Maybe I should see if I could find my old *Cat in the Hat* costume and wear that. I could just picture her face. Although, I could also imagine the comments she wouldn't be able to stop herself making on how tight it was – that was even if I could do it up after all this time – so, then again, probably best not.

'Well, Mum, we'll see you in the morning then.' Jonathon looked at his watch. 'Stella and I are off to the cinema, so we'll have to go now, or we will end up being those annoying people who wander in after the film's started.'

As I darted behind the counter to get my bag, I found Joyce, like a particularly annoying shadow, at my elbow. *What now, for God's sake? Was she going to nag me about the fat content of popcorn? Instruct me to do bottom clenches whilst sitting through the film in the hope of tightening up my flabby rear end? Veto kissing in the back row as unladylike behaviour and not fitting for a future Hazard?*

'You know, Stella dear,' Joyce stage whispered to me, looking at my hair with what was clearly thinly disguised disapproval. 'If I were you, I would keep a little comb in my handbag, and maybe some lipstick. Then you could have a quick freshen up before Jonathon comes to pick you up from work.'

I wondered if she could hear my teeth grinding. It was on the tip of my tongue to say that I had just been about to do that when she'd turned up and interrupted me, when she added, 'You can get quite handy little handbag size bottles of scent nowadays, too.'

Great! I thought. Now, according to my future mother-in-law, not only do I look like a dog's chewed up and spat out dinner, apparently I smell like it, too. Brilliant. Wonderful, Fan-bloody-tastic!

Chapter Twelve

Jonathon

It must have been halfway into the film and I still didn't have a clue what was going on. My mind just wouldn't stop going round and round on a loop. Those blasted Sitwells had been on my back all day long and their grating voices just wouldn't get out of my head.

Firstly, I had made them an appointment to look at a stunning five-bed property just outside the village of Beaulieu. It was more than perfect. I had called and let them know about it mid-week, as soon as the place had become available for viewings. Mrs Sitwell had been very excited, if the squeal that had nearly shattered my eardrum down the phone was anything to go by. She'd demanded that I show it to nobody else until they had seen it as it sounded "perfect". I couldn't believe we might actually be in agreement on something. I should have recognised the kiss of death the moment I heard the P word.

They had arrived forty five minutes late and hadn't even bothered to apologise, which hadn't put the newly widowed, septuagenarian vendor in the best of moods. Then, with her stiletto heels click clacking against the beautiful parquet floors, they'd marched all over the house as if they already owned it, loudly proclaiming how they would have to rip out this, move that, and pull down the other. Of course, a three-year-old would have known what they were up to, claiming there were so many things they would need to do to the property to bring it up to the required standard, in order to put in a lower offer. The lemon the vendor looked as if she was sucking seemed to be getting more and more sour by the minute. Her steel grey hair was matched by a steeliness in her eyes that had me cringing inside as I tried to smooth things over with her. But by the time I managed to get them out of there, I knew, in no uncertain terms that there was no offer on earth that the Sitwells could make on this house that would ever be accepted. They had pompously assumed that Mrs Henson, a retired Justice of the Peace and mother of the local constabulary's chief inspector, was just some gaga old lady who was downsizing because she needed the money. In their ignorance and arrogance they'd completely shot themselves in both feet.

The second property I'd had to show them was nearer to Brockenhurst. If the Sitwells had noticed that the places I was showing them were getting further and further away from the Netley villages, they hadn't said anything, so I guessed they hadn't, as they certainly weren't in the habit of keeping their opinions to themselves. They almost couldn't be bothered going to view it, as they were so gung ho about the Beaulieu place but, knowing that that was never going to happen, I'd started pushing the desirability of the Brockenhurst one's thatched roof and the private area of parkland attached. They had paid it scant attention as they'd wandered through its spacious rooms. Even the huge walk in wardrobe, complete with rotating shoe cupboard had failed to elicit the response I would normally have expected.

The third property I had taken them to see, I'd done so with my tongue firmly in my cheek. The guide price on this seven-bed country house, set in nine acres, in Emery Down had been three quarters of a million over and above the budget they'd given me. Hazard's has never been one of those estate agents where people were automatically shown homes only at the top end of, or a little above their price ranges, in the hopes of seducing the buyers into spending more than they were originally planning to. But this was an incredibly modern property, and it had occurred to me that it might be an idea to show them around something that they might not want to rip apart and change.

She had fallen in love with the place before she even got out of the car. He was too busy calculating how low his offer for the Beaulieu house could be, to give it more than a cursory glance. It was the first time I had ever seen them disagree. The wife pouting, the husband snarling, I had never been happier to see the back of them.

Except that once I was back at the office they kept on phoning. First it was her, telling me how much she loved the third property and how I mustn't show it to *anyone* else, while she made her husband see that it was the *only* house for them. Then it was him, with his more than insulting offer for the first one. Then her again, then him again. Then her again, then him again. By the end of the afternoon, I was wishing that I'd decided against following Dad into the family business and chosen a career as a traffic warden, or a tax inspector. Right then, a career of being the person who dons the latex gloves and does the cavity searches at the airport seemed an improvement on this one.

The one positive thing that I had managed to accomplish today was booking us a couple of tickets to see *Warhorse*. It seemed that I'd been panicking unnecessarily about the restricted view thing, and I'd been able to get a couple of cancellations, so the seats we'd got were better than the ones which I would have booked if I had just gone ahead and bought them when I looked anyway. I knew Stella was going to be thrilled and I planned on telling her after the film. I was thinking we could make a little weekend trip of it. It would be so good to get away, just the two of us. We could get the train up to London on the Saturday morning, have a nice meal, do a bit of pre-wedding, or pre-honeymoon shopping, and see the show. And then maybe on Sunday we could go to Regents' Park or the Serpentine or something like that, have a nice lunch there and get an evening train back.

I glanced at Stella, her full attention on the screen, her small tub of popcorn on her lap, barely touched, chuckling away at what must have been a funny scene that

I'd completely missed. She has always had a very sexy chuckle. It was one of the first things I noticed about her, that and the way her smile lit up everything around her, even dressed up in her sexy *Cat in the Hat* costume. And how many women could carry that off? Not that she's ever believed me when I've told her that. Stella must be the least vain woman I've ever met. As well as being the sexiest. And the most caring.

How much more of this film was there? I found myself wishing that we'd got seats on the back row. I leaned in to her and helped myself to some popcorn.

'I thought you didn't want any,' she mouthed, holding the tub out to me to offer me more, one eye still on the screen.

'It's not really your popcorn I'm after,' I whispered in her ear, starting her off chuckling again. 'How much longer does this film go on for?'

'It's about half way through …'

'We could always guess the ending ... Or make up our own …'

Two women sitting in front of us turned round. One shushed and glared at us while the other just glared. Without another word, Stella grinned, handed one of them her popcorn, and we both shuffled, as quietly as we could, out of our seats.

The door barely closed behind us, the dimly lit corridor all but deserted, I pulled my gorgeous girl to me for a kiss.

'Mmmmmm,' Stella mumbled after we came up for air. 'Let's go home ...'

'No, I've got a much better idea,' I told her, grabbing her hand. We rushed down to the lobby, out of the building and towards where I'd parked the car.

'Are you thinking what I think you're thinking?' Stella gasped, as we jumped in and yanked the doors shut.

'I don't know ... You'll just have to wait and see, won't you ...'

It was ages since we'd been to our special place, a secluded little thicket of New Forest trees with a stream running through, just far enough off the beaten track for us not to be bothered by dog walkers, just the odd, inquisitive pony. And most of those had no interest in us at all. It hadn't been long after we'd started dating that we'd gone for a perfectly innocent picnic on a summer's day pretty much like this one, and ended up having al fresco sex for the first time. I don't know who'd been the most surprised that day, the usually straight laced estate agent, or the shy librarian. Neither of us had ever done that before, but we had been back a few times since. And I've always kept that picnic rug in the boot, just in case.

Grabbing the rug, I took Stella's hand and we weaved our way through the branches, avoiding the patches of gorse that had become our friends, because they kept our place private. There was an indent in the ground, between two trees, with ferns and then a gorse bush behind it, and the stream in front. It was where Stella had laid out our picnic blanket that first time and it was just like an outdoor four poster bed. I couldn't think why we didn't come here more often when the weather was good enough. We really should. We really, really should.

Stella took the rug from me and shook it out on the ground, while I started unbuttoning her shirt. Thank God she was wearing a skirt and not jeans; that made it so much easier. She turned to face me, she was wearing my favourite bra – a lacy front fastener – it was almost as if she'd known.

We pulled each other down onto the rug and she started unbuckling my belt, while I reached for that clasp. One twist and I had my hands full. I buried my face, inhaling the scent of the orange blossom body lotion she wore, and the crap day that I'd had just melted away. This estate agent was a very happy man.

Chapter Thirteen

Stella

I needed to go to the loo, but didn't want to wake Jonathon and, untwining my legs from his, and pulling my arm out from under him, however gently, would be sure to. My skin was still tingling. First, the forest – a thrill has always run through me whenever I think of us there, half naked – what if some lost hiker were to stumble across us! Then, the shower – all hot, soapy and slippery. And then the bed, where we'd finally managed to exhaust ourselves. Three times in one night – not what anyone would expect from a book worm librarian and a country estate agent.

And he'd surprised me with tickets to see *Warhorse*. I would have thought it was all booked up months in advance, but my clever, thoughtful fiancé had managed it. I couldn't wait for our little London mini break. And if we got a really early train on the Saturday morning and then the latest one we could get back on the Sunday evening, it would be almost two whole wonderful days, just the two of us. And none of this you-know-who trying to force a "suitable" timetable on us and telling us how we were doing everything wrong, and how she would be doing it if she were us. A happy little sigh escaped my lips. Although, right at that moment, I'd be even happier if I could get to the bathroom!

Jonathon made a contented little snuffling sound in his sleep. He had slipped from sizzling sex god to slumbering teddy bear in a very short space of time, almost as if someone had flicked a switch. How did he do that? I reached a finger down and toyed with a sweat dampened lock of hair, curling on the side of his neck, just behind his ear. The greedy half of me hoped he would wake up and want to go for a fourth round. The other half, probably the half which included my bladder, wanted him to stay asleep so I could untangle myself and get to the bathroom. It was starting to get urgent now.

I managed to co-ordinate the retrieval of my arm with the next snuffle, tilting him ever so slightly away from me. Unfortunately, the sweat which had stuck our tangled legs together now seemed to have dried like superglue, and not the sort you buy in the cheap shops that doesn't live up to its title. No, this was like the sort they advertised by attaching someone to the wing of an aeroplane and watching them get flown around without falling off. This felt like the sort that caused people to have to go to hospital to have bits of semi-repaired ornaments detached from their hands with special solvents. It was going to play havoc with the hairs on Jonathon's legs. And the skin on mine.

At the next snuffle, I tried a little gentle prising and had to stifle a yelp. The one excruciating time Alli and I had experimented with leg waxing it had felt something like this – except that Alli and I had been able to numb the pain with a vast quantity of Pinot Grigio and, tonight, not a drop of alcohol had passed my lips. I tossed the lightweight duvet aside to survey the damage.

What was the name of that game where you had to pick up straws, or sticks from a dropped bundle, without disturbing any of the others? *Jack Straws*? *Pick Up Sticks*? How had two pairs of legs turned into a giant, *Krypton Factor* style game of that? With added, extra sticky Velcro, just to make it even more fun.

The urge for the loo was pressing now. I decided to give it one more go before giving in and waking him up. The notion that, after a few years, or maybe even months, of marriage, I would be waking him up without even giving it a second thought, flitted across my mind. But after the three good times he'd just shown me, I thought he deserved a good sleep. So I pressed down on the skin on the inner side of my right lower thigh and started to peel it, as gently as possible, from Jonathon's knee. So far so good. It was just Sod's Law that he decided to turn over in his sleep at just that moment and take all plans of gentle peeling right out of my hands.

I squealed. He awoke with a yell, probably thinking we were being attacked by burglars. Jumping up off the bed, taking the top layer of skin from my right shin with him, he grabbed the first thing to hand, which was the bedside lamp. Standing there, holding it out, he looked like a rather confused, naked, male version of the Statue of Liberty.

After one of those freeze-frame moments, we both found ourselves vibrating with laughter. And I only just made it to the bathroom in time.

An hour or so later, Jonathon was fast asleep again and I still wasn't. So I opened my laptop, checked my emails and read Mum's latest one.

From: astrid@thainet.com

To: stellamoon@librarymail.co.uk

Subject: **Re: Greetings from Mum and Dad!**

Friday ...

Hello Stella darling,

We've been having such a busy time of it here. You know I've been helping Tasanee out with her Thai cooking classes. Well, I forgot to tell you that the other day we had a girl with a nut allergy like yours, learning how to make Pad Thai. The poor thing didn't like to make a fuss, so she cooked it with the nuts in it and then couldn't eat it of course, so I helped her make another one without them so she didn't go hungry and she wolfed it down. Anyway she must have really enjoyed herself, because today a load of others from her holiday apartment building came along and booked classes, so we're going to put on a couple of extra ones — Tasanee is really pleased. I'm having a great time doing it, it's such fun! You and Jonathon will have to give it a go when you come out. You'll love it. And then, when you get back to the UK you'll be able to make all your favourite dishes without having to resort to packets of readymade seasoning mix!

Your father's been in a bit of a grump at the moment because we've got a dog staying with us. The poor old thing nearly sliced his foot off (the dog, not your father) on some jagged glass, so somebody's got to look after him. He's already lost an eye. He's an endearing little chap, with long floppy ears and a determined look in his remaining eye.

Talking of your father, Thaksin's been teaching him wood carving between mending sun loungers and things. He's making you and Jonathon something as a surprise (your father, not Thaksin) but I don't know what it is yet. Anyway, I just thought I'd warn you so you can practice looking delighted when he gives it to you.

I hope all the wedding prep is going well. The not so reverent Reverend Marianne sounds lovely, though I can't imagine Joyce being happy about a woman vicar marrying you and Jonathon! Please let your father and I know if there is anything we can do to help, won't you? Anything at all!

Give our love to Jonathon,

Bye for now,

Love from Mum and Dad xxx

Hmm, I thought, was there anything they *could* do to help? Short of one of them flying back here, kidnapping Joyce, taking her back to Thailand and keeping her with them until the wedding, I couldn't think of anything really.

Jonathon gave a gentle snore next to me while my finger wavered between logging off, and clicking on Solitaire or Patience for a game or two to relax me before trying to doze off again. It was alright for him, fast asleep at half past two in the morning, without a care in the world. He could sleep peacefully. He didn't have to come on Joyce's mysterious surprise in the morning – apparently it was to be *just us girls*. Kill me now. Please.

I shuddered to myself as I logged off, got out of bed and tiptoed back out of the bedroom and down to the kitchen. Maybe some warm milk and honey would help. I doubted it but it was worth a try. God only knew what horrors my torturer had in store for me – Golf lessons perhaps, dressed in some hideous diamond-patterned plus four type outfit? Having my jaws wired so I could fit into a smaller wedding dress – of her choice – and be less of an embarrassment to her in front of her friends? I couldn't really imagine it would have anything to do with leg waxing, but I honestly wouldn't put anything past Ma Hazard. Whatever her plans though, unless I could contract a mysterious illness in the next few hours, I would find out in the morning. At ten thirty. Sharp. Oh ... and wearing something *nice*.

Chapter Fourteen

Stella

'It is *so* not funny!' I threw a cushion from the sofa at Jonathon, whose lips were twitching as he tried not to laugh out loud. I aimed for his head.

'Oh, go on, Stella,' he caught the cushion easily and risked getting another one chucked at him by adding, 'it is a *little* bit funny.'

'One of them offered me a shampoo and set,' I squeaked in indignation. '*A shampoo and set!*' I squeaked again, about an octave higher, when I clocked the baffled expression on his face. Did my future husband not know anything about women?

'But isn't that just another way of saying wash and blow dry?' My clueless fiancé shrugged. Apparently not, then.

'Yes, if you're an elderly lady with a blue rinse and a poodle perm.' I picked up the next cushion as menacingly as I could. 'Are you suggesting that I look like I'm ready for a little old lady makeover?'

'God no,' he chuckled, ducking as my second missile flew past his ear and hit the wall behind him, falling to the floor with a pathetic little flump.

'Five minutes in that place and I wanted to 'mace'

the so-called stylist, with a can of their extra-strength, hurricane-proof, helmet-hair lacquer. Ten minutes and I was seriously thinking about running into the barber's place next door and having him shave all my hair off, just so I could use baldness as an excuse to get out of there ...'

'But how would your veil stay on?' Jonathon interrupted. 'Wouldn't it just slide off a shiny bald head?' The love of my life really did seem to have a death wish today. 'I suppose you could glue it in place, like they do with false beards and moustaches and things in the theatre. Or you could have bought a wig, I suppose. Or you could get a whole range of them and then you could have a different hair style every day ...'

I picked up the last cushion and, not wanting to risk missing him this time, marched over and biffed him as hard as I could on the head with it.

'Ouch,' he laughed, edging away from me ever so slightly, holding up the first cushion like a kind of droopy shield. 'I hope this isn't a hint of things to come. I've heard about women like that – they start off playfully whacking their men with the soft furnishings and then they move on to the crockery. Then the next thing you know, there are knives flying about and frying pan-shaped dents appearing in the backs of those poor, unsuspecting husbands' heads ...'

'Oh, don't worry, love,' I said sweetly. 'I'll give you plenty of warning first.' I didn't bother to add that the way I had felt, coming out of that hairdressing house of

74

horrors, I would be more likely to aim missiles in his mother's direction than his. And there wouldn't have been anything soft about them. He might not have seen the funny side of it. Although right at that moment, I wasn't so sure that I'd have been joking.

Jonathon eased my fingers from the last cushion, edged me towards the sofa and sat me down.

I mean, what on earth had Joyce been thinking of, I fumed silently, dragging me along to talk wedding hairstyles at a hairdressers that had probably been old fashioned when Princess Anne got married? Was there any aspect of our wedding that she wasn't going to try and mess up for us?

He sat slightly behind me, on the arm rest, and started to rub my shoulders. It was going to take a lot more than that to calm me down. She had already had her choice of the reception venue (her golf club), the catering *and* the cake (her ladies' lunch club, including one lady who had just done a Wilton cake decorating course and was keen to show off her newly honed skills), the flowers (her church flower ladies), and most of the hymns. Now it seemed she wanted to make me look like a 1970s' horsey princess.

I felt his fingers brush the back of my neck. Yeah, nice try, mister, but I was so not in the mood. So far, Alli and I had managed to keep her away from the dress fittings, but she had tried, oh so many times, and with varying degrees of subtlety and, well ... no subtlety at all, to muscle her way in on those too.

One of his hands started to wind its way into my hair. And then stopped. That would be all I needed – her standing there, commenting on my size and my choice of style, and how my choice of style would emphasise the apparent enormousness of my size. And all the while she would be smugly reminding us all, ad infinitum, how she had a twenty-one inch waist the day she got married. Well bully for her.

I felt a tug as Jonathon tried to pull his hand out of my hair. Then another one, this time taking my head back with it.

'Ouch! What are you ...'

'What the hell have they done to you?' He put his other hand to my head to keep it still while he tried to retrieve the first one.

'Do you *still* think it's funny?' I grumbled, my head going back and forth like one of those stupid nodding dog ornaments. Suddenly I caught sight of our reflections in the TV screen and a snort of laughter burst through my grumbling.

'It sounds like I'm not the only one!' He tilted my head back and started planting little kisses on my forehead, while he wriggled and teased his fingers out of the birds' nest of backcombed and lacquered straw my hair had been turned into. The steam coming out of my ears must have been a dead giveaway that he was about to get a sharp elbow in the ribs.

'It's going to take more than a few pecks on the forehead to ...' I started to say before the breath was knocked out of me by him rolling off the arm rest and onto my lap, a bit like somebody mounting a horse for the first time, or ... 'You look like you're about to give me a lap dance,' I giggled.

'Only too happy to oblige!' Jonathon reached behind him for the remote for the iPod dock, fiddling about with it for a moment until Joe Cocker's *You Can Leave Your Hat On,* came ringing out of the speakers. Slowly, in time with the music, he started pulling his t-shirt, playfully, up and down, up and down, a little higher each time, then up and over his head, before tossing it across the room. My hands reached out to stroke the thin line of hair that ran down from his chest, at the same time as his reached to slide down the straps of my dress.

'Er ... I thought it was the person on the lap that took their clothes off, not ...'

'That's the old fashioned way.' He put his finger briefly to my lips to silence me. 'This is how they do it in all the most exclusive lap dancing clubs now.'

'Oh, is it? And you'd know that how, exactly?' I chuckled, picturing my sensitive fiancé in a lap dancing establishment, red faced and not knowing where to look, whilst I wriggled to help him with the dress. 'So we take it in turns, do we, Mr Exclusive Lap Dancing Club Expert?'

The dress came off over my head with a flourish

and went flying after the t-shirt.

'Hmm,' Jonathon mumbled. 'Nice bra. Even nicer than yesterday's' He ran his fingers over the coral satin, sending goose pimple fireworks rocketing through me.

'Uh uh,' I slapped his hand away. 'If we're taking it in turns then it's your turn now.' I leaned back and watched in anticipation as his hand went to his belt buckle. 'And the belt on its own doesn't count. It comes off with the jeans.'

'Are you sure about that?'

'Off with the jeans!' I commanded. 'Off! Off! Off! Off! Off!'

Jonathon knelt up while he undid his jeans and slowly pulled them down towards his knees, then he leant forward and gave me a long, passionate kiss, before hefting himself to standing position. I tugged them down to his ankles and he shook out first his right foot, then his left. Then he picked up the jeans, knelt back down and made a lasso motion with them, round and round, above his head.

He was about to hurl them over the back of the sofa, towards where I'd thrown my dress, when he froze, his face white, his jeans flopping down over my head like elongated denim rabbit ears

'Dad!' he yelped, dropping back down on to me, horror now splashed in bright red across his face. 'What are you doing here?'

Chapter Fifteen

Jonathon

'Er, Mum ...' I went to take a sip of the scalding hot tea that she'd just poured for me, later that evening, and stopped myself just in time. Looking out of the window, trying to look nonchalant, I prayed that nothing would happen to shorten Dad's game of golf and bring him home while I was still here. The picture of his face burned into my mind, making it hard to remember how I had decided to word what I was about to say. I put the cup down and then found that I'd picked it straight back up again.

'How about a nice piece of home-made treacle tart with that?' Mum had a tea plate and a cake fork in front of me before I had even opened my mouth to say yes. It was too busy watering at the smell of her *pièce de résistance*, and my childhood favourite. Crisp, crumbly pastry and just the right gooiness, just the right sweetness filling. I couldn't tear my eyes away as she cut a picture perfect triangle and slid it onto my plate. Someone had given me a piece of shop bought treacle tart once, at a school-friend's house – the pastry had felt like soggy, thick, tasteless cardboard in my mouth, and the filling had been sickly sweet with a vaguely chemical after taste. I think that had been the first time I had realised what a good home cook my mother was.

'Thanks.' I inhaled the rich aroma of cooked golden syrup and breadcrumbs. I knew exactly what was in it – I'd seen her make it enough times throughout my childhood.

'Well we can't have you wasting away,' she added, as she moved the cream jug, like an over-sized chess piece, across the table towards me. She sat down. 'I'm sure you're not eating properly. You work hard, Jonathon; you need a few more home cooked meals inside you. I did offer to give Stella some cookery lessons and teach her how to make all your favourite dishes, but of course, she wants to do everything her own way. And it's such a stressful time for you, what with the wedding just three weeks away and all the preparations so far behind. I can't believe you're not more worried about how slowly everything is progressing.

'And I wouldn't have thought this was the best time to go swanning off up to London for fancy theatre weekends. Still,' she sniffed, 'you and Stella must do as you think best. Your father and I haven't been to the theatre in donkeys' years. It might have been nice if the four of us could have gone up as a family. I could have taken Stella shopping in the West End. And you and your father could have gone to a nice museum or something ... That reminds me, your father tells me that you've got some dreadful client and his, what did he call her, his "trophy wife", who keep coming down from London and trying to turn people out of their homes. Is that true?'

Was my mother trying to put me in hospital? For a brief moment, I completely understood how Stella felt after spending time with her. I nearly choked on one mouthful of pie at the thought of Stella putting up with my mother trying to give her cookery lessons. Then, a second mouthful nearly went down the wrong way at the thought of my mother and Stella going shopping together anywhere, let alone the West End of London. And that was without even mentioning the mental image my mother had just put in my head, of the Sitwells arriving in one of the villages in an armoured tank, shouting eviction orders through matching loud hailers – designer ones of course. And what did my father know about trophy wives?

Right now though, I really didn't want to think about what my dad knew about anything other than the things we expect our dad's to know about, like the safest way to change the blade in the lawn mower, or the best route to drive from A to B without using any motorways, a Sat Nav or a map.

No, the subject of the Sitwells was one Dad and I had managed to not talk about at work at all. One of the perks of his easing himself into retirement I supposed. Linda would be passing on as much as she felt he might need or want to know. And I didn't even want to think about that ghastly couple right now, either. All I wanted was to concentrate on keeping the peace between Mum

81

and Stella in the run up to the wedding, and Mum wasn't making it easy. Taking Stella shopping indeed! I decided I wouldn't mention that idea to Stella. After the disastrous morning they'd had at the hairdressers, the thought of another trip with my mother might make my future wife decide that marrying me really wasn't worth all this trouble after all.

'Actually, Mum...' I washed down my mouthful of pie with a gulp of tea, 'it was the wedding I wanted to talk to you about.'

'Well, you know me, Jonathon, anything I can do to help. It's not as if Stella's parents are here, and Stella doesn't seem to have much of an idea about what she wants or ...'

'Well ... actually,' I dived in, half expecting to be told off for interrupting, but doing it anyway, 'Stella does have some good ideas, really good ideas. The thing is ... well ... they are quite different from yours, and ... she doesn't want to hurt your feelings, so she ends up not saying anything ...'

'Well, I'm sure I'd be the last person to force unwanted advice on anyone.' My mother literally bristled. If she were a cat, her fur would have stood so far on end she would have tripled in size. She picked up the teapot and topped up her cup which was still full from when she'd poured it in the first place. 'If she doesn't want any help from me, she only has to say so ...'

'No, Mum! She does want your help – we both do.'

I was beginning to wish I hadn't started this conversation; it seemed to be making things worse rather than better. 'It's just that ... well ... things like that trip to the hairdressers this morning ...'

'Don't remind me, Jonathon!' Mum huffed. 'Anyone would have thought I was forcing the girl to have a root canal, rather than spend a perfectly pleasant hour or so getting bridal hair advice from an expert ...'

'Well ...'

'Stella was most ungrateful, Jonathon, *most* ungrateful. She doesn't seem to care what she's going to look like on the day. I just dread to think what sort of dress she's chosen, as she's seen fit to exclude me from having anything to do with it ...'

'But ...'

'I blame that mother of hers, with all her hippy dippy ideas. It wouldn't surprise me in the least if Stella turned up to get married in a cheesecloth kaftan and flip flops, with a daisy-chain in her hair.'

'It's not that she's ungrateful, Mum.' I managed to get a few words in as soon as she paused for breath. 'Really. It's just that ... well ... the place you took her to this morning ... it was a bit ...'

'A bit what?' My mother's right eyebrow shot up in a way I remembered from when she'd given one of my school teachers a dressing down after I'd received a B minus for some piece of work I'd done.

'Er ... a bit ... a little bit ... old fashioned?' It

suddenly hit me that I was criticising the very place my mother had always gone to have her own hair done, for as long as I could remember. 'Not in a bad way,' I rushed on, 'just a bit ... mature? For someone in their twenties?' *Mature!* That was a better word! Why couldn't I have thought of *mature* before I said *old fashioned*?

My mother wasn't looking any less cross. 'I mean ... your hair always looks really lovely ... but how you have it wouldn't really suit someone of Stella's age, would it?' I thought I heard a trace of a "humph" in the silence that followed, but I probably imagined it. Still, at least that eyebrow had gone back down again.

'What about Cordelia?' I blurted out, whilst wondering where the hell that had come from. Stella had her own friends; she didn't need me foisting my old family ones on her. Especially ones she wasn't all that comfortable with, even if I didn't really understand why.

'Oh, Cordelia always looks exquisite, even when she's been out with the horses and wearing a riding hat all day.' My mother looked wistful and half of me wished that I'd kept my mouth shut. But then, I was sure Stella would be happy enough to have a quick chat about wedding stuff with Cordelia if it meant she didn't have to put up with my mother rolling up and telling her what to do.

'Maybe you could ask Cordelia where she gets her hair done?' I didn't know where that had come from either. I certainly hadn't been planning on suggesting that at all. But if I could just get Cordelia to act as a sort of buffer between Mum and Stella, then maybe there would be a few less ruffled feathers. And maybe we could make it to our wedding day without either of the women in my life trying to throttle each other after all.

I could but hope.

Chapter Sixteen

Joyce

Of course, I rang Cordelia the moment Jonathon left to go back to Stella's. There was no answer, so she was probably still out giving riding lessons or something. She works so hard at that stable of hers. I left her a message, telling her it was to do with Jonathon's wedding and asking her to call me back.

Everything felt so much clearer as I put down the phone and went to make a fresh pot of tea. How clever of Jonathon! Cordelia was the obvious answer. She was practically the same age as Stella, but much more with it and stylish, very much more on the ball. Yes, Stella would listen to her.

How silly of me, not to have thought of her myself. And how clever of Jonathon. There was no day dreaming, dawdling, and dithering about with Cordelia. She got things done and she got them done efficiently.

I remembered an incident with a lame horse once. There hadn't been any of that sentimental hand wringing about what to do, which there would have been with Stella. Cordelia knew exactly what had to be done. The horse had to be shot, before it suffered any more. She just picked up the gun she was handed and pulled the trigger.

Yes, Cordelia would be the person to help me. She'd be the perfect person to help me sort out Stella. I couldn't imagine why I hadn't thought of her myself.

Chapter Seventeen

Stella

It was Sunday, and I was cooking lunch at my place. Alli and her boyfriend, Harry, were coming and Jonathon's best man, Rupert, might or might not be bringing his current squeeze. And nobody was going to end up in hospital with anaphylactic shock, or anything else.

'Mmm, something smells gorgeous,' Jonathon sniffed the air as he came in through the kitchen door and started moving things about in the fridge to make room for the three bottles of white wine he'd had tucked under his arm. I finished putting the cutlery out. 'Roast chicken, your fabulous roasties and cauliflower cheese – my favourites.' He kissed me. 'They smell almost as good as you.' He gave my ear lobe a little nibble. 'No orange dress today?' He gave a laugh, tinged with an embarrassed cringe that looked exactly like what I could feel my face doing.

'I can never wear that dress anywhere around your parents again! Well, at least not your father anyway. You don't think he would tell your mother about it, do you?' I pulled a handful of the eco-friendly, unbleached, chorine free, compostable napkins my mother had bought me on her last trip back, out of their equally eco-friendly wrapping. They weren't the most attractive things.

'No. She'd have let me know last night, or at breakfast this morning if Dad had said anything. He doesn't tell her everything, you know – he's not as under her thumb as she thinks he is – she knows nothing about the little whisky collection he keeps stashed behind the lawn mower in the shed. Or the nuts and toffees he's got hidden in an old *Quality Street* tin in there that she thinks is full of old washers and nails and stuff...'

'I thought he was always very scrupulous about cleaning the grass box every time he mowed the lawns,' I giggled. Good for James. I was glad he had a harmless but enjoyable secret or two of his own.

'Anyway, back to that dress. I was thinking you should bring it on our honeymoon ...'

'Oh yes? And next time we can embarrass ourselves in front of *my* dad instead of yours?'

'Your parents won't have a key to our room will they?' Jonathon looked almost as horrified as he had the day before. 'Your mum and the notion of boundaries have only ever had a fleeting acquaintance, haven't they?'

Luckily I didn't have to answer that, with what might, or might not be the truth, because the doorbell rang. 'That'll be Rupes and ... er ...' he looked at me blankly.

'Don't look at me,' I shrugged. 'He's got a different girl with him every time I see him. How am I supposed to keep up with all their names?'

Jonathon went to open the door while I put a napkin in each place and imagined the expression on Joyce's face if I had insisted on using these at the reception instead of the fancy three ply, colour co-ordinated ones she had ordered. He came back with Alli, who had a box of mille-feuille from my, and her, favourite cake shop in Wintertown in her hands. Harry, her boyfriend, was carrying a couple of bottles of Pinot Grigio, and a solitary Rupert was carrying his jacket and wearing a slightly bemused expression. It must have been the first time I had ever seen Rupert without a girl at his side and, by the look on Alli's face, I could see she was thinking the exact same thing. It felt a bit like seeing just one half of *Ant and Dec*. 'Rupes is flying solo today,' Jonathon grinned, 'seeing as he forgot who he'd invited and went to pick up the wrong girl.'

'*Mea Culpa.*' Rupert had the grace to look sheepish as he whipped out a bottle of white port from under his jacket. Then he went and ruined the effect by winking like a pantomime baddy at Jonathon and Harry.

Alli and I just shook our heads. It didn't make much difference to the food, as most of Rupert's female friends only toyed with tiny portions anyway, before handing back plates that were virtually as full as when I'd dished them out in the first place. We shooed the men into the lounge as Alli did some more moving about of things in the fridge and slotted Rupert's port and her cake box carefully in. I poured us both a drink.

'So,' she clinked her glass against mine. 'Shampoo and set, eh! Did they ask you if you wanted a blue rinse and a special offer on hair nets, too?'

'Don't,' I winced, taking a big mouthful of wine and glugging it back. I had already promised Jonathon that I wouldn't tell Alli about his dad catching us yesterday until another time when he wasn't around. He did not want Rupert getting hold of it – there was far too much Stag night ammunition there for a man of Jonathon's sensitive middle class up-bringing to cope with. 'The only good thing to come out of yesterday was that I know for sure now that I don't want some fancy up-do. And nobody, not even Ma Hazard pointing a gun to my head, is going to get me to have one.'

'Good for you,' Alli grinned. 'Your future monster-in-law is getting far too good at telling you what to do. You really need to put your foot down with a firm hand.'

'But gently,' I countered. 'The last thing Jonathon needs is an atmosphere between his mother and me.'

'Okay, so firmly but gently. Oh, and diplomatically,' Alli added.

'Diplomatic is my middle name,' I rolled my eyes. 'It's had to be ...'

'Mind you,' Alli giggled, 'you did have plenty of practice, growing up with your mum's nut roasts and lentil stews. And what was that disgusting thing she made once when I was staying over?'

'Do you mean the couscous cake?' I shuddered at

91

the memory of the horrific birthday cake concoction my mother had made me one year out of couscous and vegan gelatine.

'Oh God!' Alli exclaimed, 'I'd forgotten about that. That was even worse than the green sludgy thing I was thinking of. We were hiding handfuls of it all over the place. Do you remember?'

'And I had to go round the house and find it all and get rid of it after everybody left, before Mum realised what we'd done. It took me ages to flush it all down the loo, and even then I kept worrying that some of it was going to float back up and give the game away.' We both laughed.

'Nice napkins, by the way,' my best friend grimaced at me. 'A present from your mum by any chance?'

Everyone was sitting at the table and I'd just dished up the last of the hot from sitting on top of the stove plates, when we heard a tap tap tap at the kitchen window.

'Hello,' trilled Cordelia, 'is anybody home?' Great. That was all I needed. 'Oh, goodie, you *are* in.' She slid through the slightly open back door like a slender cat who'd smelled the freshly cooked chicken. 'Oh, I'm so sorry,' she dimpled round the table, looking anything but. 'I'm disturbing your lunch.'

'Come on in,' I did my best to sound welcoming rather than sarcastic, seeing as she was already in. 'Would you like some chicken and cauliflower cheese?'

'How kind, Stella,' she purred. 'I'll have a tiny bit of chicken if you've got enough. But no skin, just plain white meat. And some plain veg. But no potatoes and nothing with any cheese or sauce.' Instead of licking her hand and rubbing it over her ear like I half expected, she wriggled her tiny rear end into the gap that had magically opened up between Rupert and Harry, and onto the seat that had also magically materialised. Did little furry forest animals follow her, like they did *Snow White*, magically making sure everything was just right for her?

No chicken skin? That was the best bit! No potatoes? No cheese or sauce? Of course not – God forbid a nasty old carbohydrate should pass those perfect lips. I snuck my own warm plate back onto the counter, scooped my cauliflower cheese onto a fresh, but cold plate from the cupboard and wiped the residue of the sauce away with a piece of kitchen roll.

'You're an absolute life saver, Stella,' she gushed as I put the half empty, warm plate of just white chicken meat down in front of her. She could help herself to the carrots, peas and sweet corn. 'I had a very early first lesson so I skipped breakfast this morning, and I haven't stopped since. Mmm – it smells delicious!'

As I sat down, I saw her out of the corner of my eye pick up a piece of her chicken, reach across the table, dip it in Jonathon's gravy and pop it into her mouth, while he smiled at her, as if it was the most natural thing in the world for her to do, and with me standing right there. Why didn't he just cut up her food, hand feed it to her and then let her lick his fingers, and have done with it? After all, why mind me?

Don't rise to it, Stella, I told myself, forcing a swig of wine through my gritted teeth. Then I caught Alli rolling her eyes at me.

Don't rise to it, Alli's eyes said as well. Then my best friend tapped her wine glass with her fork. 'A toast to Stella and Jonathon! Not long to go now!'

'Stella and Jonathon!' the rest of the table joined in. Well, I heard most of their voices. But was it my imagination, or did Cordelia just mouth the words, as she smiled her crocodile smile at my fiancé?

Chapter Eighteen

Stella

From: stellamoon@librarymail.co.uk

To: astrid@thainet.com

Subject: **Re: Greetings from Mum and Dad!**

Monday ...

Hi Mum,

I'm so glad you're doing well with the cooking classes – they sound like fun! I'm sure Jonathon and I will want to come along to a couple of them – you know how much he loves Thai food. And he'd be sure to want to learn how to cook some of our favourite dishes. We both would.

Talking of Jonathon, he gave me a lovely surprise the other night. He has booked us tickets to go and see *Warhorse*, in London. Remember I told you that Mrs P and Mrs J had been to see it and told me how much they loved it? Well, he has booked us a hotel for the night and we are going up on the Saturday and making a little weekend break of it. I'm so looking forward to it. We don't get enough time on our own with the wedding coming up and his mother panicking that there are still some things which haven't been co-ordinated with military precision – basically just the few things I've been able to manage to keep her away from!

We have been having fun and games here though – on Saturday Joyce took me to her hairdressers – by the time I got out of there I looked like a reject from a 1970s' Princess Anne lookalike competition! And that wasn't even the worst part of the weekend – you'll never guess what Jonathon's dad walked in on us doing on Saturday night – we were so embarrassed, especially Jonathon ... (Maybe don't read that last bit out to Dad ;))...

P S. Is that dog just staying until he's better, or has he moved in with you permanently?

The library was empty apart from myself and my two most regular ladies. Mrs Poole was scouring the needlecraft magazines for a pattern she was sure that she'd seen in one of them but couldn't remember which. Mrs Jenkins was returning a couple of Ruth Rendell's *Inspector Wexford* books, a Frederick Forsyth and a Dick

Francis.

'Have I read *The Babes in the Wood* recently, Stella?' Mrs J peered over her glasses at the blurb on the back.

'Last year I think,' I smiled, bringing her name up on the screen. It was so sweet that on top of borrowing more books than she could possibly get through, she worried about borrowing the same books too many times in case the computer flagged it up and gave the game away to my employers. All this silver haired subterfuge seemed to be agreeing with her though. A long time stalwart of both the Wintertown Women's Institute and the Netley Mallow Mother's Union, a good cause was a thing to be enjoyed. I hadn't seen her looking this chipper since the council had foolishly tried to replace the school lollipop lady with a pelican crossing. She had organised a sponsored sit in and knitathon, combined with a stall selling lollipops, on the site of the proposed crossing. They had raised a lot of money for charity and a lot of publicity for their cause and the council certainly wouldn't be trying that again in a hurry.

'What about some *Inspector Morse*?' Mrs J moved back along the shelves from R for Rendell to D for Dexter. 'If you've got the whole collection, I could start at the beginning and work my way through the lot. What was the first one called again, Stella?'

'*Last Bus to Woodstock.*' I tapped the title into the computer. 'We don't have it here, but I could order it for you.'

'Would that be seen as a good thing, or a bad thing?' A worried frown crossed Mrs J's face.

'Any demand for books is a good thing,' I reassured her.

'Then that would be lovely. Can you order any more of them that you don't have? Goodness me!' She'd just opened the cover of an *Inspector Morse* that we did have. 'This one hasn't been out in donkeys' years. Still, I suppose with them all being televised and shown so many times on those repeat channels, nobody can be bothered to read them any more ...'

'I wonder if it was at the Post Office that I saw it.' Mrs Poole sighed, interrupting our conversation...

'If what was at the Post Office?' I turned my attention to the other half of the double act.

'It was such a lovely pattern. It had two of those funny little yellow men on it, from that film. I wanted to knit it for little Arthur's birthday.'

'Do you mean the Minions?'

'Oh, I don't remember what they're called, dear. Chattering little fellows.' Mrs P put her head on one side. 'They dash about like the Keystone Cops, speaking complete gobbledegook and getting into all sorts of mischief. Little Arthur loves them. Can't stop laughing at them ...'

'Yes, those are the Minions. You must have seen the adverts for their film that's about to come out. It's a spin off from the *Despicable Me* films ... '

'*Despicable* ... Despicable! That reminds me,' Mrs P interrupted again. All this interrupting was most unlike her, so I guessed it was something important. 'There was something I meant to tell you, Stella, but what with one thing and another it went straight out of my head.'

'Oh dear,' I sympathised. 'What happened?'

'Well, Stella, it's little Arthur's birthday coming up, and I was looking for a pattern to knit him a jumper.'

'There was something you wanted to tell me?' I tried to gently remind her.

'I remember seeing the pattern for the jumper, but I must have been on my way somewhere and couldn't pick it up there and then. I thought I would just go back and get it later, but then I couldn't remember where it was that I'd seen it.' She looked so flustered. I didn't like to stop her, but if I didn't, this conversation could go on for a very long time.

'No, Mrs Poole,' I tried again. 'There was something you remembered that you meant to tell me. The word *despicable* reminded you.'

'Despicable? Despicable! Oh yes! The council, Wintertown council ...'

'What's all this?' Mrs J marched over to the desk, fictional murder mysteries for the moment forgotten.

'What about the council?' I asked, a feeling of foreboding crawling down my back. The local council had been very quiet since our town hall march. I suddenly

99

wondered if they'd maybe been a bit too quiet.

'Well, I overheard two ladies talking on the bus, you see, and I think they must work at the town hall. One of them said it was despicable the way the council were determined to cut local services, when they were spending so much money going abroad on all these twinning trips …'

'Just an excuse for a free holiday at the tax payers' expense, if you ask me,' Mrs J harrumphed. 'That new councillor, tall skinny, copper haired fellow, he's the worst.' Then she took the words right out of my suddenly dry mouth. 'And did they say anything about the library?'

'Well, that's just it.' Mrs P looked from one to the other of us, clearly hoping she'd got hold of the wrong end of the stick. 'They said something about the new councillor trying to get some plan through to shut down the single staffed libraries as soon as the librarians go on their summer holidays, but they can't do that, can they?'

'Of course they can't!' Mrs J barked. 'If they're cutting down on temporary staff, then we'll just step in and run the place as volunteers while Stella's on her honeymoon. They can't close it down then. And we'll make sure all the other single staffed libraries in the area have people to do the same for them …'

I didn't hear much of what else she said. I was too busy trying not to give in to the sinking feeling that was enveloping me. I should have known that a gaggle of grey haired old ladies and a few librarians and their friends marching on the town hall was not, in the grand scheme of things, going to achieve any more than a coop full of chickens clucking and shaking their feathers at the fox eying them determinedly from the other side of the wire.

It was very kind of them to try and help, but I had a pretty good idea what the outcome of that would be. If it looked like the library could be run by volunteers, the council would see no reason to keep on paying a librarian to do the job. And if they didn't step into my shoes while I was away, the council would just close it anyway and save on the electricity. And I wouldn't be here to do a thing about it.

Either way, it looked like by the time I got back from my honeymoon the library would be shut, the locals would have lost a much used service, and I would be out of a job.

Unless we cancelled our honeymoon. What would happen then? What would happen if all the single staffers at the local libraries just refused to take their annual leave?

But then most of them had children and summer school holiday childcare to worry about. They would have paid for hotels and made travel arrangements. There would be non-refundable tickets and other things I couldn't even think of. No, for some of them, not taking their holidays might just not be possible.

I was pretty sure Jonathon wouldn't mind about us missing out on our honeymoon for now and going away

101

some time later when it had all been sorted out. Obviously though, I would never make plans like that without talking to him about it first.

What on earth were we all going to do?

Chapter Nineteen

Jonathon

I had given Alli's suggestions a lot of thought over the weekend, and spent as much time as I could online, checking out my options. This morning I tried very hard to concentrate on whatever the Sitwells were saying – the gist of it seeming to be that they were at an impasse and that each thought it was somehow my responsibility to wave a magic wand and make the other change their mind. They really were a pair of over grown spoiled brats and I couldn't wait for them to be on their way so that I could get on with my own plans.

As soon as they were gone, I clicked onto the Burgh Island website again and looked at all the different rooms and suites. The Agatha Christie room was the obvious one to go for, but of course, it was one of the most popular choices. Then there was the Noel Coward.

They did special events too – murder mystery weekends – of course, how could they not? But their Christmas and New Year's Eve dinners looked sumptuous and I thought it would be a wonderful way of spending our first Christmas or seeing in our first New Year together as husband and wife. And Alli was right. It would give Stella all the pleasure of looking forward to it and packing for it.

Each and every room exuded style and class – Stella would love staying in any one of them, but I really thought it had to be the Agatha Christie one. I had put myself, at once, on their mailing list for the Burgh Island Bugle newsletter and on the waiting list for Christmas, New Year's Eve and, for good measure, all this year's murder mystery weekends. But I wondered if I should just go ahead and book one of them for next year, so that I had something definite to run with. That way I could print out the reservation and have something physical to give Stella on our wedding day, rather than just the promise of a trip at some unspecified date in the future.

My parents kept asking me, or rather my mother kept asking for both of them, what I had got Stella for a wedding present and I had to keep telling them that it was a surprise. They were already fairly bemused by Stella's laid back approach to the wedding and to life in general. Mum would be horrified at how much of that laid back attitude had already rubbed off on her son. I have a sneaking suspicion that Dad would be quite envious, although, after Saturday night, I had a feeling that Dad might be quite envious of a lot of things about my new life. Although the thought of him and Mum doing anything like what he caught Stella and I doing on Saturday afternoon was one I did not want in my head.

Chapter Twenty

Stella

From: francis@thainet.com

To: stellamoon@librarymail.co.uk

Sawadee Krub – Greetings from Thailand!

Tuesday ...

Dear Stella,

Your mother is out on a hen night tonight (a complete stranger's hen night I might add, but you know your mother!) so I thought I would drop you an email and see how you and Jonathon are doing.

I am stuck in, babysitting that dopey mutt I told you about. She has only gone and given it a name now – Nelson. (Nelson, if you please!) And of course, she is feeding it better than she feeds me. Now the blooming mutt will think it never has to leave.

How is the library doing? Is there any more news on that front? If anyone can put a stop to the closure plans it is you my clever girl. And I know that Jonathon's support will keep you strong. We are both there with you in spirit if not in body.

By the way, those apartments I was telling you about – it seems the problem wasn't with the apartments themselves, but with one of the letting companies that some of the new owners signed up to, to rent them out for them. Something dodgy has been going on apparently, although I haven't been able to find out all about it yet.

Well, it looks like somebody wants to go for a walk, so I had better go and let him out or I might end up with a puddle or a pile to clean up before your mother gets back!

Keep smiling, my lovely girl,

Lots of love,

Dad xxx

How absolutely typical of my mum, inviting herself along to some random stranger's hen night. Still, she wouldn't be here to come to mine, so it would be nice for her to be able to let her hair down, dance embarrassingly and sing *High Ho Silver Lining* at the top of her voice in front of people who hadn't even been born in that decade and who she would never have to see again anyway.

I just hoped she wouldn't have too bad a hangover

in the morning, or poor Dad would be babysitting both Nelson and her – Nelson, I ask you! That injured cat that Alli had reminded me about had clawed Mum's arms to bits while she was rescuing it and had ended up being called Clawdia!

As to how the library was doing, I had still heard nothing other than rumour and speculation about what might, or might not, have been overheard by one of the world's least reliable eavesdroppers. And I didn't want to worry Jonathon by sounding him out about possibly postponing our honeymoon until I had something a bit more concrete to go on. But, of course, nobody at the town hall was returning any of my calls.

Strangely enough though, I had had a call from Cordelia. She wanted to meet up with me and have a chat about something, but she wouldn't give me any clue as to what it was.

The only other person who had been calling me was Joyce. Not once, not twice, but three times today. Three "quick" phone calls which had each lasted over half an hour. No matter how many times Jonathon and I had given her our final choices for the reception food, she kept on coming back to me with new suggestions. I'd had to be really firm with her in the end, whether I offended her or not. But at last it seemed she had finally got the message. And where our wedding reception was concerned, there would absolutely, categorically, and one hundred percent definitely not be a melon ball in sight.

Chapter Twenty-One

Stella

The swirly handwriting on the posh writing paper reminded me of my Grandma's on my early birthday cards. *First course – prawn cocktail, melon and Parma ham, or melon balls.* Melon balls! I gritted my teeth as I read what was clearly supposed to be the ultimate, final and absolutely the very last version of the reception menu. One of Joyce's lunch club ladies had popped it through my letter box with the stealth of a ninja who had also joined a convent and taken a vow of silence. Probably one who realised just how far away this was from what Jonathon and I actually wanted – sadly though, one not brave enough to attempt to tussle with Joyce over it – unless it was that pesky vow of silence getting in the way.

And how many vegetarian options had I suggested to her, which had been completely ignored? I had spent ages looking online for that marinated figs stuffed with mozzarella recipe that my dad had liked so much that one time I'd tried it out before managing to lose the recipe. It was quick and easy and looked as good as it tasted. It wouldn't have been any more work than stupid melon balls and would have gone down a hell of a lot better.

I could almost see them poring over Joyce's range

of 1970s' cookbooks. Well, vegetarian food had moved on a lot since then, and I wasn't having the non-meat eaters at my wedding made to feel like they were a nuisance to be tolerated. Quite apart from the fact that the veggie option was destined for most of my parents' friends, they were also destined for the mother and father of the bride – fairly important members of the average wedding party I would assume. And yet half an hour with a melon baller, or whatever the stupid implement was called, and the off cuts from the other melon dish was all Joyce thought my family were worth.

I could just hear Jonathon's key in the lock over the sound of my grinding teeth. His idea of having one Thai-themed element in each course, giving a nod to our honeymoon destination, had been treated as if he had suggested they throw some chicken wings, burgers and hot dogs on a barbeque and serve them wearing cowboy boots, ten gallon hats and pink and white checked neckerchiefs. At least we could look at the main course choices together. They would probably be meat and two veg, fish and two veg, or just plain veg and two veg anyway.

'Oh dear.' Jonathon studied my face. 'You look like you did that time someone returned one of your favourite books and one of her kids had scribbled in purple felt tip all over it.' He looked down at the sheet of cream Basildon Bond I was holding, probably in much the same way as I had held that book, and a frown of worry wiped away his cheery, end of the work day grin. 'Not bad news?'

'Depends on how you feel about melon balls.' I kissed him, a bit more distractedly than a bride just weeks away from her wedding might be expected to and showed him the offending page.

'Oh,' was all he said. It was the 'Oh' of someone who'd just ripped the wrapping paper off their Secret Santa Christmas present and found it was a pair of *Odour Eaters*. 'You weren't joking. What happened to your nice figgy, cheesy things?'

'Probably eloped with your Thai crab cakes and found themselves a reception in this decade to go to. I haven't even been able to bring myself to look at the main course choices yet ...'

'Well...' He kissed me on the forehead as he put an arm round my shoulder. 'Let's see them then. It might not be that bad.' He gave me that "chin up" smile he always saves for when his mum has said something so tactless that even he has noticed. 'Beef Wellington – Dad's favourite.' Surprise surprise, I wanted to say, but didn't. I liked James, and it wasn't often that he got the chance to have a say in anything, where his wife could save him the bother by deciding what it was and saying it for him. 'Poached salmon. Oh.' There was that *Oh* again. Jonathon and I had both put in a vote for griddled or grilled salmon. With a nice crispy skin. He had elaborated with an oriental style vegetable salad to accompany it, but that seemed to have gone by the wayside. 'That's a bit ...'

'Yeah,' I agreed. 'Isn't it just.'

'And vegetable tart ...'

'Which I suspect will be Quiche Lorraine without the bacon.'

'What happened to all those vegetarian recipes you gave them?'

'They'll have followed the figs and the crab cakes and the oriental vegetable thing, I expect.'

'And the griddled salmon with the crispy skin. I was looking forward to that.' He looked so disappointed I put my head on his shoulder and brushed my lips against his neck.

'I'll make you some at the weekend,' I said. 'Shall we see what they've done to the desserts?'

'If there's apple crumble and custard, the wedding's off!' Jonathon kissed the side of my forehead to soften the blow.

'And if they've got rid of my mini Banoffee pies, the wedding's off!' I kissed the side of his neck again. There was just a vague hint of his aftershave left on his skin, just enough though ...

'We could run off to Gretna Green,' his arms went round me, his right hand heading south. 'We could get married in jeans and t shirts ...' He nibbled my earlobe.

'And I could carry a bunch of dandelions,' I giggled, my fingers weaving their way into the hair at the back of his neck, 'and wear my hair in a scrunchie and no

111

makeup ...'

'And we could find a pub that served crab cakes and crispy skinned salmon and Banoffee pie ...' He nibbled a bit harder.

'Feeling a bit peckish, are we? I could make you a sandwich,' I teased.

'There's only one thing I want right now,' he whispered, lifting me up onto the kitchen counter, 'and it's got nothing to do with food.'

Later that evening, after a relaxing soak in the bath tub – sadly alone as Jonathon had been expected back *chez Hazard* – I wandered back into the kitchen in my pyjamas to make myself a low calorie hot chocolate drink. The little tub of no sugar, no fat, no recognisable taste powder had appeared a few weeks ago, courtesy of Joyce, along with a packet of cardboard crisp breads, a tub of disgusting low fat spread, and another of zero fat cottage cheese which both looked and smelled as if some poor demented soul had already eaten it and thrown it back up again. That had gone straight in the bin as soon as she had left and it hadn't taken the spread long to follow it.

A smile tickled my lips as I caught sight of the marble effect counter, scene of our earlier bout of passion. I ran the tips of my fingers along it. It wasn't nearly as uncomfortable as it looked. Although I should probably give it a good wipe down with a hot soapy sponge before preparing any more food on it.

While I waited for the kettle to boil, I did just that, and stooped down to pick up the offending menu list that had ended up on the floor – even if that was one of the best places for it. Picking it up, I realised we hadn't even noticed the list of canapés on the other side of the now crumpled page.

Joyce's favourites, the Scotch quails' eggs with mustard mayonnaise dip, and the smoked salmon wrapped asparagus tips were straight in at numbers one and two. The mini sausage rolls which James had put in a request for were nowhere to be seen – probably too similar in mashed up porkiness to the classier, miniature Scotch eggs his wife wanted – she must have been planning to buy up every quails' egg in the county. But his chicken and mushroom vol-au-vents were there, only renamed as chicken and mushroom puffs. This had to be because, in a rare moment of bravery brought on by a not so rare moment of wanting to scream, 'Whose sodding wedding is this, anyway?' I'd growled that I hated and detested vol-au-vents as much as I hated and detested melon balls, and that I didn't want to see one anywhere near my wedding. I didn't hate them. I've never actually nursed any kind of strong feeling towards a vol-au-vent, but there are times when it's important to your sanity to just slam that foot down. And a fat lot of good it did me.

The vegetarians were to be offered plain old asparagus tips – those would be the ones left after over they run out of smoked salmon. There were also stuffed

113

quails' eggs, although it didn't say what they were going to be stuffed with. The cherry tomato, basil and bocconcini cocktail sticks were the only one of my suggestions that had been taken up. Probably because they were extremely quick and easy to prepare, leaving the catering ladies more time to devote to the things that Joyce considered more important and therefore wanted done.

I could feel my teeth grinding again as I switched off the kettle, got some milk out of the fridge, poured it into a mug and put it in the microwave. While it went round and round, I reached into the very back of the cupboard and pulled out my beloved tin of *Charbonnel & Walker*, a present from my even more beloved Jonathon. As I opened the lid and inhaled deeply the rich chocolatey aroma, my fingers wrapped themselves round the nearest teaspoon.

Chapter Twenty-Two

Stella

The dreaded letter arrived the very next day. It came in a brown envelope with the Wintertown Council logo stamped along the top, just screaming out to be noticed. There was an air of gloom about it and my stomach plummeted at the sight of it.

Dear employee, began the very standard, utterly non-personalised missive – dismissive more like. Dear employee? How long had I, or indeed any of the other Wintertown librarians, worked for them? And they couldn't be bothered to even leave blank spaces and have some unpaid work experience intern write their employees' names in them. They might just as well have put Dear John, or Dear Nobody. Or just sent out a collective email and saved themselves the cost of the postage. With a heavy, sick feeling in the pit of my stomach, I forced myself to read further.

Dear employee,

Wintertown Council is working hard to improve local services in the New Forest. This includes our library service ... Really? Had Mrs P got it wrong? With that tiny spark of hope trying to catch a hold in my brain I read on ...

We aim to extend this service further afield, to serve the smaller, more remote communities, as well as the larger villages and towns ... Hang on a minute though – that sounded an awful lot as if they're talking about library vans ...

Wintertown Council wants to take the library to the people! To this end, over the coming months we plan to roll out a new mobile library service ... They were talking about library vans. So, would this be in addition to, or instead of the existing libraries? Or did I already know the answer?

We would like to offer all our existing library staff the opportunity to participate in this exciting new enterprise ... Yes, but what about this place?

All current library employees with clean C1 driving licences will be given the chance to apply first for these new mobile librarian positions ... Yes, but ...

It is hoped that the transfer from static to mobile libraries will be a smooth one, and that all the mobile units will be ready to function fully by the start of the new school year ... And?

Wintertown Council would like to thank all its library employees for their hard work, and to wish those choosing not to take advantage of this wonderful opportunity, the very best of luck with their future careers ... So ... get a C1 driving licence, whatever that is, and reapply for the mobile version of the job you've already been doing, or get lost? It had taken me four tries to pass my ordinary driving test, and I was pretty sure I'd only passed it on the fourth attempt because the examiner was sick of the sight of me. With my parking skills, there was no way on earth I was ever going to pass anything more advanced than that. And besides, what about this place? I looked down and read the last line.

Please see enclosed schedule of closures ...

I scrabbled at the other sheet of paper. Mrs P had got it exactly right. There were the words, the dates. This library was going to close on my wedding day. In just over two weeks. And it looked like there was absolutely nothing I could do about it.

Chapter Twenty-Three

Jonathon

Poor Stella was in tears when I got to her place tonight. All this worry about losing her job, and the timing of it, so very close to our wedding, had got completely on top of her. She seemed to think that she needed to take an HGV driving test to be able to drive a library van, but I looked it up online. I tried to explain to her that a C1 was part of a normal driving licence anyway, and so that wouldn't stop her from applying, but I think we both knew that the chances of her being able to park, or do a three point turn in one of those things were pretty slim. She would be a nervous wreck just thinking about steering something of that size round all the country lanes. And she would probably have to drive it past the old oak tree out by Hatchet Pond, where she'd scraped her very first car – that wasn't going to help her confidence at all.

In an effort to try and cheer her up, I very nearly told her about the surprise trip to Burgh Island that I was planning for her. But I just stopped myself in time, realising that she would only worry about how much it was going to cost, and if we could afford it while only one of us was working, and that would make her even more anxious. Technically we were still only on a waiting list, but she would probably ask me to cancel it, even though it's something she would really love. No, I was going to stick with the original plan on that one.

There had to be some other way I could help her. Had we really exhausted all other avenues? Something was niggling at the back of my mind, if only I could catch it.

How did the council think that running a fleet of mobile libraries was going to be cheaper than keeping the existing libraries open? Firstly they had to buy, or hire the vans. Then they had to tax them, insure them, fuel them, maintain them etc. They still had to staff them, at presumably the same level of one librarian to one van, as they now had one librarian to one library – unless they were planning on only having one or two vans to cover the entire area and they just hadn't bothered to disclose that fact.

Of course, what they were doing to Stella and the other staff amounted to Constructive Dismissal. I was pretty sure that meant they wouldn't have to pay out any redundancy money to the staff who couldn't take up the new positions. It was a sneaky way to get rid of loyal employees without it costing anything. I would have to look into that for them.

And what were they going to do with the library buildings themselves? Were they planning on renting them out as commercial spaces? Leasing them? Selling them off to developers with plans to turn them into

119

something tacky and trendy and totally out of keeping with the area? I would have to look into that, too.

Dad and I were usually the first to hear of anything like that around here, but there hadn't been even a hint of any of them making an appearance on the market. I just wished I knew what was going on.

Chapter Twenty-Four

Stella

From: astrid@thainet.com

To: stellamoon@librarymail.co.uk

Subject: **Re: Greetings from Mum and Dad!**

Friday ...

Hello Stella darling,

Just a quickie. It's absolutely peeing down at the moment here, so the restaurant and the beach are empty, but give it half an hour and the sun will have dried up all the puddles and we'll be back in business again.

Your father and Thaksin are in Thaksin's little shack doing something with a saw, so I hope nobody comes back minus a finger.

I got invited to a hen do the other night. It was such a scream! A middle aged bride getting married for the fourth time. The first three husbands have all died on her (well not literally on her, at least I don't think so anyway) so it's nice that she's found someone else brave enough to risk it! Her friends are all taking bets on how long this one will survive, but he's apparently a few years younger than her, so they reckon he's got a fighting chance! Although there were plenty of jokes about life insurance. Bless her, she's a size twenty, red as a lobster and she's having a beach wedding in a white strappy sun dress! I didn't manage to get an invite to the wedding itself, but it sounds like it's going to be a lively affair.

How are your wedding dress fittings going? You've got one this weekend haven't you? I wish it was me going with you, although I'm sure all this time you're spending with Joyce is helping you to bond. Have she and Alli driven each other completely bonkers yet?

You will let us know if there is anything we can do, won't you? Anything at all?

Give Joyce and James our best wishes, and Jonathon our love.

Bye for now,

Love from Mum and Dad xxx

It was absolutely peeing down here at the moment, too, which just about suited my mood. I had to make the effort though, as it was indeed my final dress fitting and not a time for doom and gloom. I was surprised though that Mum had remembered the dress fitting I was about to go to, even though, at the moment, it was the last thing I felt like doing. Less surprising was the fact she'd clearly forgotten my telling her that I'd put my foot down about letting Joyce anywhere near my wedding dress. This was one aspect of my wedding that I was taking charge of – there would be no puffed up meringues, no frills, no corsets, no seed pearls, sequins or Swarovski crystals. A little devil on my shoulder had tempted me to not even have a white, cream or ivory dress and see just how big a fit of the vapours Ma Hazard would have as I came through the church door in bright scarlet, electric emerald, or deepest midnight blue-black, but I actually wanted to get married in white – well, creamy, ivory off-white to be exact – but it was what I had chosen and I loved it, and I wasn't going to cut off my nose to spite my face on my wedding day. I was having what I had always pictured myself in, a simple shift style dress, only long – no train. I wanted a veil – just a short one – that Jonathon would be able to fold back from my face when I reached him at the altar. And these were exactly what I was getting.

'Well...' Natalie, wedding dress maker extraordinaire mumbled through a mouthful of pins, before removing them in one swipe and stabbing them into the pin cushion strapped to her wrist. 'I know most brides lose a bit of weight with all the pre-wedding stress, but you've somehow managed to lose almost an inch and a quarter all over,' she said more clearly. 'So, what's your secret? We could market it and make a fortune.'

I just stood there, motionless, surveying the pleats of material nestling between Natalie's fingers that proved I had indeed lost weight, or at least width. Under normal circumstances this would have spread a silly grin across my face because, even though my weight had never bothered me that much – or Jonathon for that matter – all those barbed little comments my future mother-in-law seemed to find it appropriate to make could really sting sometimes. But right now I couldn't summon up any kind of emotion about it. Ma Hazard might be delighted. Well whoopee doo for her. She would be even more delighted when she found out that I really was going to lose my "little job". I wondered how long it would be before she started knitting little baby bootees and force feeding me foods that were high in Folic acid.

'Well, quite apart from the usual pre-wedding stress, have you met her future mother-in-law?' Alli quipped, over brightly, keeping well away from the subject of the library closure situation.

'Not personally, but I have had a couple of customers who are members of the golf club.' Natalie's raised eyebrow said it all. 'Seriously though, Stella, I know this is supposed to be your final fitting, but I think we might need to make this a pre-final fitting and schedule a final *final* fitting. What do you think? What are the chances of you not losing any more weight before the big day?'

That was a question I couldn't answer. I was too busy hoping that the old adage that said things went in threes wouldn't prove to be true in this case. I'd lost weight. And I'd lost my job. I didn't even want to think what the third thing I could lose might be.

Chapter Twenty-Five

Joyce

I decided against playing golf this morning. It was a beautiful morning for it, but I wasn't happy with one of the hats that I'd bought for the wedding and so, with just a fortnight to go till the big day, I decided to go into Winchester to look for something more suitable.

It would, of course, have been so much easier if I knew what Stella's mother would be wearing. Astrid hadn't even shown me the courtesy of letting me know what colour she had decided on although, knowing her, she probably wouldn't even know that herself until she got here. Then she would just turn up at the church in whatever fell out of her bag the least creased, or at least I would hope she'd give that minor consideration some thought, but you never could tell with that family. I wouldn't normally have needed to buy two outfits, but I had to be prepared in case whatever she ended up in clashed with what I was wearing. It was the very least I could do. One of us had to be organised. And of course, that *had* to be me.

Jonathon let it slip that Stella went for a dress fitting last night. Of course, I wasn't invited. And I got the distinct impression, from the look on his face, as soon as he'd said it, that the words had accidentally slipped out of his mouth, and that he thought he was going to be in the dog house with Stella for having told me. I didn't like the way that girl was changing my son. He never used to keep secrets from me. Now he barely told me anything anymore. That was Stella's influence and I didn't like it one bit.

If only Cordelia could have managed to go along with her and make sure Stella hadn't chosen something too awful, it would have gone some way to putting my mind at rest. But even if she had known about it, Friday evenings are so busy for the poor girl. It was such a shame Stella couldn't have picked a more convenient night, when Cordelia could have joined them. Then I would know what was what.

Chapter Twenty-Six

Stella

Stan, the plump, slightly greasy haired landlord of The Badger's Inn looked up from his already crumpled Sunday paper as Jonathon and I walked in. He always wore a woolly cardigan over his shirt, even in the middle of summer. Today's was bottle green.

'Morning,' he nodded, from his stool by the bar flap. 'Church service finished then, eh?' Instead of getting up he called over his shoulder, 'Pauline! Got customers!'

'It looks like there are going to be quite a few of us,' Jonathon said, as Pauline, Stan's equally plump, but glossily clean haired daughter sprang out, like a cuckoo from a cuckoo clock, through the door to the back room.

'Morning, Jonathon, Stella,' she flapped towards us, draping the glass cloth she had in her hand over her shoulder. 'Pint of Badger's and a glass of Pinot Grigio?' As always, she pronounced Pinot *peanut*.

'We'd better make it a bottle, Pauline. Is it still alright if we take over the snug for our meeting? The church ladies will be here in a moment, as soon as they've finished putting the prayer and hymn books away. Give them a drink, will you, and put it on our bill.'

'You go on through,' she nodded, picking up a pint

glass and holding it under the Badger's Ale pump.

Jonathon had kept himself very busy on Friday and Saturday, phoning round what had, since the planning of our town hall march, become the Save the Wintertown and Netley Libraries committee. This consisted of all my library customers, my fellow librarians from the other branches and as many as possible of their customers, and anyone else he could think of who might have an interest in what was going on. Straight after the ten o' clock Holy Communion service and before Sunday lunch had been deemed the earliest and best time to get as many people as possible together for a village meeting. We had gone along to the service ourselves, where we'd seen Mrs Jenkins reminding members of the congregation about it and chivvying them along to come and support our cause. Needless to say, Joyce wasn't at all happy about us jeopardising her Yorkshire puddings, although after the last Sunday lunch we'd had at her house, I thought it was rather brave of me to agree to go there afterwards at all. If there was carrot cake, I certainly wouldn't be having any.

Instead of going to church, James had told his wife he was going to play eighteen holes. In actual fact, he was rather bravely planning to play the front nine holes and then sneak in and join the meeting on his way home. I've told Jonathon that if he ever feels the need to lie to me about where he is, or what he's doing, or hide things from me in the garden shed, in case I give him a hard time about it, then he has my full permission to bat me over the head with the nearest frying pan. Mind you, if I were ever to find him doing anything so terrible that playing golf would actually sound like a good alibi, it would be my hand that would be reaching for a heavy kitchen utensil.

Claire, the chief librarian from the main Wintertown branch came bustling in, giving me a hug and clasping Jonathon's hand. She was a divorcee with a couple of children in Wintertown Primary school, one in the Secondary, and an ex-husband who thought maintenance was a dirty word. She needed her job even more than I did. And although the Wintertown library wasn't a single staffed one, and none of the staff there had received the dreaded letter, what affected us was bound to affect them. Plus they wanted to support us as much as they could anyway.

Alli was next through the door, towing a more than slightly hung over looking Harry in her wake. I was willing to bet that she'd only managed to get him out of bed with the promise of one of the Badger's particularly lush sausage or bacon sandwiches and a pint of the hair of the particular dog that had bitten him last night. Right now, he looked like he would sign his name to just about anything we put in front of him, in order to get this over with quickly so he could crawl back to bed. He was quite a greenish shade of grey and his forehead was a bit on the shiny side.

'Just a small, sweet sherry for me, Pauline,' Mrs Jenkins followed them in. 'What are you having, Doris?'

'Ooh, I don't know,' Mrs Poole dithered. 'What are

130

you having, dear?'

'A small, sweet sherry,' Mrs Jenkins said again, louder and more slowly.

'Shall I have the same? Or will it mess about with my tablets?'

'No, dear, it won't affect your tablets,' Mrs J sighed.

'So, shall I have that, then?' That was a conversation that could go on for hours. I happened to know for a fact that the staff in the Wintertown tea rooms had taken to making bets on how long it would take Mrs J to get Mrs P to choose between a scone, a hot buttered tea cake and a slice of whatever the sponge cake of the day was.

'Let me get these, ladies,' Jonathon jumped in before Stan and Pauline felt the need to do the same, ushering them gently through to the snug and picking up a tray from the bar. Stan was still perched on his stool, nodding at people as they came in, some to join us, others for their regular pre Sunday roast dinner pints. I sometimes wondered if the seat of Stan's shiny trousers had been super-glued to that stool – I certainly couldn't remember ever having seen him serving anyone with a drink in all the years he and Pauline had been running the place. I could just picture him, after closing time, getting up and going upstairs, the stool bobbing along behind him like a badly thought out experiment in wooden udders. Pauline, as always, was doing her impression of a Swiss army knife, carrying out half a dozen tasks at once, and all of them with supreme efficiency.

The murmur and hum of late Sunday morning conversation was starting to build up. The organist playing the wrong intro for the second hymn got a few mentions, as did whether the Reverend Marianne had had her hair dyed a different shade of red. A few of the elderly ladies asked me how the wedding plans were going and a couple of the men were discussing various methods of getting rid of the grey squirrels that had been making a nuisance of themselves in their gardens. I was so glad my mother wasn't here to hear some of the suggestions they were making on that particular subject – particularly the one about drowning the little so and so's in the water butts – we wouldn't have been able to stop her going round the area gathering them all up and making a sanctuary somewhere for them, unpopular as they were. And I didn't even want to think what she would do to the man who'd suggested the water butt method of execution – he might be found, days later, floating face down in it himself.

Jonathon and I looked at each other. He tapped the corkscrew against the wine bottle on our little table – yes, our local pub still served bottles of wine with corks in them – and the conversation rattled to a halt.

'Ladies and gentlemen,' he began. 'Thank you all for coming here today …' There was a brief hiatus as Harry's sausage sandwich turned up and every nose in the

132

room started twitching away like those of the *Bisto Kids*, mine included. 'As you all know,' Jonathon pushed on, although I could see him trying not to look at the sandwich too, 'Wintertown Council have decided to close down almost all of the local libraries, over the course of the summer ...'

'It's an absolute disgrace!' Mrs Jenkins exclaimed.

'Ah, but is it?' A tall, gangly, ruddy faced man, nursing a pint of something that looked like cider was standing in the doorway. I didn't recognise him.

'Of course it is,' Mrs J argued, a few of the others joining in with her.

'But what about them people who can't get to the libraries, eh? What about people living out in places like Hatchett's Bottom? Apple Garth End? Lower Lymebury? Eh? They pay their taxes just the same as all of you ...' He had a commanding voice. And was making a valid point. I looked at Jonathon.

'You're not wrong,' Jonathon spoke up. 'They should have access to a library. Everyone should. What we need to do is to find a compromise and ...'

'The council can't conjure up money for mobile libraries out of thin air. Something has got to go, and that something's ...'

'The council members could do without their expensive, freebie, town twinning junkets!' Mrs J stood up and faced the man at the door, her cheeks bright pink. 'If they spent less of the taxpayers' money buying

133

themselves Business Class tickets to fly off around Europe enjoying themselves, or if they paid for them themselves, then they would be able to afford to buy a library van without closing the existing libraries …'

'I'd like to see you sell that idea to them …' Mr Gangly Ruddy Face interrupted.

'You just bring one of them here and give me the chance!' Mrs J fired back at him. 'You bring me that new one, the tall skinny one with the red hair. He's at the bottom of this. Don't think we don't know all about it …'

And so it went on. It was like watching a three handed game of table tennis, with Jonathon and Mrs J hitting the ball on one side and the tall, ruddy faced stranger on the other, walloping it back at them with one hand tied behind his back and without even breaking a sweat, until time and the rumbling of people's stomachs brought the meeting to its disappointing non conclusion.

Alli gave Claire and myself a hug each and I downed the last of my drink, as Jonathon went to the bar to pay the bill. The last thing I needed right now was to have to go and hear Joyce pontificating about what she thought of it all over the roast beef. James hadn't turned up yet and while one half of my brain wondered if we should stay a little longer and wait for him, the other half was trying to work out the odds on whether or not I would be expected to play Russian Roulette with a couple of carrot cakes again. The way today had gone, so far, I'd be bound to pick the wrong one.

Chapter Twenty-Seven

Stella

She steered clear of the nuts today. Her weapon of choice, on this occasion, was a cherry stone. A very carefully concealed missile in my slice of pie – just mine, no one else's slice had one in it. And it was, most definitely, the slice of pie that was destined for me, and me alone – I could see her keeping a firm watch on it as she handed out the dishes. My portion was cut from the quarter where that porcelain blackbird thing she always likes to stick in the middle of a pie she's baking to stop the top going soggy, was facing.

The thing about those pesky cherry stones is that they have two chances of getting you. Firstly, you can choke on one – that's easy enough to do – and it was exactly what I did. Until Jonathon messed up her plans by thumping me hard on the back, sending the little red projectile shooting its way back out of my mouth and landing at the far end of the snowy white table cloth – that would teach her – she loved that table cloth. I think it had been a wedding present, and she'd managed to keep it snowy white all these years. It seemed like a small punishment for attempted murder, but as said attempted murder would be very difficult – if not impossible – to prove, it would just have to do.

I wondered just how many people died each year in choking related accidents? Well, I don't know the answer to that, but it must be quite a lot and I wasn't planning on being sent to join them any time soon.

Secondly, although you would need what would probably look like a suspiciously large quantity of them for this, cherry stones contain tiny traces of cyanide, just like apple pips. I know this because I looked it up – you do look up things like that when you've got an unlikely looking homicidal maniac for a future mother-in-law – after all, knowledge is power. The victim would have to swallow a huge amount of them and I don't know quite how anybody would get someone to do that – hypnosis possibly – but if anybody could manage that, Ma Hazard could. I was going to have to keep a firmer eye on that woman.

Chapter Twenty-Eight

Stella

From: stellamoon@librarymail.co.uk

To: francis@thainet.com

Subject: **Re: Sawadee Krub – Greetings from Thailand!**

Monday ...

Hi Dad,

I'm sorry it has taken me so long to reply. A lot has been happening here.

Please don't tell Mum any of this yet, but the council are going to be closing the library – get this – on my wedding day! They have now sent out letters offering all their staff the "opportunity" (big fat huh!) to re-apply for their old jobs, just as long as they can drive a great big mobile library van. And they have managed to make it sound as if this was some great new service that they were going out of their way to provide for the community, rather than a cost cutting exercise that would put at least half of us out of work.

So it seems our march didn't do any good after all. And Jonathon spent most of Saturday organising a meeting at the pub after church yesterday morning, which was hijacked by some man none of us had ever clapped eyes on before, making a very good case for the other side – I mean, people in the smaller villages and hamlets must find it hard to get to the libraries where they are now – he really did have a point. Am I being selfish, do you think, just worrying about my job and my customers, who have, of course, all become my friends over the years?

Joyce is being a bit of a pain in the proverbial, but nothing I can't handle.

I hope Nelson is behaving himself and not making puddles (or leaving piles) in the apartment! Do you have to watch Mum giving him juicy chunks of rare steak while you munch on your bean sprouts and tofu? I will have to get Jonathon to distract Mum so I can sneak you a beef Wellington at the reception. Maybe if we find a long song for him to dance to with her, that will give you long enough to eat two …

So if you had bought one of those apartments, did you mean that you would have been alright because you would have been living in it rather than renting it out with some unscrupulous rental agent?? You could have started up your own holiday let business out there – you would be really good at that ...

There was a lump in my throat as I came in to the library this morning. I stood for a few minutes, just inside the door, breathing in the bookish smell and fighting back the tears that were prickling away behind my eyes. This place wasn't just my job, it was a part of the community – just as big a part as the pub, the church, the post office – something else there had been rumours about being closed although, thankfully, nothing had come of those yet.

The top half of a poster on adult literacy had come away from its Blu Tack over the weekend and I pressed it back in place with my thumb, half of me wondering why I was bothering. The other half immediately stuck its chin in the air, cross with the first half for such a defeatist attitude. Where would the people who needed help with their reading go now? Had the council even given a thought to that or to all the other services the local libraries had been performing over the years? Or was saving money so that they could reallocate it to their own pet projects all any of them cared about?

There had to be more we could be doing, something

we hadn't tried yet. The petition, right back at the beginning after we had heard the first rumours, had gathered pages and pages of signatures. The many, strongly worded letters of complaint the council offices would have received would, I had no doubt, have gone straight into the recycling bins, unread. And then our much publicised march on the town hall had brought traffic to a halt for a whole afternoon. None of these things, however, had achieved anything other than using up a lot of paper. What would it take to change the council's minds? And whatever it was, why couldn't one of us think of it before it was too late?

I was just picking up the phone to call Jonathon for a quiet grumble, when Mrs Jenkins and Mrs Poole came bustling in like a pair of silver haired, cardigan wearing, avenging angels.

'Stella!' Mrs J plonked her basket down on the counter with a lot less care than she usually did. 'Put that phone down, Stella and get your address book out. Then call everyone on the Save the Wintertown and Netley Libraries committee and get them all here. In fact, just call everyone you know! It's time for an emergency meeting!'

Chapter Twenty-Nine

Jonathon

It was such an utter pleasure to be able to tell the Sitwells that I had somewhere else important I had to be and that it was therefore necessary to cut their usual Monday morning meeting short today. The looks on their faces had said that they couldn't believe I could possibly have anything more important to do than making them happy. And also that I was failing spectacularly on that score. In fact, Mrs Sitwell's mouth was still hanging unattractively open as I dashed out of the door, feeling a tad guilty for leaving Linda with the task of trying to smooth their ruffled feathers, but knowing that she would understand. Hell, I half expected that as soon as she had managed to get rid of them, she would be closing up the office and coming to join us at the library. She felt just as strongly about this library closure business as any of us did.

There were already a dozen or so villagers, mostly elderly ladies, at the library when I got there. Old Mrs Jenkins seemed to be in charge, rather than Stella, who slipped round the counter as soon as she saw me, side stepped between a Zimmer frame and one of those indoor wheeled mobility contraptions that one of them was manoeuvring about as if it were a go cart, and came over and gave me a hug.

'Aren't they wonderful?' my fiancé nodded towards the indomitable Mrs J and her rather woolly friend who were greeting what looked like they might be the Women's Institute or the Mothers' Union. Then she grinned a very Stella like grin at me. 'I was just wracking my brains trying to think up some kind of last ditch type idea and drawing a complete blank. Then in they both came, all guns blazing, just like …'

'Yes, but what is this amazing idea of theirs?' I couldn't help interrupting her.

'Well … now this'll make you laugh,' she chuckled. 'It all came about from Mrs Poole falling asleep in front of the television after her lunch yesterday afternoon and waking up to find herself halfway through an old episode of *The Vicar of Dibley*…'

'*The Vicar of Dibley*?'

'Yes, you heard me right,' Stella grinned again. 'Now we'd better nip over to the pub – Pauline said they can lend us as many extra chairs as we need. I don't know how many people are going to be able to turn up at such short notice, but then again, I don't know how many people would dare to disappoint Mrs J!'

No, I thought. Neither did I.

Chapter Thirty

Stella

We chose The Shining Moon restaurant as it was usually quiet on a Monday evening, and fortunately for us, tonight turned out to be no exception. In fact the staff looked amazed to see such a large party walking in.

'I'll just order some steamed vegetables,' Cordelia, who had annoyingly invited herself to join us, purred as one of the waiters led us to our row of hastily conjoined tables. I guessed she would be passing on the deep fried banana fritters and ice cream, drizzled with chocolate sauce, at the end of the meal then. And doing her best not to look horrified when Jonathon and I shared a portion, him demolishing most of the banana fritter, while I scooped up most of the chocolate sauce – we were usually pretty much fifty-fifty on the ice cream front.

'Steamed veg? That sounds absolutely revolting,' Rupert teased, winking at the willowy girl in the very tight fitting dress who he'd brought along with him, a girl who, for the first time since I'd known Rupert, was one we had actually seen him with more than just the usual once. In fact, I thought this might be the third time that I'd seen him with her. And the soppy expression on his face caused Alli and I to exchange glances. This version of

Rupert was a new one on both of us. Normally he would have loved her, left her and moved on to the next one, or even the one after that by now. Was our Rupert in love by any chance? Or had the lust he usually fell in and out of on an almost daily basis managed to keep a hold on him this time? There must be something very special about this one. Probably nothing at all to do with the fact that there was definitely no visible knicker or bra strap line breaking the smoothness of that extremely tight dress. Jonathon and Harry were, of course, oblivious.

Alli had been brilliant as always, rounding up as many of her fellow teachers as she could at such short notice. Harry had brought his brother and his brother's girlfriend. And Jonathon had only had to mention it to Linda, when she had called him from the office to check everything was alright. She hadn't been able to join us as Jonathon had hoped, as unfortunately for her the Sitwells had stayed on for the rest of the morning, wanting to go over every possible suitable property on Hazards' books with her, just in case, as they suspected, Jonathon was actually a complete idiot. Although that wasn't the word Mr Sitwell had used. She and her husband had both come along and brought a couple of their friends and neighbours too. It took quite a while to get everyone seated.

A trio of smiling waiters handed us our menus and started taking our drinks orders. And although the food was really of secondary importance tonight, I hadn't had time to eat my lunch, so I really hoped this wasn't going to end up being one of those awful communal meals where everyone chose a dish and then we all dipped in and shared each other's random choices. Jonathon knew how much I hated that. He did too. The Shining Moon had been a favourite of ours right from the start of our relationship. The waiting staff knew about my allergy. They were very careful about shaking their heads at me – and sometimes even driving the point home with a comically waggled index finger in my direction – whenever they put a dish on the table that I shouldn't eat. Equally, they nodded with a smile – and similarly sometimes a big thumbs up – when it was a dish that was safe for me to eat. It served an eclectic mix of Chinese, Thai, Vietnamese, Korean and other South East Asian dishes and so had an extensive, and somewhat confusing for the first time visitor, menu. But of course, with a group, somebody always chose the inevitable, hideous sweet and sour dish, somebody else would choose something so spicy that only those with asbestos roofs to their mouths could stand to eat it, and a few somebody else's would, of course, choose dishes with nuts in them – chicken with cashew nuts seeming to be the most popular. Then they would all tuck in to my choice and I would end up munching on prawn crackers and steamed rice for the rest of the evening. Jonathon would always choose something he knew that I'd like and be able to eat, as would Alli, but their choices would always prove popular

145

and be hoovered up by everyone else before any of us got a look in. Perhaps we were all just blessed with friends with exceedingly bad table manners.

'Mm, sweet and sour pork balls for me.' Harry snapped his menu shut with barely a glance. He didn't need to look at it anyway. He always ordered the same dish. And it always looked revolting, which was no reflection on The Shining Moon's kitchen, it was a revolting looking – and tasting, from my point of view – dish, whatever restaurant anyone ordered it from.

'I reckon I'll go for the hot and spicy chilli beef with extra chilli.' Rupert practically licked his lips as he winked at the willowy girl, whose name I still couldn't remember, and didn't like to ask now in case she was offended that I'd forgotten it. Of course he would. And there would be a competition as soon as it arrived at the table, for who could eat the most without any accompanying rice to absorb any of its spiciness. That would soon be followed by another to see who could drink their bottle of Tsingtao, Chang or Tiger beer the quickest, and poor old Jonathon would come third in both. Well, usually he came third. Tonight there were more potential competitors. If my head counting was anywhere near the mark, he could come twelfth, thirteenth, or even fourteenth.

The first of the waiters returned with a heaving tray of assorted cold beers, and wandered around the elongated table letting people help themselves. The second one followed him a moment later with a couple of ciders, some soft drinks and Cordelia's bottle of room temperature mineral water with a slice of lemon. The third came along a few minutes later with a couple of bottles of house wine and a few cocktails and mocktails, and glasses of whisky and ginger ale. All three trays looked so heavy I couldn't imagine how the waiters managed to balance them without dropping or spilling anything.

'Good evening,' the manager greeted us with a warm smile, having just made an appearance. I wondered if he'd been reading the newspaper out in the kitchen office or, as was more likely the case with it being a Monday night, had been upstairs in his flat, and had hastily pulled his jacket and tie on at sound of a sudden deluge of diners. 'We can take your food order now? Or do you need some more time?'

There were some mumbled yes and no responses up and down the table. Linda's husband called him over to ask a question about one of the dishes. Cordelia, at the other end of the table, also called him, probably to ask if the steamed vegetables were organic and had been handpicked at dawn, this morning, and steamed in spring water which had been filtered through volcanic rocks.

Jonathon rolled his eyes at me. 'Don't worry. This was a good idea. Once people have ordered and relaxed with their drinks, we can tell them all about Mrs J's plan. I'm sure that everyone who physically can will agree to come and help us.'

As I listened to the little pockets of good natured argument about who was ordering what and how many portions of fried or steamed rice would be needed, running up and down the length of the table, I began to wonder if he was right, or if this had been such a good idea after all.

Chapter Thirty-One

Stella

From: stellamoon@librarymail.co.uk

To: astrid@thainet.com

Subject: **Re: Greetings from Mum and Dad!**

Tuesday ...

Hi Mum,

Well, you will never guess what Jonathon and I, plus almost everyone in the entire village are going to be doing tomorrow afternoon. In the absence of any railings to chain ourselves to, we are going to be making a human chain around the library! Doesn't that take you back to your Greenham Common days? Hopefully we can get the council's attention and show them that the people who elected them do actually care about their libraries. And guess who came up with the idea? Mrs Jenkins and Mrs Poole! Those two are priceless! You and Dad are going to love them when you meet them.

The weather forecast says it is going to be a

hot day tomorrow, so it will be sun hats and factor thirty all round, I should think. Plus plenty of cold drinks. The Badger's Inn have promised us as many of their garden chairs as we might need for the older volunteers and some awning type things for shade, so hopefully we won't need to have St John's Ambulance at the ready for any fainters. :)

I will email you afterwards and let you know how it all goes.

So, what have you been up to since that hen night? And has Nelson completely taken over the apartment yet? Please tell me he isn't sleeping between you and Dad, or worse, he hasn't taken over the bed, leaving you and dad sleeping on mats on the floor ...

I'd had to reword the original email I was going to send Mum as I remembered that I'd asked Dad not to tell her about the letter from the council.

I just hoped that it didn't turn out to be too hot a day, especially seeing as our oldest volunteers tomorrow would be in their seventies and eighties, with one in her nineties. This had to work. It *really* had to work.

Chapter Thirty-Two

Stella

'So, we are all going to chain ourselves to the railings,' Mrs Poole had announced prematurely at our emergency meeting of the Save the Wintertown and Netley Libraries committee on Monday. Her cheeks had been pink with excitement, her eyes shining, her hands clasped in front of her chest, and the words were clearly unable to keep themselves in any longer. It was Mrs Jenkins who had, just as patiently as always, reminded her that neither our own little library nor the one in Wintertown actually had any railings.

'But in a way she's right,' Mrs J had added, pausing to let her words sink in. 'We are going to make a human chain around the building. We are going to make human chains around each of the Wintertown and Netley library buildings,' the indomitable lady had finished with a flourish. They were both fairly bristling all over with what was probably a heady mixture of indignation and excitement. My mother would love these ladies.

And so that was how we ended up at midday on Wednesday – Jonathon, his secretary Linda and her husband who had taken the day off work, the friends and neighbours of theirs who had joined us on Monday night and myself. Nearly all the mums from our various children's reading groups had come along to join us, and with a couple of dozen assorted and very determined pensioners, we were all linked arm in arm around the perimeter of the library. Rupert and his willowy, underwear free girlfriend were a surprise addition to our number – I suspected that was her doing and I was determined to find out her name and get to know her a bit better – as were Cordelia, Marianne the vicar, what looked like most of the new family who had moved into the old vicarage, and the entire, if small, congregation from the local church. I had been worried that, as small as the library building was, we might have to stretch our arms as wide as possible and just hold hands, or even just touch finger tips in order to go all around it. But with the swell in numbers we were able to stand much closer together and actually link our arms in the manner that Mrs P and Mrs J had suggested. A sing along of *We Shall Not, We Shall Not be Moved,* was soon underway and what it lacked in tune and musicality, it more than made up for in enthusiasm and volume.

At exactly the same time, the staff of the Wintertown library and all the supporters they had been able to gather together were doing exactly the same thing. The average age of the Wintertown contingent was, however, considerably lower than ours. Alli, who we felt would be needed more at the bigger branch than here with us, along with Harry, who was feeling and looking much better than he had on Sunday, had turned out, taking with them more of Alli's fellow staff than I would have expected on a week day. Although of course, it made sense for them to care about the libraries and try to keep them open. In fact, now I thought of it, the head master or whatever he was called had probably given them all time off to attend. There were also about half of the college's students, some of whom had probably only turned up to take advantage of a day off from their studies, but that didn't matter – they were there – they were swelling the numbers and helping the cause. That branch also had its own group of library-using pensioners, attendants of the Wintertown church's congregation, staff and members of the local youth groups and a pair of traffic wardens who'd had the misguided impression that they'd had any chance at all of writing out parking tickets for any of the people involved and had then found themselves roped in.

All in all, we had a much better turnout than we could have expected. Mum and Dad would be so proud. Joyce would be just horrified – particularly if she got wind of the fact that it was an episode of *The Vicar of Dibley* that was responsible for Mrs J's and Mrs P's idea in the first place. Dawn French's ears would be burning for weeks, if not months. And poor old James would probably get it in the neck for allowing Linda the day off to come along and join in. He had looked a little wistful, as if he would have come along himself too, if only the thumb print on the top of his head had been a little less embedded. But of course, if we got the local newspaper coverage we were hoping for, Joyce would be bound to spot her own husband in among the throng.

It was just gone half past one when I got a text message from Alli, saying that a couple of council officials had finally turned up at the Wintertown branch and suggested that everybody go home. I relayed that information to our team and was rewarded by another rousing sing along, again in various keys, of *We Shall Not, We Shall Not Be Moved*.

Another message from Alli at about quarter past two said that the council members had returned and threatened to call the police if the crowd didn't disperse. She added that at this point the two Mrs Hensons – one the retired JP and mother of the local chief constable, the other his wife who was a stalwart of many Wintertown committees and a leading champion of one of the local youth centres – had chosen this moment to make their presence known to them. The council members themselves had dispersed at this point and the two Mrs Hensons had been on the receiving end of hearty cheers and whistles. This news brought a fresh wave of cheers as it made its way round our own chain. Mrs P, who was inside the library on a bathroom break, came rushing out to find out what had happened, complete with a couple of feet of toilet paper stuck to the bottom of her shoe, which

Linda's husband gamely trod on, as she rushed past and back to her place in the chain.

'What do you think will happen next?' Linda asked me over the reactivated noise of the crowd.

'I don't know,' I shrugged. 'I can't imagine the fact that Chief Inspector Henson's wife and mother are on our side is going to get them to do a sudden U-turn, once they sit down and think about it. What do you think?' I turned to Jonathon.

'I haven't met Mrs Henson junior, but Linda and I have had dealings with Mrs Henson senior, and she isn't a lady to be messed with. I wouldn't want to be in the Chief Inspector's shoes tonight, if she's displeased with the outcome of the protest.' He shrugged. 'I don't know what he can do, but if there is anything, I would imagine he'll be busy doing it.'

Not long after that, a couple of police cars and a police van drew up on the village green. The look on Jonathon's face reflected the jolt of fear and worry that was rushing through my own mind. We didn't have any Mrs Hensons of our own to keep us from being arrested, if the police had a mind to make an example of us. And as wonderful as Mrs Jenkins, Mrs Poole and all their friends had been, I didn't imagine any of them having the same clout as them. What on earth were we going to do now?

Chapter Thirty-Three

Stella

I quickly dialled Alli's number, crossing my fingers that she had remembered to put her phone on vibrate, as she might not be able to hear it over whatever noise was being made at her end. She answered almost straight away.

'Stella? Is everything alright?' she yelled down the phone.

'Two police cars and a van have just pulled up,' I shouted back. 'I think they're going to try and move us on and if we don't move, they might start arresting some of us.' My guess being that, not wanting to appear too heavy handed, they would arrest the youngest and least frail of us, which would be Jonathon and myself, Cordelia, Rupert and his girlfriend, some of the reading group mums ... I could hear Alli shouting my news to the protesters at her end and muffled voices shouting back at her, but I couldn't make out what they were saying.

'Stella! Don't worry,' she yelled back down the phone again. 'Help is on its way. Just try and stay put and hold your ground for the next ten to fifteen minutes ...' Ten to fifteen minutes? A quarter of an hour? Most of our group were sweet little old ladies whose only experience with policemen would have been asking them what the time was, or how to get to such and such a place. I couldn't see any of them risking being arrested. And why should they, at their time of life.

'Alli, we'll do our best, but I don't know if we'll be able to hold out for that long ...' Anything she might have been trying to say back to me was drowned out by the sound of feedback from a loud hailer.

'Ladies and gentlemen! Would you please disperse! You are causing a public nuisance! You have two minutes to start dispersing, or we will have no choice but to start arresting you!'

Well, at least they were being polite about it. I suspected that had a lot to do with what they guessed was the average age of our older protestors, along with the fact that a local television news crew had also just turned up. They must have realised that the possibility of more action that they had been hoping for in Wintertown had now relocated to here and come along looking to get the next part of the story.

The many keyed chant of *We Shall Not, We Shall Not be Moved* started up again, with Mrs Jenkins and Mrs Poole's voices and those of the church congregation ringing out above the less melodic ones of most of the others. Jonathon and I looked at each other, caught the eyes of Linda and her husband, Cordelia, Rupert and his girlfriend, and as one, we all linked our arms together more firmly and joined in with the less tuneful end of the singing.

The TV camera swung around, getting a good view of those of us on three sides of the building. James would be so relieved he hadn't been here to be filmed, when he and Joyce watched this on this evening's local news. I, of course, would get it in the neck from Joyce for leading Jonathon astray, but hey, if it wasn't this she was holding against me it would only be something else. And nobody could say this wasn't a good cause.

It felt like a lot more than two minutes later, when the loud hailer was raised again and the feedback once more whistled around our ears. 'Ladies and gentlemen, you have been warned. If you do not disperse immediately, we will have no choice but to start making arrests.'

I felt Jonathon grip my arm more tightly on one side and Linda's neighbour do the same with my other arm. I was probably doing the same back to them too. We could see the police officers looking at us. It was all too obvious who they were going to come for first.

Chapter Thirty-Four

Jonathon

There was no way I was going to let them arrest Stella. I'd do something to make sure they took me. Maybe they would head for me first anyway. Surely that would look better for them on camera than arresting a woman first? Or was that just me being hopelessly old fashioned?

I swung my head round to look at Rupert, as we were the youngest adult males here. He raised his eyebrows at me. On his right, his girlfriend looked ready to battle for a community she had only just come into – I was impressed. On his left, Cordelia looked like she had just realised she'd bitten off more than she could chew. There must have been quite a struggle going on inside her head with half of her wanting to be seen to be doing the right and community spirited thing, while the other half worried about what all those pony club mums and dads would think about the woman teaching their little darlings to ride being arrested for public disorder.

On either side of me, Stella and Linda looked determined to stick this out for as long as they would be allowed to. I knew Stella would stay put until the police dragged her away – her mother's Greenham Common spirit was alive and kicking inside her. And what Stella was prepared to do, I was prepared to do too.

'This is your last chance!' The officer holding the loudhailer announced, minus the feedback this time, so he must have got the hang of the thing now. 'Please disperse immediately!' They so clearly didn't want to be here, getting heavy with a group which consisted mostly of elderly ladies – some of them probably even agreed with our cause. I wondered how many more warnings we were going to get before they felt they had to come closer and actually start arresting people.

The TV camera started to zoom in on Stella as one of the news reporters approached her. I was surprised it had taken them so long to actually initiate an interview.

'This young woman is Stella Moon, the librarian in charge of the Netley Mallow branch,' the reporter said facing the camera, 'which, as you can see is completely surrounded by a human chain of support. Tell me, Stella,' she turned towards Stella, giving her a smile which didn't quite reach her eyes, 'how do you feel about all the loyal support you've received here today?'

'It's been wonderful,' Stella beamed back at the camera. 'It just goes to show how high public feeling is running about the closure of such a vital local service. It's been really heart-warming ...'

'And talking of warm, it is indeed a very warm day for so many of our senior citizens to be standing outside in the sun. How do you feel about that, Stella?' The reporter smiled her crocodile smile. 'How do you feel about having all these elderly ladies standing about in the heat on what could very well be one of the hottest days of the year? Is that not a little bit ...'

'This human chain protest wasn't Stella's idea,' I spoke out as loudly as I could, seeing the smile on Stella's face flounder at the accusatory tone of the question. 'It was in fact the idea of a couple of the library's longest standing customers, who are indeed two of the very senior citizens you're talking about ...'

'Three cheers for Mrs Jenkins and Mrs Poole!' Linda shouted. 'Hip hip ...'

'Hooray!' shouted those nearest who had heard what she said. 'Hip hip ...'

'Hooray!' The shout spread round the building like a fire taking hold. 'Hip hip ...'

'Hooray!' The third shout was deafening, as every single person around the building joined in, including the two ladies themselves, who probably hadn't realised that they were the ones being cheered.

'Why don't you ask the ladies themselves how they feel about standing here today to support a cause which is obviously very dear to them?' Linda challenged the reporter. I could have kissed her.

'Yes!' Linda's husband joined in. 'Let them tell you in their own words. Mrs J? Mrs P?'

A chant of *Mrs J ... Mrs P ...* started up and quickly built. There was clapping too, from those who were close enough to the people on either side of them to be able to put their hands together. *Mrs J ... Mrs P... Mrs J ... Mrs P ... Mrs J ... Mrs P ...*

The policemen just stood there, looking at each other. They could clearly see what a PR disaster this could turn into for them. I almost felt sorry for them. Almost, but not quite.

Chapter Thirty-Five

Stella

I shot Jonathon a look full of gratitude, hoping that he could read the message in my eyes which said that I would show him just how very grateful I was, later.

The village's two favourite old ladies were just a little way further along the line from Linda's husband. They were both looking quite flushed at all the sudden attention they were receiving. I wasn't the only one looking in their direction and so the reporter didn't need to ask who Mrs J and Mrs P were. The camera followed her around to just in front of where they were standing.

'I believe you are the ladies behind today's protest?' I couldn't see how far up her face the reporter's smile reached this time, but I hoped for her sake she wasn't going to try and make a fool of Mrs Jenkins and Mrs Poole, the way she had clearly been trying to do with me. On the other hand though, it would serve her right if she did give it a go. There was no doubt at all in my mind that Mrs Jenkins would make short work of anyone who tried to make her or any of her friends look foolish.

'Oh ...Well ...' Mrs Poole looked like she might start to witter.

'Yes, we are,' Mrs Jenkins took charge and the

battle commenced. 'We have been members of this library since it was built back in the nineteen seventies ...'

'Have you? That's ...' the reporter started to say.

'Our children were members while they were growing up here and until they moved away from the area. And their children would be members if they still lived near enough; but they are very loyal members of their own local libraries.'

'Yes, that's all very admirable, but ...'

'The local library isn't just a place from where people can borrow books, you know.' Mrs J was getting into her stride now, bless her. 'It is an important part of the local community. The library runs early learning and play groups for preschool age children, reading groups for adults. It provides adult literacy classes and computer classes for those of us to whom these things arrived a little too late in life to learn about them at school ...'

'Yes, but ...'

'How are mobile library vans going to be able to provide these services? How are mobile libraries going to cater for the disabled? The blind and partially sighted who know their own libraries like the backs of their own hands? How are they going to provide courses for people with learning difficulties by driving around once a week or however often the council deem fit?'

'Yes, these are all valid questions, but ...'

'Yes, young lady. They are all valid questions. And

there are many more valid questions which needed to be asked before this hare-brained scheme was slipped past us by council members with their own private agendas. And yet the council haven't seen fit to provide an answer for any one of them ...'

'You mention private agendas Mrs J ...'

'Mrs Jenkins,' the lady herself bristled. Only her friends and those she respected were allowed to call her Mrs J.

'Mrs Jenkins. You mention private agendas. Do you have any proof of anything of that nature? Because without proof, you could be accused of slander ...'

'I believe I can answer that question, if the good lady you are currently harassing has no objection?' A smartly dressed woman with a thick crown of steel grey hair, whose face was familiar from the local newspapers was stepping out of a Mercedes which had just pulled up, right in front of one of the police cars. I looked at Jonathon.

'Mrs Henson,' he mouthed back at me. The Chief Inspector's mother no less.

'No objection at all.' Mrs Jenkins gave a gracious smile in the retired J P's direction.

'Ladies and gentlemen, members and friends of the Save the Wintertown and Netley Libraries committee,' Mrs Henson enunciated beautifully. She sounded a bit like the queen only in a slightly lower tone. I wouldn't have wanted to face her across the bench, or wherever it was that she had done her J P thing. 'It has been brought to my attention that certain members of the local council have been trying to rush through the closure of the local libraries and their replacement by just a pair of mobile library vans ...'

'A pair,' I mouthed to Jonathon. That was news to me. He shrugged back at me.

'It is not possible that the correct council procedure has been followed,' she carried on. 'Therefore, the council is currently undertaking an emergency meeting to go through the procedure leading up to the announcement of the closures. My daughter-in-law is in attendance at that meeting and will be letting me know the outcome as soon as there is one.'

A babble of comment went round the three sides of the building from where she could be seen. The people who had been at the back had broken the chain and moved round so that they could hear what was going on.

'I will stay here with you and we will wait for that phone call together,' she declared. 'And, as this is a peaceful meeting of community minded people, I see no further need for a police presence.'

As if she were their superior officer, rather than her son, and she had issued an actual command, the policemen looked at each other and almost immediately started to get back into the cars and the van.

'Three cheers for Mrs Henson,' Mrs Poole piped up, obviously thinking it was only fair as she'd been the recipient of some earlier. 'Hip, hip ...'

    'Hooray!' everyone roared.

    'Hip hip ...'

    'Hooray!'

    'Hip hip ...'

    'HOORAY!'

Chapter Thirty-Six

Stella

From: stellamoon@librarymail.co.uk

To: astrid@thainet.com

To: francis@thainet.com

Subject: **Re: Greetings from Mum and Dad!**

Thursday ...

Hi Mum and Dad,

Well, you will never guess how our protest turned out (although you probably could, Mum, with all your experience of doing them!)

It was a scorcher of a day, for here, and I was worried about the more elderly of our protesters, but I needn't have worried. The Badger's Inn had done a great job of fixing up awnings all the way round the building so nobody was actually standing (or sitting) in direct sunshine. They also provided loads of garden chairs and some tables too and kept sending out trays of cold drinks, which, when Jonathon went to settle up the bill for them at the end of the day, they wouldn't accept any money for. Stan and Pauline insisted that it was their contribution to the protest, as neither of them had actually been able to come and physically take part in it.

Anyway, I'm rambling. Alli let me know what was happening at the Wintertown branch and she told me when the police turned up there both the wife and the mother of the local Chief Inspector had sent them away with a collective flea in their ears. So then they must have decided it was our turn, and the police turned up at our protest. I don't think they had realised just how much older most of our protestors were than at the Wintertown branch, and once they had seen us, it was so obvious that they didn't really want to have anything to do with it. It was quite funny actually. They kept issuing us with final warnings to disperse or be arrested, and then doing nothing at all about it, other than stand there looking embarrassed. Especially when a reporter and a cameraman from the local news programme started shooting footage of the protest and trying to interview me ...

    ... Anyway, the upshot is that due to the two Mrs Hensons getting behind our protest and demanding an investigation into the council trying to rush the library closures through before anybody could rally round and stop them, the whole closure business has been suspended, along with the new councillor, the one who was behind the plans. So it isn't a definite, definite "yes, the libraries are closing" or "no they're not". But it is a stay of execution which we all reckon could last from six months to a year. They certainly won't want to be caught doing anything else that isn't by the book, not now they know who they're being watched over by!

Jonathon send his love ...

It took me most of the day to get my email to Mum and Dad written as the library was so busy, and I only managed to send it at closing time. Last night's evening news and the late edition of the local paper, plus this morning's paper and an interview on the local radio with Mrs Henson senior, seemed to have brought half the county out to have a little look at what all the fuss was about.

During the course of the day I had twenty seven new customers sign up to join and at least as many old customers who hadn't been here in years had come along and borrowed a book or two. It was the busiest I had been in a very long time and all I wanted to do at the end of the day was go home, put my feet up, open a bottle of wine and watch some soppy old rom com with Jonathon. But alas, that was not to be.

I had been summoned by Cordelia. I couldn't imagine what she wanted with me, but Jonathon had seemed pleased that she had called me, so I couldn't very well get out of it. He probably thought it was nice that his fiancé and one of his oldest friends were going to spend the evening together.

So why was I feeling a lot like I had when his mother commanded me to meet her on Saturday morning?

Chapter Thirty-Seven

Stella

I had been to Cordelia's stables before, of course, but never without Jonathon. In fact I hadn't
ever spent any time with Cordelia, without Jonathon around, and I couldn't begin to imagine why she wanted to meet up with me on my own now.

She greeted me like an old friend and poured us each a dainty glass of perfectly chilled pink Zinfandel. Then she made what was probably just the right amount of small talk about yesterday's library protest. She proclaimed Mrs P and Mrs J to be a wonderful pair of old ladies, and congratulated me on the unexpected boost our cause had been given, both by Inspector Henson's wife and mother, and by the local evening news coverage we had received, whilst sipping hers delicately. Feeling like a big, clumsy elephant next to her, I just smiled, nodded whenever it felt appropriate, and did my level best to concentrate on not spilling mine. Then, before I even realised what was happening, we were outside and in her car, and zooming through the forest lanes at what felt like much higher than the speed limit, towards Wintertown, where she had some friends she said she wanted me to meet. All kinds of alarm bells were ringing in my head at the thought of meeting anyone who'd managed to gain entry into Cordelia's close circle of friends, but the constant monologue she kept up, as we skimmed the hedgerows, managed to make them a lot harder to hear.

She parked her car, which I'd never had reason to notice before but was very similar in both colour and model to Ma Hazard's, and then lead the way along the high street, before turning off down an alley. I didn't even begin to associate our trip there with the tanning salon she was walking me towards, until she opened the door and practically pulled me inside. There, she air kissed a couple of slender, glossy, pony-tailed young things who could almost have been clones of herself, except for the long, painted and bejewelled talons they sported, compared to her more practical short ones. The she introduced them to me as Amelia and Cinnamon, or Cinnabar, or something like that.

I wondered where we were going now that she'd found her friends, but there was an open bottle of Prosecco in an ice bucket with four champagne flutes next to it on a little table, and none of them seemed to be in any hurry to be off anywhere else.

'Here, Stella, why don't you have a look through this?' Cordelia said, handing me a glossy brochure. I took hold of it by reflex and to be polite, rather than through any wish to read its contents, but now she had also handed me a glass of fizz, she'd turned away from me. She started chatting to an unnaturally mahogany skinned woman in a startlingly white jacket, made all the whiter by the contrast to the sideboard coloured face, neck, arms and legs poking out of it at various angles. And so rather than stand there looking as much of a spare part as I felt, I did as I was told.

"What else can 'set off a gorgeous and stunning wedding gown like a dazzlingly radiant, vibrantly glowing tan ..." What? I read the opening line again. Was this supposed to draw potential customers in? It sounded to me like an advert for a wedding in Sellafield. Why on earth did Cordelia think that this was something I might be interested in? We hadn't spent that much time in each other's company but how had I given her the impression that I would be up for this? Maybe instead of a wedding dress, she thought I should be thinking about wearing one of those Hazmat suit things. Jonathon could wear one too. I couldn't imagine what had put this idea into Cordelia's head, but it was an utterly ridiculous one. Quite apart from anything else, Jonathon hated fake tans, just like he hated fake eyelashes and fake boobs – he had a real thing about it – surely someone who had known him for as long as Cordelia had should have known that.

'I really don't think a fake tan is me,' I started to say, trying to put the brochure back where Cordelia had picked it up from. She wasn't, however, having any of it, and pressed the brochure firmly back into my hands.

'Nonsense,' she shook her head. 'Pale and interesting has its place, Stella, but no bride should walk down the aisle looking like *Caspar* the friendly, or whatever it is, ghost, should they, Ames?' She turned to address the others.

'Ghastly!' one of the girls, presumably Amelia, shrilled in my face as she leaned over and topped up my glass. 'Down the hatch, Sheila!' She clinked my glass before half draining her own and topping it straight up again.

'Er ... It's Stella,' I tried to correct her, knowing without a doubt that my words were falling on deaf and disinterested ears. 'To be honest, I don't really want to walk down the aisle looking like an *Oompa Loompa* either,' I tried to reason with her, although quietly, hoping Mahogany Woman wouldn't hear – she looked like she'd started sampling the wares a long time ago and had forgotten to stop, and I didn't want to risk offending her. Cordelia just looked at me blankly – clearly *Charlie and the Chocolate Factory* wasn't her cup of tea.

She clearly hadn't told Jonathon that she was bringing me here, or he certainly wouldn't have looked so pleased about it. And he would never believe that I'd allowed myself to be dragged along to a fake tanning salon. How had that happened? And how did I appear to be undergoing some kind of consultation I hadn't even agreed to, as to what colour I might like to be sprayed? Mahogany Woman, whose white jacket – yes, the whiteness was definitely exaggerated by the dark orange skin sticking out of it – was probably supposed to look clinical but she wasn't fooling anyone, least of all me. She seemed to see my lack of excitement at the thought of being doused in saffron coloured chemicals as proof of some level of insanity. She obviously thought that every sane and sensible woman between the ages of seventeen and seventy should want to look as if they'd been *Tangoed.*

'Now this shade would look perfect with your eye and hair colouring,' Cordelia cooed, pointing to one of the less orange shades before topping up my glass again. The phrase *over my putrefying, maggot-infested corpse,* danced on the tip of my tongue, held back only by my heavily ingrained politeness – something I was beginning to curse my parents for – and the thought that she could have picked one a lot worse. 'Ames? Cinny? What do you think about this one for Stella?' Both girls gave a quick flash of their attention before the one who I thought was Amelia whinnied something that sounded like 'Super!' The other one brayed a quick 'Yah!' Then they turned back to the far more interesting job of choosing their own shades – even though they both looked to me like they'd already been cooked quite enough. Judging by the look on Mahogany Woman's face, Cordelia, or Cordy, as her clone friends called her, had clearly picked a shade that was for the wimpiest of wimps. Well, that was fine by me – it wasn't as if I was actually going to do this, but if I were going to go through with this thoroughly unnecessary performance, well – the wimpier the better.

There was something decidedly odd, I thought fuzzily, an hour or so and a couple more bottles of Prosecco later, about being handed a disposable black paper thong to wear. Especially one that looked quite so much like a pirate's eye patch. I fought back the fit of the giggles that threatened to escape me as a picture of Johnny Depp wearing this over his eye as Captain Jack thingummy bob flashed up in my mind and refused to budge. I fought even harder to resist the urge to pull it on over my own eye and run back out into the little corridor and shout, *Yo ho ho and a bottle of rum,* or *Ooh arr, me hearties,* at the three of them. Or were there four? Whatever. I got the distinct impression they were all far too cool to go to the cinema and wouldn't have a clue what I was talking about anyway.

My newly topped up glass and I seemed to have been more or less frog marched to the changing cubicle like a reluctant child and its teddy bear being taken into the dentist's waiting room. Having read the instructions Cordelia had given me, I'd grumbled that if she had shown me them before she'd brought me here, I would have known to bring an old bikini along with me to wear for my ordeal – not that I was really going to go through with it, of course, but it seemed like a good idea to make the right sort of noises. Her reply was that if she had let the cat out of the bag about where we were going, I would have chickened out of coming along. And I couldn't really argue with that as she was bang on about it. It was for my own good, she'd said. When I looked back at my wedding pictures I would thank her, she'd said. I supposed I couldn't really argue about any of that, either, I thought, as I took a sip or two of my rapidly disappearing drink. She did seem to know what she was talking about.

There were also instructions about painting finger and toe nails in a clear varnish so they wouldn't get stained by the colour. That would have been information I could have done with knowing beforehand, if I had actually been going to do this. Ditto the plucking of eyebrows, shaving of legs, underarms and anything else that might need plucking or shaving, plus the exfoliation of everything that could possibly need exfoliating in order to ensure completely smooth coverage. Although, on those scores I was alright, as I always exfoliated in the shower twice a week, my legs and underarms were pretty much as smooth as they were ever going to be and I had never plucked my eyebrows in my life and so saw no need to start now. And, much as I was still completely sure that this was something I wasn't going to be doing, if there was any chance there was going to be any kind of coverage, then smooth sounded a much better alternative to … well … whatever the other alternative was.

I hiccupped slightly as I lifted my glass to my lips again – Oh! There was only a trickle left. This fizz was very moreish. And ever so light – I'd have to remember what make it was and tell Alli. Then we could get the manager of Nettles to get a case of it in for us to have on my hen night. We could have little pink umbrellas in it.

The instruction about not wearing any make up wasn't a problem as I never wore that much anyway but, of course, I had put my usual body lotion on after my shower, which was something that I apparently shouldn't have done. So far, so not very good. It was a good job I wasn't going to go through with this, as I seemed to have done most of the things I shouldn't have and not done most of the things I should have.

I would much rather have had a bikini with me if I had been going to do it. An all over tan wasn't necessary. It wasn't as if I was going to go topless on the beach or anything. I wondered if I should just keep my bra on. It wasn't one of Jonathon's favourites – as I wasn't going to be seeing him tonight – or one of mine really, so it didn't matter if it got ruined.

'Come on Stella!' Cordelia barked through the door, putting me immediately in mind of Ma Hazard and bringing on another fit of the giggles – just imagine Jonathon's mother in a place like this – she'd be horrified! Cordelia and the other two girls were getting one at the same time, although what Cordelia needed a spray tan for, when she spent so much time outdoors with her horses anyway, I couldn't fathom. 'How long does it take you to strip off and pull on a thong?' An unladylike snort of laughter escaped me as I heard that question in my future mother-in-law's voice rather than Cordelia's, to be rewarded with, 'Stella? Are you alright in there?'

There was no more time to dither about. With the image of my future mother-in-law's glare of disapproval in my head, I stepped out of my knickers and picked up the hideous, stringed black triangle. A rather fuzzy part of my brain was yelling *Bring it on!* A less fuzzy part was grumbling, *this is going to be the longest ten minutes of my life.* But the fuzziest part was doing a very good job of drowning it out.

Chapter Thirty-Eight

Stella

Something shrill and screechy pierced my eardrums and reverberated right through to the backs of my eyeballs. What the hell was that? And where was I? And why was it so dark?

I opened my eyes – or rather I tried to – something was holding them tight shut. Had I been blindfolded? Had Joyce finally freaked out and locked me in the attic? What was she planning on doing to me here? I raised my hands to my face – so she hadn't tied them behind my back then – and scrabbled at my eyes.

There was no blindfold. There was a pair of hairy spiders – hairy dead spiders – stiff with rigor mortis, and they seemed to have spent their final moments of life enjoying a game of Hide and Seek in my eyelashes. I gave what felt like the longest leg of one of them a tentative tug and instantly regretted it, as a gritty pain gouged its way from the front of my eyeball through to meet the vibrating one at the back. That felt like a severely unfair amount of pain for such a small organ to have to cope with. I kept myself completely still as I waited, hopefully, for the pain to subside, and tried to remember how I came to be in this state. Nothing. Not a sausage. Complete memory meltdown.

Once my eyeballs felt a little less like they were in danger of spontaneously combusting, I tried to sit up. A wave of nausea washed over me and I flopped back down again, the back of my head connecting with something that felt more like a well stuffed sand bag than a memory foam pillow. I lay still again and took a deep breath. What was that disgusting smell?

I gave a gentle sniff, and the nausea gave me a gentle reminder that it hadn't completely gone away. It was a chemical smell, a sort of cooked, chemical smell. As if someone had microwaved some chicken flavoured biscuits in Chernobyl and, for some reason, left them here with me. Mum would be furious about the chicken bit. Although she probably wouldn't be best pleased about any of it.

The screechy, piercing sound shattered the silence again and I clamped my hands over my ears. And there was that smell again. Was I imagining it, or did it seem to be coming from one of my arms? Whatever it was that I'd obviously brushed against, why on earth hadn't I washed it off before going to sleep? Bringing my arms closer to my face I gave another gentle sniff and then really, really wished I hadn't – they were both where the smell was coming from – and they both smelled just like the panels of the wooden garden fence had always done after Dad had painted it with that horrible black stuff that was so toxic they had to stop making it. That thought stirred

182

something in the back of my brain, but it floated away before I could catch it.

I had to have a shower and wash off whatever it was. Maybe some hot water would unglue my eyelashes and then I could get my eyes open, too. As I forced myself to slowly sit up again, the alarm clock shrilled for the third time. Fumbling to switch it off before it tortured me for a fourth time, I pulled myself upright and, using the bedside table and then the wardrobe door to guide me, felt my way out of my bedroom and along the corridor to the bathroom. Clutching the sink with one hand, I turned the mixer tap on and towards hot with the other, and as soon as it was as hot as my hands could stand, started sloshing it over my face and scooping handfuls of it against my eyes. And it didn't seem to be doing any good at all.

My still aching forehead, desperately wanting icy cold water to cool its pain, rebelled against my actions by doubling the number of drummers doing band practice on the backs of my eyeballs. I had to get some painkillers down my throat, but until I could see which packet was which, I daren't grab at random from the cabinet and hope I was giving myself the right tablets – I could end up swallowing a couple of laxatives or some of those night time cold and flu things that knock you out so you don't wake yourself up sneezing – and if today was a work day, which I was pretty sure it was, then neither of those were going to be a good idea.

Just when I was starting to think I was never going

to be able to open my eyes again, one of the spiders started to loosen its grip. A moment later, the other followed its lead. Another couple of scooped palms full of hot water held against each softened their hairy, long legged hold further and blurry chinks of daylight started to find their way through. I took a deep breath before attempting to tug at one of them again, but when I did, it actually started to come away. It felt a bit like back tracking to undo a zip where the teeth had somehow caught unevenly, but at least it didn't feel like it was taking all my eyelashes out with it.

I repeated the process with the other one, splashed a bit more water in both eyes and tried hard to focus. Then I tried even harder to un-focus, panic highlighting and enlarging every horrible detail of what I was looking at. Because the image peering back at me from the mirror looked like a grotesque parody of my face. It was caked in what looked like enough makeup to kit out a Katie Price wannabe for a year. The only thing missing was the pair of ridiculous tarantula eye lashes – which were, of course, what I'd just pulled off.

But that wasn't the worst of it, I realised, as my stomach went into free fall. I could scrub all that off. But the face beneath the makeup, and the body underneath the face. They were bright orange. *I was bright orange!* What the hell was I supposed to do about that?

Chapter Thirty-Nine

Stella

A kaleidoscope of memories about last night started shooting in and out of my mind like criss-crossing fireworks, as the full horror of my reflection shot into it and stayed there. Cordelia. The tanning salon. Her ghastly friends. The delicious Prosecco – Oh God! How much of it must I have drunk to have let them do *this* to me?

I hadn't been going to go through with it. I'd only been going along with them until I could find a good moment to tell Cordelia so. I mean, there had been a moment when I could remember thinking how much it would wind Ma Hazard up for me to go through with it, but I'd never really have actually *done* it. Jonathon hated fake tans. Just how much of that Prosecco had I downed? A whole case?

An image of a tiny black paper thong flickered across my consciousness. Had I really put that thing on and ... Pulling my clothes off, I looked in the mirror. My entire body was indeed orange all over.

I hurled myself into the shower and turned the water on full blast, not caring if it was ice cold, or if it scalded the top layer of my skin off. In fact, the scalding option sounded like a really good idea right now.

Squeezing out whatever was left in the tube of exfoliating body scrub, I rubbed, scrubbed and scoured my skin with it until the orange glow was completely hidden by the red rawness. Was it my imagination, or was the water running towards the drain a murky shade of bronze? Dare I hope that I could step out of this shower looking like my usual self? Was it possible that this had only been some sort of test with some kind of wash off-able product to see what colour they thought would look best on me?

But as soon as that bubble of hope started to rise, another memory of last night pricked it out of its soapy existence. There had been some kind of mix up with the timer, or the lock on the tanning booth door, and I had somehow ended up being sprayed with whatever this stuff was for longer than I was supposed to be. There was also a vague but horrifying notion teasing my brain, that someone had shrieked something about the wrong shade, but my being hastily reassured through the door that this had been somebody else and nothing at all to do with me. I felt very cold and very sick all of a sudden.

If the hot water hadn't eventually run out, I don't know how long I would have stayed in that shower, but once it ran too cold, even for me, I had to get out. Delaying the moment of truth, I spent ages rubbing my skin dry with the towel in a last ditch attempt to get rid of a few more bright orange skin cells. But when there was nothing else to be done, I bit the bullet, offered up a silent prayer, took a deep breath, closed my eyes and forced myself to move in front of the mirror.

When my eyes eventually opened, the sight in front of me was every bit as bad as I had thought it was before I got in the shower. I looked like I'd overdosed on *Tango* and then rolled naked around the floor of a *Wotsits* factory.

It wouldn't just be Joyce who would have a fit. Jonathon would, too. Even his overly tactful, mild mannered father would have something to say about the state I was in. I could wring Cordelia's neck for letting this happen to me. What had she been thinking, leaving me to come home looking like this? Surely if there had been something that could have been done to lessen the *Ready Brek* glow, then straight away last night would have been the time to do it.

Marching back to the bedroom I grabbed my mobile and, with no idea what I was actually going to say to her, I rang Cordelia's number. It went straight to voicemail – yes, I'd be willing to bet just about anything I owned that she wouldn't be too keen to talk to me right now – if I were her, I'd be screening my calls, too. Probably from my seat on the first available flight to Australia.

Then I noticed the time. Orange skin or no orange skin, I had to get dressed and go to work. After all the publicity our protest had received, the library was more than likely going to be as busy today as it had been yesterday. This was not the time to call in sick and take a day off. It was Friday, the end of the week, and if yesterday was anything to go by, there would be a lot of people coming and going at the library. I searched the wardrobe for my longest sleeved shirt. It would have to be trousers too, and shoes rather than sandals. That just left my face, neck and hands to try and disguise as much as I could. And I really didn't think the tiny amount of makeup I owned was going to be up to the job.

Chapter Forty

Stella

'Oh my God!' Alli squeaked as I opened the front door to her. 'I thought you had to be exaggerating when you called me! You look like you've been ...'

'If you dare say *Tangoed*, you and I are officially no longer friends.' I pulled her inside and shut the door tight on the outside world, leaning back against it as if expecting some sort of marauding hoards to try and batter their way through it to get a good look at the village freak. 'Now, what did you bring? Is there anything you can do? Please tell me you can make me look normal ...'

'Stella, calm down,' my annoyingly sanguine friend soothed, shaking her music and drama department's make up case at me. 'If I can't do something with this little box of tricks, then there's no hope at all ...'

'No hope at all is not what I want to hear right now ...'

'Then it's a very good job I was paying attention the week we covered stage make up then, isn't it ...'

'One week? Was that all you did? One measly week?' My confidence in Alli's ability to save my skin – a little too literally for my liking – took a sudden nose dive.

'I'll have you know my Geisha Girl got me the highest marks ever awarded on that module ...'

'Geisha Girl!' I squeaked in such a high pitch I could probably only be heard by dogs. 'Your solution is to turn me from pumpkin orange to chalk white? I'll look like Widow bloody Twanky!'

'Honestly, Stella!' Alli rolled her eyes. 'That was just an example. I did a really good werewolf too, but I'm not going to start sticking bits of false hair all over your face either. Now, come here and sit by the window and let me get a proper look at what I've got to work with.'

I did as I was told whilst sending up a hundred silent prayers and hoping that God didn't take it personally that I hadn't been to church as often as He would probably have liked me to...

'Blimey!' My best friend recoiled dramatically, sending what was left of my hopes plummeting to the floor. 'Just kidding,' she teased, 'just kidding. Now tilt your head back a bit and relax and let aunty Alli make you look beautiful again.'

I tilted my head and tried to relax. The relaxing part was nigh on impossible.

'Oh my God!' Alli squealed, causing me to almost bang my head on the window behind me.

'What now?' There were times when I had serious misgivings about my friend's sense of humour and her sense of timing.

'We're supposed to be going to Natalie's tonight, for your final, final wedding dress fitting!' The panic in her voice mirrored what was running up and down my back.

'And I'm supposed to be going to London for the weekend tomorrow with Jonathon, to see *Warhorse*,' I groaned.

Bloody Cordelia. Bloody, bloody Cordelia. Apart from the night before the wedding itself, she could not have picked a worse time to have me turned into some kind of circus freak.

Chapter Forty- One

Stella

From: astrid@thainet.com

To: stellamoon@librarymail.co.uk

Subject: **Re: Greetings from Mum and Dad!**

Friday ...

Hello Stella darling,

Your father and I have just finished reading about you online! There was a small piece in the Daily Echo, but the Wintertown Warbler had you and your fellow protestors on the front page! Although I expect you have already seen it by now.

Whatever did Joyce have to say about it? Plenty about what her golf club ladies will think about it all, I should imagine. Although isn't Mrs Henson J P a member of the same club? That might keep her quiet, as I can't imagine she would want to upset somebody like her. Anyway, whatever Joyce says to you in private about it all, don't you listen to a word of it. Your father and I are very, very proud of you, and Jonathon. You tell him a great big Well Done from us, as I know he won't hear one from his own mother.

But I do wish we had known just how serious it was, darling. Why didn't you tell us that the council had sent out those letters? We could have changed our flights and come home early and supported you. We could have been two more in your human chain. Not that it looks as if you needed us. That Mrs Henson sounds like a woman not to be tangled with – you should introduce her to Joyce, if they haven't met already – that would set the cat among the pigeons, wouldn't it!

Well, I have to go and set up for today's Thai cooking class. Tasanee has a group of Scandinavian ladies coming. She doesn't know if they are Danish, Swedish, Finnish or Norwegian, not that it would make any difference to her as she won't be able to understand a word they say, so I'm going to have to be on my toes, not that I'm going to be much help, language wise!

Well done again my darling!

Bye for now,

Love from Mum and Dad xxx

I had seen Mum's email as soon as I logged on to the library's computer in the morning, but there had been a steady stream of new potential customers all morning and so I didn't get a chance to read it until I closed the doors for my short lunch break.

Alli had gone above and beyond the call of best friendly duty by giving me what she had considered suitable for me, in my delicate condition, out of her own packed lunch, as I hadn't been in any fit state to make a sandwich or have any breakfast this morning. I hadn't really thought I could face the cheese, tomato and cucumber sandwich she had given me as I sat down with what must have been my twelfth cup of tea of the day so far. Once I had taken a nibble at one of the corners however, I had found myself wolfing the rest of it down and fantasising about the mini packet of shortbread biscuits, the shiny red apple and the black cherry yoghourt she had kept for herself.

If only the afternoon could be a little less noisy. Hopefully, the headache I had finally managed to get under control with the help of a couple of doses of extra strong, extra quick painkillers washed down by the afore mentioned bucketfuls of tea, would decide to keep a hold on itself. Then all I would have to worry about was the fact that my entire face and body were bright orange. And that on one of the hottest days of the year so far, I was melting away under far too much fabric and several layers of makeup. Oh, and not forgetting the fact that anything I touched ended up with little smudges of old fashioned, five and nine stage make up smeared all over them. And me a librarian.

Chapter Forty- Two

Stella

It was now Friday afternoon and the drummers had taken up residence in my head again. Whatever it was they were practising, they must have been doing it very badly, as they kept on starting from the beginning and repeating their out of time sequences over and over again. And they weren't getting any better at them no matter how many times they tried. Plus, I was sweating all over from my body being so completely covered up and my face, neck and hands being caked in make up on what had turned out to be if not the hottest, then certainly one of the hottest days of the year so far. I felt like a melting candle and had to keep nipping to the little staff toilet to check my appearance in the mirror. The last thing we needed at the moment, after everyone's efforts on Wednesday, was for me to start scaring away any customers, journalists or council officials who walked through that door, by looking like a waxwork model who had been left too close to a heater.

The human chain protest, and Wednesday night's and yesterday's newspaper and local radio and television coverage of it had certainly boosted interest in the library, thanks in a very large part to the Chief Inspector's wife and mother. I had worried that Mrs Jenkins and Mrs Poole might feel a little side-lined by what had happened in the end, but I needn't have worried.

'Hasn't it all worked out wonderfully well?' Mrs Poole gushed, as she came in to change one of her knitting patterns and saw the number of people in the building.

'That Mrs Henson is a good one to have on your team,' Mrs Jenkins nodded, coming in behind her. 'Somebody who gets things done properly. If she wanted to run for the council, she would get my vote.'

'Oh, mine too!' Mrs Poole exclaimed.

'Mine too,' I agreed.

The kid's section had been overflowing with a whole new load of toddlers, three and four year olds that I hadn't set eyes on before. Half of them seemed to have come from the newish housing estate on the way to Wintertown, and part of me wondered what their criteria had been for choosing to come to Netley Mallow, rather than going to the larger Wintertown library – not that it mattered, as long as they came along to one of them. The quietly spoken mums, grandmas, and a couple of dads of these new little customers looked tired and pale.

The other half, I supposed, hailed from some of the more upmarket houses that had started springing up on the outer outskirts of Netley Magna. Their loudly spoken, glossy haired, scarily long nailed, yummy mummies all seemed to know each other. I struggled to keep my gaze from their arms and legs – they had a lot of tanned and toned flesh on display, probably even more than usual, thanks to this mini heat wave. They all looked so cool and comfortable. While all I wanted to do was pull the top layer of *my* skin off and dispose of it one of those hospital bins they keep for toxic waste.

And I could be wrong, but I got the distinct impression that they all thought this was going to be some kind of great free crèche for the afternoon. If there was any chance the library was going to stay open, and if there was any chance these were going to be regular customers, I would have to give serious thought to running *Story & Rhyme Time* twice a week. From now on I would have to split them into two, easier to manage groups – although how this would fit in with the socialising plans of the yummy mummies I had no idea. But that was their problem not mine – I had quite enough of my own to be going on with for the moment, thank you very much.

Still, worrying about that could wait until Monday morning. I had my final, final dress – or at least I hoped so – fitting tonight with Alli. The thought of unveiling my tandoori skin in front of Natalie who, even though she claimed to have seen it all before and to be completely un-shockable, I would be willing to bet had never before been confronted with a bride to be in quite this shade of orange, made me want to pull two layers of it off just to be on the safe side. I sincerely hoped there was going to be a nice, chilled bottle of Pinot Grigio with our names on it. Or two. Or even a whole case. Although, as having too much to drink did play its part in my ending up in this state in the first place – although not quite as big a part as bloody Cordelia – maybe not.

And then Jonathon and I were supposed to be going to London in the morning for our own version of one of those theatre break weekends. No Joyce, no library worries, no wedding plans, no Cordelia, just lunch in a fancy restaurant, a Saturday evening performance of *Warhorse*, a romantic supper, a king-sized bed and Jonathon. Was there any way I could persuade him to wear a blindfold for the whole weekend? It would be nice and dark in the theatre though, so he could take it off for the play …

Everyone had finally gone and I was just about to shut down the computer when the door half opened and what could only be termed a *handsome stranger* put his head round it. Well, his head was handsome anyway and, going on that I assumed that the rest of him was as well.

'I'm not too late, am I?' the handsome head enquired with a disconcertingly diffident smile. He was a cross between Jonathon when we first met, and Hugh Grant in *Notting Hill,* well Hugh Grant in any of those nineties Richard Curtis films. I suddenly felt goose-pimply all over my orange skin.

'Too late for what?' I heard my voice ask, foolishly, as if he might have mistaken the library for a pub at last orders, or an airport and he was worried he might have missed check-in.

'I read about your protest in the paper and I wanted to come along and register as a new customer.' The rest of him followed his head through the door and proved me right – he was indeed handsome. And quite strange in the fact that we don't get that many good looking, non geeky men in their twenties coming in here. In fact, Jonathon is the nearest we've got to that and if he weren't my fiancé I doubt even *he* would ever set foot inside the library. 'Sorry, I couldn't get here any earlier.'

'No! No that's fine!' my voice blurted out as I moved my glowing hand away from the mouse, in case my finger accidentally clicked on shut down. I really should have put some more of Alli's five and nine, or whatever it was on it – the colour was starting to show through again. 'The more the merrier!' *The more the merrier?* Seriously? What was wrong with me? Just because this man looked a bit like Jonathon crossed with a *Notting Hill* Hugh Grant with slightly less floppy hair, there was no need for me to gush like a St Trinian's schoolgirl. I was going away for a romantic weekend with the real thing tomorrow – Jonathon of course, not Hugh Grant – although you never knew who you might bump into in the big city. Mind you, just how romantic it was going to be once Jonathon had clapped eyes on me remained to be seen.

'I'm working in Netley Magna at the moment, you see,' he explained, 'and I usually just download books onto my e-reader, but I left it on charge at home and left in a rush and forgot to bring it. I was going to go into Wintertown and buy something to read in bed but, having seen the article about them trying to close the library here, I thought I should come along and borrow a few and kill two birds with one stone.' He had a warm, friendly but shy smile and hadn't recoiled as soon as he'd caught sight of me, so was obviously in possession of tact and, or, impeccable manners.

'So, where's home?' my voice nosily asked, as if it was any business of mine. Except that it sort of was, as he would have to put his home address on the temporary membership form. I pushed the image of him reading in bed straight out of my head and firmly replaced it with one of Jonathon.

'London. St John's Wood. We've got an enormous library in Swiss Cottage. Lots of staircases everywhere. But then, you probably know that.'

'Are you a member?' I asked, busying myself locating a temporary membership form whilst ignoring the annoying voice in my head. It was saying that if anyone else had assumed that because I was a librarian I must know every library in the country, I would have groaned inside and thought them a halfwit. The voice sounded remarkably like Joyce, but then it would, wouldn't it.

'Have you worked here long?' he asked, getting his wallet out and pulling a pristine Camden libraries membership card out of one of the tight little spaces.

My mind went blank. I couldn't, for the life of me remember how long I had worked there. 'It feels like it sometimes,' I said, because it would be rude not to give any kind of reply. 'You just need to provide some proof of identity, and fill in your home address and your temporary address.' I passed him the form and a pen and took the card from him. It was spotless and shiny and didn't look like it had been used much. A bit like his fingernails. He was no stranger to a manicure. I wondered what he did for a living.

'There we are.' He handed me the form and I started to tap the details into the computer. 'Can I whizz round and grab something for the weekend?'

'Sorry?' I coughed, as an image of those barbershops in old films popped into my mind, where the barber offers his customers something for the weekend and he doesn't mean books.

'A couple of Ken Follett's should keep me out of mischief,' he grinned. 'Where would I ...'

'Oh, spy thrillers are on the back wall, on the right hand side,' I directed him, thinking he must be some kind of speed reader if he thought he might need more than one Follett for the weekend. It had taken Jonathon over a month to read *The Pillars of The Earth*, and that was after watching it on TV so that he would have some idea of what was going on.

I was just finishing putting his details into the

computer when the door opened again and Alli flounced in.

'Wine,' she gasped, 'I need wine and lots of it. Possibly not quite as much as you do, but still … lead me to wine!' She laid her head down on the counter and covered it dramatically with her arms. This was her default position after a really stressful day and nothing short of the sound of a bottle being opened would prize her head off that counter. Unfortunately there was no wine in the library and so the promise of it on the way to Natalie's would have to do.

'Bad day?' I chuckled as sympathetically as I could, given my own less than wonderful one.

'Bad cellist,' she groaned, opening one eye and fixing it on me. 'You remember the one I was telling you about? The one the clarinet players were fighting over and he wasn't paying either of them the slightest bit of attention? Well,' she carried on, turning her head so that just her chin was now resting on the counter, as the vague recollection of her telling me about them in the wine bar the other night crept up on me, 'it turns out he was secretly giving them *both* plenty of attention!'

'What a pig!' I exclaimed, indignant on both their behalves.

'Oh that's not the worst of it,' she lifted her head completely off the counter now and looked at me over her now ever so slightly smudged eye liner. 'When they found out about each other and went round to his place to have it out with him, he only went and managed to persuade them that instead of fighting about it, it would be a much more fun if they all got together and had a threesome ...'

'No!' I squeaked. That sort of thing didn't happen in the New Forest. Well, not our part of it, anyway.

'Oh yes,' she shuddered. 'The three of them have been at it for weeks. He lives with his dad who's never at home, so they've been using his place ...'

'Oh my God! Just imagine if his dad had come home and caught them ...'

'I don't need to imagine it,' she groaned, closing her eyes and then instantly snapping them open again. 'They decided to up the excitement level a few notches and use the percussion cupboard down the corridor from my office.' Poor Alli looked like a character from a Jane Austin novel who was suffering from a fit of the vapours.

'No!'

'Oh yes!' she groaned. 'I went to see what the funny noises were and ... there they were. God, Stella! I want to gouge my eyeballs out, only there's no point because every time I close my eyes I can still picture the three of them. I want to go back in time and walk past that cupboard door, put my fingers in my ears and ignore those noises.' She scrunched her fingers through her hair, leaving the elfin cut she wore attractively dishevelled. 'I'll never be able to use a triangle in orchestra practice ever again.'

'The mind boggles.' My new temporary customer

appeared from the end of a line of bookshelves with his couple of Ken Follett's and a copy of William Boyd's *Waiting for Sunrise*. I dreaded to think how much he had just heard and what he might be thinking of the good people of Wintertown and Netley. 'I thought I might read this again,' he indicated the Boyd, as he put the three books down on the counter, treating us both to his warm but shy smile. 'Hello,' he said to Alli, who looked torn between wanting to meet the handsome stranger in front of her and wishing the ground would swallow her up whole. 'I'm Craig, I'm a new temporary resident. It sounds like you've been having a right old day of it.'

'Let's just say thank God it's Friday. I'm Alli.'

'Well, Alli and ...' he looked questioningly at me.

'I'm Stella ...'

'Oh yes, of course, I should have remembered your name from the piece in the newspaper! Well, ladies, I'm new to the area and hardly know anybody here yet. Is there any chance I could persuade you both to join me for a drink? That pub across the village green seems very nice ...'

'Oh believe me, Craig,' Alli smiled at him, 'after the day we've both had we would have loved to. Unfortunately, Stella has a final wedding dress fitting to get to and, as her best friend and chief bridesmaid, I have to be there too.'

'Oh, never mind. Maybe another time?'

'You never know your luck,' she grinned at him.

Chapter Forty- Three

Stella

'You were so flirting with him!' I stage whispered to Alli after Craig had left with his books, wishing us both a lovely weekend.

'I so was not. I was just being friendly,' she raised an eyebrow at me. 'It was *you* he meant when he asked us out for a drink, anyway ...'

'Er ... hello, best friend and chief bridesmaid – and what was that about *chief* bridesmaid? You're the only blooming bridesmaid – are we not just on our way for me to try on my wedding dress? Do you really think you should be encouraging strange men to flirt with the bride to be? And what a strange man he would have to be, what with me looking like something out of *Tales of the Unexpected!*'

Alli chuckled away to herself as I locked up the library and we walked towards her car. 'I wasn't suggesting that you do anything about it. As if you would! It's just nice sometimes to be appreciated by someone other than the person you're going to be spending the rest of your life with.' She stopped by her car. '*Tales of the Unexpected*? I thought you were going to say *Bride of Chucky!*'

'Did we say *best friend*?' I gave her my strictest, most formidable librarian look, the one I reserved for parents who allowed their children to scribble on the books, or eat sticky things whilst reading and leave finger prints all over them. 'That position can be reviewed, you know ...'

'And after I came to your rescue this morning?' she quipped, unlocking the doors and getting in. 'How was my lovely cheese sandwich, by the way?'

'Er ...' Natalie looked from me to Alli and back to me again as soon as we walked through her door. 'Have you been trying out different make up looks for the wedding, Stella?'

'Yes, that's right,' Alli said with her straightest face. 'This is one of the looks we were considering, so we thought we would see what it looks like with the dress.' There went that wicked sense of humour again.

'Oh,' was clearly all Natalie could bring herself to say.

'I'll go and get undressed then.' I made my escape to the little changing area Natalie had had curtained off in the corner of her workroom, which was essentially the downstairs back room of her little cottage. Alli could explain to her what had happened.

The deep breath I took before I could bring myself to start removing any of my clothes tonight wasn't really deep enough, but I thought I should probably leave a bit of oxygen for the other two. This was going to be so

207

humiliating. The only upside to any of this was that Jonathon's mother wasn't here and so, for now, I was being spared her opinion on the ridiculousness of women who got drunk and allowed themselves to be persuaded to do things they ought to have had more sense than to do. Of course, the fact that it was her beloved Cordelia who was at the bottom of my mortifying state would have no bearing on the matter at all as far as Joyce was concerned. No, silly me, it would all have been my fault and mine alone.

'Here you are then,' Natalie approached the curtain. She would have my beautiful dress cradled in her arms. 'Are you ready?'

There was no more time to stand there worrying about how this was going to look to Natalie. Anyway, she must have seen some sights in her time as a dressmaker, mustn't she? I quickly started pulling my top and trousers off, took another deep breath and sent up a silent prayer that it might not really be as bad as I thought. Then I pulled back the curtain.

'Oh. My. God!' Natalie's usual cool calm and professional composure slipped right off her face and fell on the floor in a puddle at her feet the moment she clapped eyes on me. 'Please tell me this is either a very late April Fools' joke, or a very early Halloween trick?'

Who had I been kidding? Of course it really was as bad as I'd thought it was. It was probably worse. I'd had all day to get used to it. Every new person who saw me was going to have this reaction. Jonathon was going to have this reaction, if not worse, although he would have it very quietly, with a great deal of tact and diplomacy. I had a combination of two of the things he disliked most in a woman, bright orange skin and make up that looked like it had been plastered on with a trowel – which it more or less had, but that was beside the point. How could we go away for the weekend tomorrow? People on the train would be pointing and staring at the man with the weird looking woman. Jonathon would be so uncomfortable. Of course, he'd try and hide it for my sake, but he would be so embarrassed. I would have to call the weekend off.

'Shall I open another bottle?' Natalie asked, a couple of hours later, having gone to pour the remains of the second Pinot Grigio bottle into Alli's glass and found that nothing had come out.

'Coffee for me please,' I begged. I couldn't do this two nights on the trot – who was I trying to kid? I couldn't do this one night on the trot.

'Yep, coffee for me too please,' Alli stifled a dainty yawn. 'Harry's helping a mate do a car boot sale tomorrow and he'll be expecting me to be up with the lark, too.'

'Ok, coffee it is.' Natalie clambered up from where she had been sitting on a cushion on the floor and took the empty bottle to the kitchen. I could hear her filling the kettle and switching it on.

She had been wonderful. As soon as we'd told her what had happened she had sent me to have a shower and wash all the makeup off so that she could see what we had to work with. She had mixed me a paste of baking soda and lemon juice and found an unopened exfoliating mitt from some hotel spa she had been to and sent me back to the bathroom again to give myself a good scrub all over. This, she told me, should be at least a bit more effective than the regular body scrub I had used this morning.

Once I'd scrubbed until I couldn't stand it any longer, I'd come back downstairs. They had studied me and both of them proclaimed that, although I wasn't back to my normal colour, they could definitely see a difference. Part of me clung on to that, while another part told me they were just being kind.

Natalie knew all about my weekend trip to London and Alli had told her I was thinking that I should cancel it. She had a much better idea, she said. That was when she opened the second bottle of wine and Alli and I sat and listened to her suggestions for my trip.

I recalled, earlier in the day, thinking that the only way I would be able to go on this trip with Jonathon would be if I were able to persuade him to wear a blindfold. It seemed that Natalie had been thinking of something along the same lines. Only her ideas for when and where he should wear it had turned out to be very different from mine. Very different indeed.

Chapter Forty- Four

Stella

Our train to Waterloo was already half full when it pulled into Southampton Central and I was so glad that Jonathon had reserved seats for us. He hitched our overnight bags up onto the rack above and we settled ourselves and the coffees we had just bought at our table. A little wave of excitement rolled through me – this was more like it – Jonathon and I off on an adventure together, just the two of us. And a selection of silk scarves lent to me by Natalie, who had promised me faithfully that their only purpose had ever been to put over her brides' faces to keep their make up off the dresses while they were trying them on.

I loved travelling by train, although I didn't really get to do that much of it. Mention train journeys to me and immediately black and white footage of glamorous women, and men wearing hats, all boarding boat trains for Southampton Docks, or the Orient Express Pullman for Paris or Venice, started playing through my head.

'Is this alright?' Jonathon smiled at me. 'I did try to get forward facing seats but they'd all gone.'

'This is lovely,' I smiled back. 'Relax, Jonathon. We're going to have a lovely time.'

'It's such a pity you've had a reaction to … what was it again? A new body scrub?'

'That's right …' I mentally crossed my fingers behind my back. As far as I could remember, I'd never ever deliberately lied to Jonathon before. Well, apart from telling him that I'd liked the scrambled eggs he had insisted on cooking for me the morning after the very first night we'd slept together. But that lie had been a very white one – pretty much like those wishy washy, cream sodden eggs he had poured onto my immediately soggy piece of toast – but then, if he'd spread butter and marmalade on a week old dog biscuit that he'd happened to have in his pocket and served it up to me I would have told him it was delicious. That's what you do, isn't it? This lie was less white though. It was for the benefit of my own pride rather than his feelings. Although there was, of course, an element of not wanting him to worry about it, which I told myself made it a bit less self-serving.

'What a good job you didn't try it out even closer to the wedding.' Jonathon carefully levered the lid off first my coffee and then his own – he never trusted that they'd been put on properly and always thought we'd end up tipping hot coffee down ourselves – although to be fair, that was just the sort of thing I would go and do. A bit like getting drunk and letting myself be spray tanned the colour of the filling in a Jaffa Cake, when the most important day of our lives was just around the corner.

'Mm … yes … isn't it …' On the off chance that he could read my thoughts through my eyes, I looked out onto the platform and fixed my gaze on the window of the little coffee shop. Strangely enough, there was a man there who looked very much like the one who had come into the library and signed up as temporary resident just before I closed up yesterday. What was his name? Greg? No … Craig! That was it. Craig. He was sitting right next to the window, reading a paper, and he looked up just as I was staring at him, caught my eye and buried his face straight back in his newspaper again. How odd!

'Is that lotion doing the trick?' Jonathon was looking at my hands, which had received a good old slathering of calamine lotion, pretty much as the rest of me had before I'd got dressed this morning. The lotion was courtesy of a herbalist friend and neighbour of Natalie's, who had knocked us up an emergency batch minus the usual kaolin clay which was apparently what gave the shop bought stuff its pink colour. So not only did it feel lovely on my skin, it also had a very useful, even if temporary, whitening effect.

'What? Oh, yes! Do you see that man in the coffee shop? The one who looks as if he's hiding behind his newspaper?'

'Where?' Jonathon peered past me out of the window.

'There. Behind that newspaper?'

'All I can see is a newspaper with a pair of hands

213

that look like they could be a man's, or maybe a butch woman's, holding it, but I can't see who it is. Why?' He smiled at me, obviously enjoying the little bit of intrigue and wondering which Agatha Christie plot I had in my head now. 'You've not been reading *Four Fifty from Paddington* again, have you?' His smile turned a little too indulgent for my liking. God help me if I ever came across a real life mystery – everybody I know and trust would just think I was imagining it. 'Because this is Southampton, and the time is …'

'Actually this does have something to do with books.' I just stopped myself from adding *so there*! 'He came into the library just as I was about to close yesterday and borrowed three books …'

'And now he's reading a newspaper,' Jonathon shrugged. 'He's obviously a keen reader.' My fiancé then picked up his cappuccino and took a tentative sip. 'Mm, not bad for station coffee.' He looked down at my sugarless, black decaf. 'Have you tried yours yet?'

'But he came and joined as a temporary resident because he was working in the area and he borrowed three books because he didn't have his e-reader with him and he didn't have anything to read over the weekend …'

'Stella sweetheart, if you're determined to turn us into *Tommy and Tuppence* for this weekend, you're going to have to come up with a better plot than that …'

At that moment a harassed looking middle-aged couple rushed on board and started to settle themselves into the seats opposite us, just as the announcement came that this train was the ten fifty five, South West Trains, Poole to London Waterloo service from Southampton Central to London Waterloo, calling at Southampton Airport Parkway ...

'It's not some mystery plot,' I mumbled. 'I was just curious, that's all. He said he was from London and that he was going to be stuck here for the weekend. I just wondered what he was doing sitting in a café on the station platform ...'

'Well, when he comes back in to return his books you can ask him.'

'I shall do no such thing,' I exclaimed, feeling a tiny blush wash up my face as I remembered Alli thinking that he'd wanted to invite me for a drink. The last thing I intended to do was encourage that, as innocent as she had managed to make it sound.

The doors closed and a moment later the train started to move and the little platform coffee shop was left behind. That was one little mystery that would have to remain unsolved.

'What did you bring to read?' Jonathon asked as I reached into my handbag.

'I'm reading one of my favourite Libby Sarjeant mysteries,' I told him, pulling Lesley Cookman's latest, *Murder in a Different Place,* out of my bag. 'What about you?

He reached into the little carrier bag he had in front

215

of him and took out Phillip Pullman's *The Amber Spyglass*. We smiled at each other. Pullman's trio of books titled *His Dark Materials* had been the first gift I had ever given Jonathon. I loved that he still re-read them from time to time.

'What do you think you'll be doing this time next week?' I asked him.

'Why? What's happening next week?' He chuckled and I joined in. 'Knowing my mother, I'll be sitting down to an enormous full English, to keep my strength up for the gruelling day ahead ...'

'Well that's a nice way to describe our wedding!' I put on my indignant face, until he kissed me, then I picked up my book in case we were embarrassing the couple sitting opposite us.

We settled down to our journey, each gravitating towards the bit in the middle of our two seats, the corners of our books touching, our bodies leaning against each other in spite of the warmth of the day and the sun streaming in through the carriage windows. This was going to be the lovely weekend Jonathon had planned, after all, I thought. Nothing, not even a stupid spray tan was going to spoil it. All I had to do was follow Natalie's and Alli's suggestions and this would turn out to be a weekend Jonathon would *never* forget.

Chapter Forty- Five

Jonathon

The little old fashioned, independent hotel I had booked for the night, in one of the streets behind Marble Arch, had turned out to be a good choice, although that was more by luck than by any kind of hotel choosing skill. Stella just loved its creaky, dippy floor boards, its ancient, mismatched but well-polished furniture, and it's old building smell. I had mainly picked it for its location. Oxford Street was just a couple of minutes' walk away and I knew Stella would want us to have a look round the sale in the big Debenhams there. And Holborn was only a couple of stops on the Central Line, for Drury Lane and the New London Theatre. I was so glad I'd been able to get tickets for *Warhorse* for her, even if they were only the restricted view ones. Mrs P and Mrs J had been telling everyone at the protest just how much they had enjoyed it and so Stella was really excited to be coming to see it.

It was a nuisance about that scrub thing though. I had hoped we might spend some time in our room before we went out for a late lunch, but I supposed that if her skin was feeling sore, she wasn't going to be up for that, which was a shame. It was a lovely big bed and felt very comfortable when I sat down on it. But Stella didn't seem to have any intention of taking that long sleeved top off. So, lunch it was.

We ate at The Grazing Goat before heading for the shops. I'd managed to persuade Stella to look for a new bikini and sarong for our honeymoon. Not that there was anything wrong with the one she had, but she'd lost quite a bit of weight over the last few months, so I wanted to buy her something new and pretty. Anyway, she hadn't had a new bikini in all the time I'd known her, so it would be nice to see her in something else. She had said something about looking for some new lingerie too, although I suspected she would buy that when I wasn't with her. And she'd told me I needed some new shorts.

I was very lucky. Stella wasn't one of those women who could spend all day wandering round a whole street full of shops, looking at various versions of the item she was looking for. Or even worse, a woman who would go shopping just for the sake of it, with no idea what she was looking for, just waiting to see what grabbed her attention. That would have driven me nuts. No, Stella was a *Debenhams* and *Marks & Spencer* girl through and through. One trip to either one of those shops was all she needed, and so we were back at our hotel in plenty of time to get showered and changed to go to the theatre.

Stella seemed to be reluctant to get changed in front of me, or to have her shower while I was in the bathroom, which was a bit strange. She had never been shy around me before. I hoped she wasn't feeling self-conscious because of a few patches of red skin. I would have been more than happy to have rubbed some of that lotion into it for her, but she insisted she could manage, so I didn't push it.

Maybe when we got into bed tonight and the lights were out she would feel less uncomfortable about it.

Chapter Forty- Six

Stella

It was such a relief to get out of the hotel and be on our way to Marble Arch tube station. As soon as I'd started to get undressed for a quick shower, Jonathon had wandered into the bathroom. There didn't seem to be anywhere that I could get changed without him being there. And it didn't feel right, not being able to take my clothes off in front of him. Natalie hadn't thought about all that when she'd come up with her plan for tonight. I just hoped it worked. I hated to see disappointment in my fiancé's eyes.

It was a lovely warm evening with just the gentlest of breezes and I would have loved to have been able to wear something with short sleeves, but I just couldn't let Jonathon see the state of my skin until the spray tan had been able to be toned down a bit, by whatever means necessary. He looked so cool and comfortable in the new, short sleeved *Mantaray* shirt I'd just found him in the sale. It was a bit on the creased side, but Cornflower blue really did suit him.

The tube was packed and we were crushed together like sardines in a tin for the three stops to Holborn. The warm, early evening air outside as we came back up to the ground felt all the fresher for our cramped little journey, and the walk towards the theatre, hand in hand, was an enjoyable one. It only took four or five minutes to find the theatre, once we'd worked out which was Parker Street and made our way towards Drury Lane.

Jonathon had been worried that the seats weren't going to be too good as the only ones he had been able to get had a partially restricted view of the stage, but I thought that added to the atmosphere. And once the play started, we just forgot everything else around us and couldn't take our eyes off the stage. You really did forget that the horses were puppets, they were so wonderfully crafted and so skilfully worked by the actors. I was spellbound.

Chapter Forty- Seven

Jonathon

The show was amazing and I was so glad that Stella had said she wanted to see it, otherwise I would never have thought of booking tickets for it. I was relieved too that I'd booked us somewhere for a post theatre supper, as a lot of places would have stopped taking orders by the time the show finished and we had got out of the theatre. It occurred to me, as we were making our way out of the auditorium, that when a film finished everybody was always in a rush to leave the cinema, but when a play or show finished, nobody seemed in any hurry at all to leave. Stella would probably say that was part of the magic of theatre, or something like that. I could just see us in five or six years or so, taking our first child to see his or her very first Christmas pantomime and Stella explaining it all in that wonderful way she has of bringing things to life. If we had a daughter, there would be ballet shows as well, although knowing Stella, she wouldn't differentiate between a son and a daughter, and either would be taken to see *The Nutcracker* or whatever it was. She would be brilliant at all that. Anyone could see how much the kids in the library have always loved her.

We finally made it out onto the street. It was a

warm night, but the Crusting Pipe, where we were going to have supper, was only about a ten minute walk from the theatre and our table was booked for half past ten, so we didn't have to rush. Hand in hand, we sauntered in a zig zag fashion along Drury Lane, Bow Street, Russell Street and on to Covent Garden.

'Oh Jonathon, this is perfect.' Stella squeezed my hand as we were shown to our table. The wine bar's website had boasted of little nooks and crannies for semi-private dining and our little table was in just such a nook. 'You think of everything, don't you!' Encouraged by the look in her eyes, I didn't tell her that the secluded table had been down to pure good luck. That was a look I loved to see in her eyes and, what with her rash and not wanting me to see her without her clothes on earlier, I hadn't expected to see it tonight. Maybe it was that thing about the magic of theatre, but I certainly wasn't going to say anything to put a spanner in the works.

Neither of us wanted a huge supper before going to bed, so we ordered a British charcuterie board between us from the sharing items on their menu, followed by a trio of ice cream which we fed to each other. This was looking decidedly promising. They also had Stella's favourite, white port, on their wine list and she had a couple of large ones, which looked even more promising. We decided not to linger over a coffee.

The plan had been to make our way back to Holborn tube station, as we would have preferred to walk the little bit further in the warm night air, than take the tube from Covent Garden and have to change trains. All at once though, we realised how late it was and, not knowing what time the tube stopped running and not wanting to miss the last one, we sped along to Covent Garden station. No one else seemed to be in any hurry though, and I suddenly felt like a bit of a country bumpkin, panicking in the big bad city.

As if reading my mind, Stella grinned at me and teased, 'In a rush to get me back to our room are you?'

'Well, we are almost newlyweds,' I felt myself grin back. I felt I should ask her if her rash was ok – I didn't want her to be uncomfortable. On the other hand though, I didn't want to remind her about it, or make her think it bothered me in any way other than my caring about her welfare. If she thought I was going to be squeamish about it, that could put the kibosh on a night of romance. I guessed that this was one of those times when it was best to keep my mouth shut.

Chapter Forty- Eight

Stella

As we made our way back to our hotel from Marble Arch, I couldn't help thinking that while those couple of glasses of white port had been very welcome, a third one would, in fact, have rounded the other two off very nicely. It might also have put those annoying butterflies flapping about in my stomach to sleep so they could stop bothering me.

It was all very well Natalie coming up with this plan for how I could spend the night with Jonathon without him seeing what had become of his pale-skinned wife to be. And it was all very well Alli encouraging her in her deviousness. But neither of them were going to be here carrying out Natalie's plan. That was going to be me. Little old me. The shy, quiet librarian, and yes … I know the al fresco thing in the New Forest wasn't exactly shy, quiet librarian territory, but that was something which had happened very naturally the first time, and had taken us both completely by surprise. All the subsequent times had been something which had always happened by some kind of tacit agreement – sometimes just with a certain raising of an eyebrow. But what I was about to do now, well … it was premeditated. And not only was it premeditated, it was completely out of my comfort zone. It could well be out of Jonathon's comfort zone, too. I didn't know.

His hand felt so comforting in mine that a part of me thought, why don't I just tell him that his stupid childhood friend took me to a spray tanning salon, we got drunk on some really nice Prosecco and some kind of mishap with the spraying gadget turned me orange. What would be the worst that would happen? But as he pulled me in to him for a lingering kiss, while the rickety little cage of a lift jerked us up to our room on the third floor, I just didn't want to say or do anything that would spoil this trip for us. I had already seen the flash of disappointment in his eyes earlier, when I'd shied away from getting changed in front of him. No, tonight I was going to have to follow Natalie's plan. And give my fiancé the shock of his life.

'Do you want the bathroom first?' Jonathon asked, nuzzling my ear. He was probably being tactful about the rash I was supposed to have, but my having first dibs in the bathroom didn't fit in with the plan.

'No, you go first and then get comfortable in bed.' I stroked his cheek, smiling what I hoped was a seductive smile and not a reflection of the turmoil going on inside my head. 'I might be a little while ...'

'Is ... is there anything you want me to ... er ... do?' Jonathon looked like he had his own little battle with tactfulness going on. 'If you want me to ... er ... rub in some ointment?'

226

'No thanks.' I took hold of his hands in mine and gave them a gentle squeeze. 'I've got all that covered.' And with that I ushered him towards the bathroom as if he were a small child looking for excuses not to get ready for bed.

While he was in there and I could hear the shower running, I sorted out Natalie's silk scarves and put them in the draw on what would be my side of the bed – I always slept on the side nearest the bathroom when Jonathon stayed at my place and so that was what we automatically did whenever we stayed anywhere else, whichever side the bathroom happened to be on.

Then I spent the next couple of minutes trying not to bite all the skin off my lip while I waited for him to come back out.

Chapter Forty- Nine

Jonathon

Blimey. I did not see that coming. Even before she put the blindfold on me.

One minute I was lying in bed, skimming across a page of *The Amber Spyglass*, while Stella got ready in the bathroom. The next thing I knew she was telling me to close my eyes – which I did, of course, because I thought she didn't want me to see her rash. But then suddenly she was tying some kind of silky blindfold over my eyes.

'Stella?' I put my hands to my face but she moved them away, as I felt her lean over me to kiss me. Then, just as I was getting used to the idea of the blindfold, she started tying something around one of my wrists, and then the other, and then tying my wrists to one of the brass posts on the head of the old fashioned bed frame.

'Stella?' Wow! If I'd known she was going to do something like this, our supper would have been a much quicker one, or we could have just skipped it completely and come straight back here after the theatre.

'Ssh,' she whispered gently in my ear. This wasn't like anything Stella and I had ever done before and I certainly hadn't had any idea she was planning on doing this tonight. And I certainly wasn't complaining. Was it

228

some kind of dress rehearsal for something she was planning to do on our honeymoon? 'That isn't too tight, is it?' she whispered.

'No,' I whispered back, wondering what she was planning to do next, and wanting so badly to touch her, and aroused by very the fact that I couldn't.

I felt her pull back the covers and lean over to kiss me again, her hands stroking my face as her lips followed them, down to my chest, down to my stomach, down ... 'Oh God, Stella,' I gasped. 'Oh God ... Stella ...'

Chapter Fifty

Stella

I was in that warm, sleepy, snugly place, where most of me was still in the land of nod but somewhere in my head a kind of mental snooze button had been pressed. Something inside me knew I was going to be waking up soon, but I just wanted to snuggle up to Jonathon for a few more minutes until it went off again. My mind was drifting off, somewhere warm and soft and floaty and ...

'What the hell? Stella! What's happened to you?' Jonathon's voice was like a bucket of ice cold water being thrown over me and I shot upright in the bed, banging my head on the brass bedstead. I was wide awake now.

Crap! Oh crappy, crappy, crappy, crappy, crap! Natalie and Alli hadn't thought of this scenario had they? They hadn't put a contingency plan in place in case I forgot to set the alarm on my phone to vibrate, or to put it under my pillow, or I fell into such a deep sleep that I didn't manage to wake up, shower and get myself dressed while Jonathon was still fast asleep. The plan had fallen spectacularly apart. I didn't want to see the look of horror on his face but that was exactly where my eyes were drawn to. And the look was exactly that. One of horror.

'Jonathon ...' I started to say, pulling the covers up

over as much of me as possible, even though the damage had already been done.

'You're ...' he looked lost for words.

'I know ...' I couldn't tear my eyes away from his.

'Is there something wrong with your kidneys, or your liver?' He looked panic stricken. Only my Jonathon could look at me in this state and his first thought be that I must be ill and not that I must have done something very stupid, or allowed something very stupid to be done to me.

'No,' I whispered, clutching the bed covers to me and trying to remember what I had planned in my head to say if such a moment as this happened. And failing miserably.

'Is ... is this what that body scrub did to your skin? I thought it was just a rash. Why didn't you tell me it had turned you a funny colour? We need to notify the manufacturers, Stella.' He jumped out of bed and grabbed his bath robe, pulling it on any old how, which showed just how worried he was. 'They need to recall the product before it does somebody some serious damage. And we need to get you to a dermatologist ...' He was pacing the room now.

'No.' I said again, trying not to mumble, knowing I had to speak up now. 'Thursday night, when I went out with Cordelia ...'

'Is Cordelia in this state as well?' He stopped pacing. 'What on earth happened to the pair of you? And why didn't you tell me?'

'She took me to a spray tanning salon.' The words came out in a rush, as if my saying them quicker might disperse them more quickly into the universe and then they wouldn't be here anymore for him to hear.

'She took you *where*?' His look was one of genuine incomprehension. I might as well have told him we had been arrested for soliciting on the planet Gallifrey and spent the night locked in the TARDIS, before Dick Van Dyke had come along and rescued us in Chitty Chitty Bang Bang.

'She took me to a spray tanning salon where she was meeting some of her friends ...'

'A spray tanning salon?' The look on his face was there for a different reason now. 'Cordelia went to a spray tanning salon? What would Cordelia want with one of those places? She spends all day outside with the horses. If she wants a tan, the last thing she needs to do is go to one of those places.' Which was a thought I now remembered flitting through my own mind at some point in the proceedings.

'I didn't know we were going there. She drove us into Wintertown. She said it was to meet some of her friends ...'

'I can't imagine Cordelia having the sort of friends who go to those sort of places ...' Jonathon argued.

'Well, she does. They were called Amelia and Cinnamon, or something like that. And they kept calling me Sheila.'

232

'And what was this, some kind of spray tanning party?' His tone matched his look. Complete, total, and 100%, incomprehension. I could have been speaking Swahili.

'Something like that, yes.' I shrunk further down into the covers.

'But what possessed you to join in and have one, Stella?'

The words *about half a crate of Prosecco, probably,* froze on my lips as he carried on, 'You know how I feel about fake tans ...'

'Yes, Jonathon, I do, which is why I was trying to keep it hidden from you while I tried to sort it out ...'

'So that was what the thing with the blindfold and the silk scarves last night was all about?' His face took on a kaleidoscope of emotions; anger, disbelief, betrayal, disappointment. 'It wasn't anything to do with surprising the man you love, the man you're about to marry, with something you thought he might enjoy. It wasn't about trying something a bit different and imaginative. It was about tricking him and keeping secret from him the fact that you'd gone out, obviously got drunk – which is most unlike you, Stella – and done something incredibly stupid which you knew he wouldn't be happy about. Is there anything else you haven't told me about that night? Is there a dirty great tattoo I haven't seen yet that you're hoping will magically disappear between now and the wedding?'

'Of course not! And I was trying to sort it out so

that you wouldn't have to know about it, Jonathon, because I know how much you hate that sort of thing ...'

'Which begs the question of why you did it in the first place?'

'I kept trying to tell them that I wasn't going to do it, but they kept on refilling my glass and ...' I knew how pathetic that sounded. The look on his face just confirmed it.

'Well you'd better hurry up and get on with whatever you're doing to sort it out then hadn't you, because I'm telling you now, Stella, if you're thinking of walking up the aisle looking like that ... well, you might not find me at the altar waiting for you.'

Chapter Fifty-One

Stella

From: francis@thainet.com

To: stellamoon@librarymail.co.uk

Subject: **Re: Sawadee Krub – Greetings from Thailand!**

Sunday ...

Dear Stella,

How was your trip to London? Did you enjoy the show? I'm sure you will have, I've read some great reviews for it. Anyway, it must have been good to get away from the village, even just for one night, and spend a bit of time alone with Jonathon – well apart from the other thousand or so people in the theatre! Did Jonathon book you a nice romantic hotel? And I expect he found you somewhere lovely to eat after the show?

I know your mother has already said it but I just wanted to tell you again how proud we both are of you. We both knew that if anybody could save the library it would be you and, yes, we know you didn't do it alone, but all those people helped because you inspired them to. So well done, my girl. And you will be able to enjoy your honeymoon so much more, knowing that you still have a job to go back to. Jonathon must be so proud of you, too. Your mother has printed up the picture that was in the Wintertown Warbler and is showing it to everyone she comes across.

Talking of your mother, she went off to the mainland first thing this morning, with a group of golf widows whose husbands are going to northern Thalang, or somewhere like that, to play in some tournament or other. Needless to say she invited herself along and also, needless to say, I'm left looking after Nelson. Although if you ask me his paw looks perfectly fine. He isn't even limping anymore – well, not properly. I swear he puts one on though whenever your mother is around. He knows a good thing when he sees one!

I sneaked a look at that shell wind chime thing she's still working on. It's monstrous, Stella, and the racket it makes when any of the strands get moved around is horrendous! But don't ever let her know I said that!

Some of us are having a barbecue on the

beach tonight, which is great timing. I'm going to enjoy a nice crispy skinned pork chop and some spare ribs and sausages without the usual lecture and disapproving looks!

By the way, did I tell you that I found out some more about those apartments and why all the owners are up in arms? It seems that this dodgy holiday rental company, which is run by a Belgian couple, have been ripping them all off left right and centre. Apparently they have charged them all a small fortune for jobs which have never been done — things like a deep clean, which hadn't been necessary because all the apartments had just been newly refurbished, and fixing things that couldn't have been broken because they were brand spanking new and would have been covered by warrantees even if they had been. I'll let you know what else I hear about it. Jonathon will be interested, I know.

Hope all is going well with you, my lovely girl,

Lots of love,

Dad xx

Oh Dad. My eyes blurred with tears as I tried to read his

email again in the coffee shop at Waterloo. It was so tempting to email him straight back, or even to make that international phone call and tell him what a stupid thing I'd managed to do. But it was so close to the wedding, and I didn't want to worry him.

I'd never seen Jonathon so angry. And certainly never with me. We'd had minor disagreements in the past, just like any other couple did, but nothing like that. And over such a stupid thing. I would have expected him to be cross at first, but then supportive. I could imagine him getting straight on to the internet and looking up ways for calming down spray tan mistakes, just like I had, only being much more methodical about it and maybe finding some sure fire method that would work a lot quicker than what I was doing now. I just didn't know what to do, other than keep on using the baking soda and lemon paste that Natalie had made for me and keep plastering on the herbal calamine lotion her neighbour had made.

Our weekend had been ruined. Jonathon wouldn't even wait for the train we were booked to travel back on. He'd had the quickest shower I had ever known him have, and then he was dressed and on his way out of our room, while I was still huddled under the covers wondering what I could do or say to calm him down. He'd barely spoken to me as he shoved his things into his overnight bag and dropped my train ticket on the bedside table.

'The room is already paid for until check out time. I'm sure you can amuse yourself for the day here in

London, or you can change your ticket to an earlier train. Just try not to get plastered on Prosecco and come back with a couple of enormous tongue piercings.' I hadn't been able to believe the words that were coming out of his mouth. I still couldn't. It was as if somebody had flicked a switch and changed his personality to that of a complete stranger.

I'd been saved from trying to think of any kind of response by a knock at the door as he was about to open it anyway. 'Room service,' a female, Eastern European voice had called.

'That'll be the breakfast in bed I ordered,' he'd said to the door frame. Obviously I was too hideous to look at even to say good bye to. 'I hope you enjoy it. I know I would have.' Then he'd opened the door. 'Thank you,' he'd said to the slender young blonde woman carrying the tray. 'On the bedside table will do.' He'd pressed whatever tip he was giving her into her hand as she went back out again and then, without another word to me, he'd followed her out, shutting the door quietly, but firmly behind him.

I'd been too shocked to cry at first. That outburst had been so unlike Jonathon. Of course I'd always known he could be a bit disapproving and a bit snobby about things he didn't agree with. But that coldness, that quiet fury, they were things I had never seen in him before. They were things I could *never* have imagined seeing in him.

The tears had come while I was in the shower, mingling with the hot water as they ran down my face. If only I'd been stronger and said no to Cordelia straight away. I could have got a taxi home. Or I could have called Jonathon. He could have come into Wintertown to get me and we could have gone for a drink or a meal. But I hadn't thought of it then. And if I had, I wouldn't have wanted to disappoint him, he'd been so pleased that Cordelia had invited me out with her. If only I'd followed my gut instinct instead of trying to please everybody and ending up pleasing no one and hating myself.

The breakfast had been cold on the tray by the time I'd come out of the bathroom having rubbed and scrubbed myself raw again with Natalie's paste and the exfoliating mitt, and covered myself from top to toe with the calamine stuff. I couldn't have eaten a thing anyway. But the eggs Florentine which he must have ordered for me, and the eggs Benedict which would have been his, looked as if they would have been lovely. Thirsty after all the tears, I had drunk both glasses of orange juice and poured out a cup of the now stone cold coffee. Then I'd started to get my things together.

We'd been supposed to go for a wander, hand in hand in Regent's Park, maybe go to the zoo, or have a walk round the Serpentine together. And now he'd gone and I'd been left behind all alone. Never in my wildest dreams would I have imagined that our lovely weekend away together might end up like that.

Chapter Fifty-Two

Stella

I called Allie from the train and she came and met me at Southampton. She was furious with Jonathon for his reaction and the way he had behaved towards me, but I was furious with myself for being so stupid in the first place. And with Cordelia, who still hadn't answered or returned a single one of my calls. Alli was furious with her too, and was all for going round to the stables and giving her a piece of her mind.

'I mean, what the hell did she think she was playing at? I'll bet you anything you like she did it on purpose ...'

'What? Why would Cordelia do that to me deliberately?' I asked my loyal friend. 'She's gorgeous. She's got a wonderful figure, a vibrant personality and her own successful business. Cordelia has got just about everything going for her that a woman could have. Even if she is ever so slightly annoying. What could she possible have against the rather average looking village librarian?'

'Oh, I don't know ... maybe the fact that with all the coverage the library protest has got, you, who are not average looking at all, my gorgeous friend, are currently the centre of attention? Maybe the fact that you, who also has a wonderful figure, are about to walk down the aisle in what is going to be the wedding of the season around here. Maybe ... well I don't know but I'm sure I can think of something else.'

'Let's just slob out at your place with some hot chocolate and a funny DVD, shall we?' I couldn't face going home and I couldn't face seeing anyone else other than Alli.

'I've got a nice bottle of Pinot in the fridge, with our names on it,' Alli tempted. 'All nice and chilled and just waiting to be opened up and poured into a couple of glasses.'

'Absolutely not.' I closed my eyes so I couldn't see the encouraging look on her face. 'It was the demon drink that helped me get into this state in the first place. If I'd been stone cold sober I would never have let this happen to me.'

'Ah ... If I had a pound for every time I've said that about some situation or other, I'd be ... well ... I'd be a hell of a lot better off than I am now ...'

'I want hot chocolate,' I interrupted before she went off at a tangent that I couldn't get her back from. 'And none of that low calorie crap. I want the good stuff ...' I could feel my face starting to crumple at the thought of the tin of *Charbonnel & Walker* that Jonathon had bought me. He'd always been such a thoughtful boyfriend, and then fiancé.

We should have been finishing a late lunch now, and thinking about heading back on our way to Waterloo station, to get our train back to Southampton. I wondered what he was doing right now. Had he managed to calm down just a little bit, or was he still furious with me? And had he really meant what he said about the wedding? If I hadn't managed to get completely back to normal by the big day, would he really not turn up to marry me?

Chapter Fifty-Three

Stella

When I woke up on Monday morning in Alli's spare room I had to check my phone – I couldn't really believe that Jonathon wouldn't have called me. But he hadn't. Not even a text message to check that I had got back from London alright. I didn't know which emotion was uppermost in me, sadness or anger. It was like they were wrestling with each other and one moment one was on top and the next moment the other one was.

I didn't feel like going home, so Alli lent me a long sleeved tunic top and some cotton trousers and gave me the last new pair left in a *Marks & Spencer* five pack she found at the back of her knicker draw. Then, once I'd covered my face, neck and hands in the white calamine lotion, she dropped me off at the library on her way in to Wintertown. It was another hot day – hadn't they all been since I'd had to start covering my skin up while everybody else was stripping off to enjoy the sun.

The doors had only been open a couple of minutes when the voice of doom came booming in through them. 'Ah, Stella, there you are.' Great. Ma Hazard. That was all I needed after the Sunday I'd just had. I dreaded to think what Jonathon had told her. This was probably going to be painful. And all on just one cup of coffee.

I took a deep breath and turned to face her with a bright smile plastered on my face. At least I hoped it was a smile and not a grimace. I couldn't really be sure. 'Good morning, Joyce. How are you?'

'Never mind me! Now what's all this nonsense about you and Jonathon having a falling out? I've never heard anything so silly ...'

It was a bit hard for me to answer without knowing what he'd said to her about it. Luckily she didn't seem to need a reply.

'Now I know that with the wedding coming up things are bound to get a little bit on top of you both – that's only natural – but you mustn't let silly little arguments fester, Stella. You are the woman. The peace maker. It's up to you to smooth things over, just like wives all over the world have always done. So as soon as you close up this evening, go home and put on something nice and then come round and sort things out. I'll expect you for dinner. It's pork chops and baked apples.' And with that she was off again, leaving me speechlessly wondering if I'd just been briefly teleported into the 1950's – *Just like wives all over the world had done*! Seriously?

I couldn't wait to dissect that conversation – if it counted as a conversation, some might call it a monologue – with Alli, but I would have to wait until her break time. For now, I had Mrs Jenkins and Mrs Poole on their way in

245

to hear about how much we enjoyed *Warhorse*. Thank God that part of the weekend had gone well and I wouldn't have to tell them any lies.

'She said what?' Alli fairly yelped down the phone at me. 'Does she not know it's the twenty first century? Does she not know it's 2015, not 1915? Blimey Stella, are you sure you want to marry into that family ... Oh! Bugger! That was a stupid thing to say. I'm sorry ...'

'It's alright. Hey, if I can put up with her levels of bombastic tactlessness, I can certainly cope with a few tiny little slivers of it from you.'

'I'd say mine were more sliverettes ...'

'Yeah, whatever ...' I rolled my eyes, even though she couldn't see me.

'So, are you going to go?'

'I don't know,' I allowed myself a great big sigh, feeling a bit of a drama queen. 'The more I think about it, the more out of order I think Jonathon was, saying all those things to me. I don't think I should be the one to go and seek him out. I think it should be the other way round ...'

'Good for you,' she said, egging me on.

'But if I don't go, I'll only end up with her on my back. Though I don't really want Jonathon to see me again until more of this colour has come off me. I just wish I knew how long it was going to take. Everything I've looked up online has given me conflicting advice.

Some websites and blogs make it look like one swipe with a bit of baby oil on a wet wipe and it can all go away; others make it look as if you're stuck with it until all your skin cells replenish themselves naturally. I still think what Natalie has given me is the best thing to use, I just can't work out how long it's going to take to work completely.'

'Well, I can definitely see a difference. It's only Monday now and yet you definitely don't look as scary as you did on Friday morning.'

'Well, thanks for that – Oh, what a shame – I have to go – Customers – Bye!' The customers in question would be ages choosing their books before they needed me to do anything, but I thought I'd better end that call before any more of Alli's little sliverettes of tactlessness slipped out. They could be quite sharp.

Chapter Fifty-Four

Stella

I was just about to close up for the evening when the floppy haired man from Friday night popped his head round the door again. Did he ever just walk through a door, and go straight in to a room? Or did he always have to send his head in first to scout things out, a bit like a submarine periscope type thing? I should ask him that. But of course, I wouldn't. Just like I wouldn't ask him what he had been doing hiding behind a newspaper in one of the coffee shops at Southampton Central on Saturday morning.

'Not too late to change a book am I?' he asked with that same disarmingly diffident smile he'd used last time. 'Sorry. I'm just on my way home from work otherwise I'd have come in sooner.' He had his copy of *Waiting for Sunrise* in his hand and it seemed churlish to turn him away.

'No, no that's fine,' I found myself saying, even though I should be locking up if I was going to go along to Jonathon's for pork chops and recriminations – I could do without the baked apples, mine would definitely be full of pips. 'You go and choose another one.'

'Thanks so much,' he smiled at me. 'I won't be

long.'

While I waited, I tidied up the leaflet stand near the door, where some of them had been taken out and put back in the wrong slots, and a couple were upside down. Was that Joyce's car parked across the village green? Did she not trust me to turn up for dinner? Or was she going to take me home and go through my wardrobe – could I not even be trusted to *put on something nice* now? It would serve her right if I didn't turn up at all. Except that I didn't think I could bring myself to be that rude to my future mother-in-law. Although, maybe I should – she seemed to have no problem at all being rude to me.

'Sebastian Faulks this time, I see.' I took his copy of *A Broken World* to scan for him.

'Another of my favourite authors,' he said. 'Who do you like?'

'I beg your pardon?' What did he mean by that?

'Who do you like to read? You must have your pick of the bunch, working in a library all day ...'

'Oh ... well, my favourite has always been Agatha Christie, but she obviously isn't writing any more ...' I cringed inside – did I really just say that? 'And I adored Ruth Rendell's books too. Out of the modern crime writers, I like Lesley Cookman's Libby Sarjeant mysteries and Sophie Hannah and Robert Thorogood. Oh, and I just love Anthony Horowitz. And Val McDermid ...' I trailed off, thinking that I must sound like a radio advert for crime fiction.

His attention was caught by one of the handfuls of leaflets I'd been about to shove back into an empty space in the rack. 'Here, let me do that,' he offered, holding his hand out to take the leaflets while I went to take his book before he dropped it. Typical where I was concerned, the ensuing muddle of hands ended up with the book thumping to the floor and the leaflets skittering down after it like a flurry of over-large snow-flakes. 'Oh! I'm so sorry,' he said, squatting down at once to start picking things up.

'No, no, it was my fault.' I followed his lead and started scrabbling about on the floor too. 'If I hadn't grabbed at your book ...'

'No, no, it was me trying to take all the leaflets out of your hand ...' he jumped in. We were both so busy trying to apologise over each other while we fumbled about that we ended up banging our heads together.

'Now that really *was* my fault,' I laughed, as I saw him about to start apologising again. 'That is absolutely the sort of clumsy clown type thing I do all the time ...'

'I don't believe that for a moment,' he said with a grin, as he helped me up then bent down to pick up his book, and the leaflets nearest to it which he placed straight into my hands before they could cause any more mischief.

'Oh it's true, I'm afraid,' I grinned, warming to my theme. 'You should never eat a banana anywhere near me. No matter how carefully you dispose of its skin in a bin, it will find its way under one of my feet and I'll end up treating you and anyone else standing around to the least graceful display of skating without ice that you've ever seen.'

He gave a belly laugh that had a lovely warm tone to it. 'I'd pay good money to see that ... Only, of course, if you had something soft to land on though ...'

'Well, unfortunately that's the thing about those pesky banana skins, they never seem to turn up when there is something soft available to land on ...'

After the weekend I'd had, it was heart-warming to end the day with such a silly conversation. I didn't know how much longer it would have gone on for if his phone hadn't started to ring at that moment. 'Yes? Craig speaking,' he said into it. Then, 'no, it's alright, I won't be long. Just changing a library book and then I'll be on my way over ...'

I went back to the counter and scanned his book for him while he was talking, then came back and held it out so I wouldn't keep him waiting any longer. 'Here you are, hope you enjoy it ...'

'I don't suppose,' he started to say and then floundered and dithered in a very Hugh Grant, *Four Weddings and a Funeral* kind of way.

'What?' I asked, even though I knew that the answer to whatever he was going to ask was going to have to be no.

'Well, I just wondered ... a few friends and I are

251

meeting for a drink at the Badger's Inn ... I don't suppose you might be free to join us?'

'I'm sorry. I'm expected for dinner at my future mother-in-law's,' I told him, thus reminding him that I was indeed a bride to be and that, nice as it was to be asked, he shouldn't really be asking me.

'Of course, of course,' he dithered a bit more. 'I shouldn't have asked. Well ... have a lovely evening.' He turned to go and then, right in the doorway turned back again. 'I didn't hurt you when we banged heads did I?'

'No, of course not,' I smiled. 'Might have knocked some sense into me, or knocked a bit more out, but I'm well and truly used to that. You're talking to the woman who managed to fall down the stairs at her own engagement party.'

'You didn't!'

'At the risk of sounding like a trip to the pantomime, oh yes I did. Heel caught in the hem of my long dress apparently. Although I don't remember doing it. My life is like one long *Carry On* film.' My smile tightened on my face slightly as I remembered the latest *Carry On* style episode in my life, and Jonathon's reaction to it.

'Well, I really must get going now. It's been lovely talking to you, I can see why this library is popular. I bet all the customers love you.' He held out his hand as if he wanted me to shake it, so, although it felt a bit formal I did. 'Are you sure I didn't hurt you?' he asked again, as he put a finger up to my forehead and gently stroked at the place where we had bumped. I felt as if I should step away but for some reason my feet wouldn't move.

'Quite sure,' I breathed, wondering how wildly inappropriate this was, and how it would be a really bad time for Jonathon to realise how much he'd overreacted and come to pick me up from work and apologise.

'Bye then,' he smiled. Then he turned and left me standing there, wondering what that had all been about.

Chapter Fifty-Five

Stella

'I can't think where Jonathon can have got to,' his mother gave her homemade apple sauce another quick stir. 'It's *most* unlike him to be late for a home-cooked dinner. And he did know I'd asked you to come round.'

Was the home-cooked dinner comment meant to be a dig at me? It seemed that even when she was trying to smooth the waters, or whatever it was she thought we women should be wearing frilly aprons and doing, she could still find time to have a pop at me.

I wondered if Jonathon could be staying away because he knew I was going to be here and he still couldn't bring himself to be in the same room as me. Surely he wouldn't be that childish? Mind you, before yesterday I would never have expected that kind of coldness from him either. Joyce did have a point about the stress of the wedding getting on top of him. I was pretty sure, having thought about it, that at any other time his reaction would have been to try and help me find some way of sorting it out. But it wasn't any other time, it was now. And we were too close to getting married to be acting so stupidly.

'Maybe those people who keep coming down from

London at the weekends are still around and he's having trouble getting away,' I suggested, hoping that that was the case, but doubting it, even as I said it. From what Jonathon had told me about them it sounded like they normally left by Monday lunchtime, but they might have stayed later this week, or he might have had the perfect house to show them and they could all be busy viewing it right now.

'People are very inconsiderate,' Joyce remarked, turning her attention back to the boiled potatoes she had cut up to cool for her potato salad. I gave her the benefit of the doubt and assumed she meant Jonathon's awkward customers and, for a change, not me. 'Cut these spring onions up for me would you, Stella?'

I took the bunch of onions to the sink and gave them a good wash before chopping the end bits off. Joyce's car had gone from across the village green by the time I'd finished locking up the library, and she hadn't mentioned the fact that she had been there, so I didn't either. I was just happy that she hadn't found it necessary to make any comments about my appearance, other than looking my ankle length dress up and down and not saying anything at all about it. In Joyce's book, a lack of criticism was a complement and I'd take what I could get where she was concerned. The fact that she hadn't said anything at all about my skin looking funny or pale was a relief. I'd been worried that I might have put too much of the calamine lotion on and ended up looking like Alli's

Geisha girl minus the wig.

Joyce wasn't going to put the chops under the grill until Jonathon got home, but it was getting late and so she decided not to wait. James came in from the garden once the smell of cooking meat must have permeated the shed three quarters of the way down it. I smiled to myself, remembering what Jonathon had told me about the whisky and the *Quality Street* tin.

'Dinner almost ready? Oh ... Hello Stella dear, lovely to see you. That's a pretty dress.' He obviously hadn't known that I'd been summoned. 'Jonathon upstairs?'

'Your son hasn't come home from work yet, James. I can't think what's keeping him.'

Jonathon hardly ever put a foot wrong as far as Joyce was concerned, but it always amused me that the few times he might be suspected of doing so, he always automatically became *James's* son.

'I'll go and give the office a ring, although I can't imagine that he'd still be there.' James made his escape before he got blamed for anything else. He was a wise man.

'You need to slice those thinner,' Joyce said over my shoulder, looking at the perfectly thinly sliced – to my mind at least – spring onions. 'And then pop them in that bowl with the mayonnaise and stir them into it with some black pepper. From the pepper mill, not the powdered stuff.'

      With anyone else I'd have saluted and quipped *Sir, yes sir!* But I couldn't see that going down very well with her. Where on earth was Jonathon? If he didn't get back soon it was going to be just me, Joyce and James round the table for dinner. And James on his own just wasn't enough to dilute his wife's acid tongue.

Chapter Fifty-Six

Joyce

I was very disappointed that Jonathon didn't come home for dinner this evening. I wanted to get to the bottom of whatever their disagreement had been about. It was very unsettling not knowing.

And Stella had actually made an effort tonight. Much more so than she usually did, anyway. She had a nice dress on that I certainly hadn't seen before, and she looked like she had been having a go with some different make up. I didn't know why she couldn't make the effort a bit more often. It was a shame Jonathon hadn't been there to see her looking nice for once. I was sure that whatever she'd done, he would have forgiven her for it.

Mind you, I don't know what she thought she was doing, mashing that lovely baked apple around the plate and hardly eating any of it. Such a faddy eater – she gets that from that mother of hers. And you would have thought that after the lovely meal I cooked for her that she could have stayed and helped me with the washing up. Cordelia would have.

Chapter Fifty-Seven

Stella

'Have you still got that bottle of Pinot with our names on it?' I rang Alli the moment I could get away from Joyce's evil baked apples.

'No, I don't, sorry,' my friend's tone was glum. 'But ... I do have a couple of its friends in the fridge,' she whooped straight into my ear. 'Come round and help me liberate one of them. I thought Harry was coming round tonight but he's playing pool with some mates in Winchester so I'm on my lonesome and my marking's all done.'

'I'll be right over then ...'

Alli had got the little bistro table and chairs out, in the pocket handkerchief sized back garden of her two up, two down, cottage, and it was so nice to be able to relax and roll up the long, loose sleeves of my floaty dress without worrying who was going to see the state of my arms.

'How was dinner then? Has Jonathon unbent yet?' she asked, pouring generously into two of her oversized wine glasses.

'Jonathon wasn't there ...' I grabbed mine and took a big gulp to wash the greasy apple taste out of my mouth.

'You mean you had to sit there, just you and his mum and dad?' Alli looked horrified at the prospect and downed a pretty big gulp herself. 'That's what I call a cruel and unusual punishment. What did she make you eat?'

'Pork chops – which were nice, if a bit overcooked, potato salad – which I helped make, and a leafy green salad which was ... well .... green and leafy ...'

'Something with apples in it for pudding by any chance?' Alli disliked cooked apples and the need to have them in some form for dessert at almost every meal, almost as much as I did.

'Oh yes. Baked ...'

'Plenty of pips left in them?' Now she was taking the Mickey out of my theory that the woman was trying to do away with me.

'Yes, but none of them made their way into my mouth. I just ate most of the skin and did my best to make the rest of it look as small as possible on my plate so that she wouldn't be offended ...'

'You do realise,' she put her head to one side, 'that whatever you do she is always going to be offended – it's just her default setting – and there is absolutely nothing you're ever going to be able to do about it.'

'Well, aren't you the wise one.' I waved my empty glass in her direction – I must have spilled some while we were talking.

'Seriously though,' she said, when we were about half way down the second bottle, 'it's a shame Jonathon wasn't there tonight. Where was he?'

I shrugged by way of reply. His dad hadn't been able to get any answer at the office.

'You should go and talk to him tomorrow. He'll probably have calmed down by then – he can't stay angry with you forever about something that wasn't entirely your fault ...'

'He doesn't have to stay angry with me forever. It'll only take him still being angry with me when the day of our wedding rolls around for it to end up ruining everything ...'

'It won't come to that,' she dropped her head onto my shoulder. 'Jonathon loves you. He isn't going to let a stupid thing like this stop you getting married. And,' she hauled herself upright again and looked at me, 'you're definitely getting less and less orange. It will more than likely have gone completely by the big day.'

'You do realise I'm less orange because I've got about a gallon of chalky white lotion all over me ...' Not to mention the fact that Alli's eyes were getting ever so slightly crossed and so she might not even have been looking at me.

'Hey! I can do my Geisha girl make up on you,' she beamed at me as if she'd just had the most marvellous idea in the world.

261

'Just how much wine did you have before I got here?' I asked, before sliding off my chair and going back into the kitchen to put the kettle on.

I was going to go and try to talk to Jonathon in the morning before work, so I needed to have a clear head.

Chapter Fifty-Eight

Stella

Alli had been fast asleep with her head on the table when I'd gone back out with the coffees, so I'd put her to bed on the sofa and stayed the night again in her spare room. But I'd set the alarm on my phone for earlier than usual so I could go home, shower and change and go and talk to Jonathon. She was still asleep when I left in the morning, so I tiptoed past her and let myself out.

The vague hope I'd been nursing that Jonathon might have been round to my place at some point, shrivelled and died the moment I walked through the front door. Everything was exactly as I had left it on Saturday morning, even my mug, just rinsed and sitting in the sink where I hadn't had time to wash it properly. Jonathon wouldn't have been able to resist washing that, drying it and putting it away if he had been here. There had still been no text messages or missed calls from him. Maybe, in this instance, his mother was right and it was up to me to smooth things over.

I went and had a shower, following my usual routine with the baking soda and lemon and the white calamine. It looked like it was working. I hoped Jonathon would be able to see a difference.

Carefully dressed in an old but pretty, long white cotton gypsy skirt that I hardly ever wore because I always spilled something down it – and it had previously been a bit tight – I left for Jonathon's house. I decided not to call first, just in case he decided to make himself scarce, but I knew that at least he and his father would be up by now and getting ready to go to the office.

'Oh! Stella!' Joyce opened the door to me, her hair in one of those Hyacinth Bucket pink chiffon hair net contraptions. She looked over my shoulder. 'Isn't Jonathon with you?'

'Jonathon?' A cold feeling washed through me. 'Isn't he here?'

'No, dear. We thought he was with you.' She turned and marched through to the kitchen with me close at her heels, panic gnawing at me. 'James! Jonathon wasn't with Stella. Did he say anything to you about going anywhere?'

'No,' he looked up from his toast and marmalade, seemingly puzzled by all the fuss. 'He'll probably be at the office. I'll head off in a moment and call you when I get there ...'

'What if he's had an accident?' Joyce demanded. 'What if he's in a ditch somewhere? Really James! Am I the only one who cares?' She picked up the kitchen phone and speed dialled the office. The answer phone was the only reply she got.

'If he's busy, he won't have switched the answer

phone off,' James tried to soothe his wife. 'I'll head off now, if it will put your mind at rest.' He stood up, reached for his car keys, kissed his wife and made for the front door.

'If I don't hear from you in the next ten minutes, I'm going to start ringing round the hospitals,' Joyce called after him.

There was nothing I could do there, so I headed off as well. I would call in at Rupert's place and see if he'd crashed there, just like I had done at Alli's.

I'd only just left their driveway when I spotted Cordelia's car parked right by the gate to her cottage, at the entrance to the stables. She'd had quite a big hand in all of this. If anything had happened to Jonathon it would be partly her fault.

I marched past her car, through the gate and banged on the door. A moment later I heard movement inside and could see, through the mottled glass pane, the shape of someone coming down the stairs.

Then the door was flung open and there, right in front of me, stood Cordelia, naked except for one thing. With just a couple of strategic buttons done up, all she was wearing was Jonathon's new shirt.

Chapter Fifty-Nine

Jonathon

I didn't know what woke me, I had a feeling it might have been a banging sound, but I lay there, face down, wishing to God it hadn't. My eyes hurt too much to open. They felt as if someone was trying to gouge them out but from inside my head. My tongue was welded to the roof of my mouth. Was it flu? Stella would know. I'd wake her up. I'd just have another bit of a snooze first.

Stella! I lifted my head from the pillow – it might have been straight away or I might have had that little snooze first, I didn't seem to be able to get any grip on time – all I knew was that a red hot poker was searing its way through my skull. What day was it? Was last night my stag night? Rupes had promised it wouldn't get out of hand, but what the hell had we been drinking? And why the hell had we drunk so much of it? And what was that disgusting taste in my mouth?

One eye managed to prise itself open. I started to sit up but felt like I was going to throw up, so I leant on my elbow and stayed still a moment, swallowing. My eye started to focus. Then I felt really sick. This wasn't my bedroom. And it wasn't Stella's bedroom either. It wasn't even Rupert's bedroom. So where the hell was I?

Chapter Sixty

Stella.

'Oh dear!' Cordelia gave an embarrassed giggle and put her hand to her mouth. I couldn't move. My eyes seemed to be the only bits of me that could still function. Everything else was frozen. Except the beat of my heart. Ricocheting around my body. Making me shake.

She moved slightly in the doorway, looking back over her shoulder. My eyes followed hers. I wished they hadn't. Because there, strewn about her lounge like wrapping paper on Christmas morning, were Jonathon's shoes. His socks. His belt. His jeans. His boxer shorts.

And I still couldn't move.

'I'm so sorry Stella,' she simpered, sounding anything but. 'I suppose you had to know some time though. You didn't really think a man like Jonathon was going to marry someone like *you*, did you?'

A hot wave of bile rose up through me and I somehow reached the front door step before it came spewing up and out of my mouth. I was barely aware of the door closing in my face.

Chapter Sixty-One

Jonathon

A door swung open behind me, sometime later, causing an explosion in my head that made my teeth chatter, and what sounded like crockery rattling on a tray sent a wave of aftershocks through my guts. It was nothing though, compared to the sick feeling of panic in my stomach. *What the hell had I done?*

'Good morning, sleepyhead,' came a voice that sounded like Cordelia's ... Oh thank God! Cordelia! I couldn't remember what had happened, but clearly I had been drunk and incapable of getting home and either Rupes had had the foresight to call Cordelia, rather than letting Stella see me in that state, or she had just happened to be somewhere nearby. Anyway, whatever had happened, she must have brought me back to her place and let me sleep it off here. Thank God for that.

Cordelia was carrying the tray round the bed. Tea – just what the doctor ordered. She was a life saver. And hopefully juice. I bet she had brought some paracetamol with it too. She was always good in a crisis, Cordelia. I wondered if she would think me rude if I downed the tea and juice and asked for a second one of each. My throat was parched.

I opened my second eye as she came into my line of vision, smiling at me as she put the tray down on the bed. She wasn't wearing very much, just a blue shirt that looked a bit like that new one of mine, and only a few of the buttons were done up. She had probably put it on in a hurry and hadn't realised. I opened my mouth to tell her and then shut it again as my mind did as close to a double take as my aching head would let it. That was *my* shirt she was wearing, wasn't it? Oh no, please God, I hadn't been sick down her or anything like that. I might have known her most of my life, but that would be just too embarrassing.

Chapter Sixty-Two

Stella

I didn't know how I managed to stagger home, or how I got through the front door ...

I didn't know what I threw in the case, or how I drove to the station ...

I didn't know how long I waited for the coach, or where I was going ...

The first thing I knew, I was at Heathrow.

Chapter Sixty-Three

Jonathon

'Here we are then. Breakfast in bed,' she said in a funny, breathy sort of way, sitting down on the bed and crossing one leg ever so slowly over the other. An image of Sharon Stone in that film ... what was it? Where the police thought she had killed someone? No, that wasn't it. Someone had been killed. Was it her husband? – I couldn't remember if she had done it or not –*Basic Instinct*, that was it. *Basic Instinct* ... flashed into my mind. It wasn't an image I was comfortable associating with someone who was like a sister to me.

'Are you alright?' I asked her, wondering if she was feeling hungover too. She looked a bit flushed. Maybe she'd had too much to drink as well, although that wouldn't really be like her. 'You look a bit hot ...'

'Oh Jonathon,' she laughed out loud – a sort of girly, tinkling laugh that didn't sound like her – although I didn't see what was so funny. 'You silly thing! I'm the happiest I've been in ... oh, such a long, long time!'

'Are you?' I asked, genuinely pleased for her but wishing her happiness could be a little less eardrum shattering and eyeball piercing. And about an octave lower.

'Of course I am, silly. Aren't you?' Without taking her eyes off me, she started unwinding the end of a croissant she had picked up off the tray with her finger and thumb.

'Well ... er ...' I didn't quite know how to answer that question, seeing as I was currently in the clutches of the worst hangover I had ever experienced in my life. I couldn't remember what we had been drinking last night, but whatever it was, I sure as hell wouldn't be going near it ever again. And just wait until I met up with Rupert!

I looked at Cordelia, playing with the end of the croissant, felt nauseous and looked away again. Hadn't she just asked me something? I tried to remember what it was, but found myself suddenly saved the trouble by that chunk of pastry being posted, delicately into my mouth, her finger and thumb slowly and gently brushing against my lips. What on earth was Cordelia playing at?

Chapter Sixty-Four

Stella

Numbness was setting in and blurring the edges of the cine film flickering on its loop inside my head. It was as if the edges of the celluloid were melting, highlighting and giving a surreal quality to the nightmare images I was trying so hard not to see – Jonathon's cornflower blue shirt swamping Cordelia's slender, clearly otherwise naked body. Lithe, tanned, smooth as silk legs, like something out of that old chocolate flake advert. Bed-tousled hair framing her flushed face. That look of triumph as she saw me take in the scene, watched me recognise my fiancé's clothes scattered across her floor. I could even smell his aftershave on her. *Oh Jonathon. How could you do that to me?*

She barely said a few words. She didn't have to say any more. The picture in front of me said more than its allotted thousand. And all I could do was stand there, mouth open, waiting for the nightmare to end. Until suddenly I wasn't. Suddenly I was throwing up on her door step, staggering home, throwing things into an already half-packed case, waiting at a coach station. How I could see to drive there through my tears I would never know, but I had. Where I had dumped my car I couldn't remember. But I would never be going back, so it really didn't matter.

I gazed through the little window now – all the better to keep my puffy red eyes to myself – the last thing I needed was some kind stranger asking me if I was alright. I lifted my gin and tonic to my lips, but the ice just rattled against itself in the plastic tumbler. Looking down at it, I vaguely wondered where my drink had gone. That was when I noticed the air hostess, smiling at me and saying something I couldn't hear. I stared back at her.

'Prawn with rice, or chicken with noodle?' Her head tilted slightly to one side, she repeated the lunch menu choice slowly as if she thought I hadn't understood her. Or maybe she'd noticed my eyes and was just being kind.

I shook my head – speech would only bring a fresh flurry of tears. I'd had enough sympathetic glances in the Ladies' loos at the airport, when I'd finally come out of the cubicle I had hogged for what felt like hours, allowing the hot, wet tears to make silent tracks down my face. So I just held out my tumbler for a refill, not caring what she actually put in it, as long as it contained alcohol. My mind wasn't nearly numb enough. I could still smell his aftershave. I could still see her Cadbury's sodding Flake advert legs under his cornflower blue shirt.

The air hostess had either remembered it was gin, or had smelt the tumbler. Or maybe gin was the usual choice of silent females with puffy red eyes, flying alone on suddenly altered tickets. Perhaps airlines had done a study and worked out that the depressive qualities in gin would keep us quiet and render us less likely to get loudly drunk and disturb the other passengers. Anyway, the drink was put in front of me on a meal tray with a space where whatever it was she had offered me would have gone. The sight of the tiny, egg cup-sized wine glass on the tray nearly set me off again. Jonathon and I had always chuckled at those teeny tiny little glasses that looked as if they'd been borrowed from a dolls' house. One of our wedding presents had been a set of gorgeous wine glasses. They would have to go back. Fresh tears brimmed as I pictured Jonathon returning presents. Or would he be too wrapped up with his new love? Would Joyce take over that task? I could just see her, embarrassed at the late cancellation of her beloved son's wedding, but happy to be rid of the unworthy bride to be and ecstatic at her replacement – the perfect daughter-in-law – the one she had wanted all along.

***

The air hostess took away my untouched tray. That was a first. Jonathon and I had always enjoyed the food on Thai Airways – our pre-ordered, nut free meal trays had gone back empty every time – in fact it had turned into a bit of a race to finish first, as whatever was left on the tray of the slower eater became fair game for the quicker one. I couldn't imagine him doing that with Cordelia. She would probably be one of those passengers who pre-ordered a plate of fruit and then only picked at a few grapes on that. The thought of Jonathon, *my* Jonathon, going on holidays with *her* made my stomach turn over. *She* would probably only fly business class, wherever they went, even though Jonathon, like me, couldn't see the point of paying so much extra. *She* would travel with perfectly matching luggage, containing a perfectly co-ordinated capsule wardrobe, all neatly packed with tissue paper to stop everything creasing. *She* would dress for style over comfort, even for a fourteen hour flight and would, of course, get off at the other end looking like she had just stepped out of the fashion pages of one of those in flight magazines where they tell you how to do it all perfectly. They should dedicate an issue to her. In fact they should put her in charge of it and she could write the damn thing. Her and her amazing bloody legs. Did I sound bitter by any chance?

***

My feet trudged their usual path through international transit at Bangkok's Suvarnabhumi airport. Except that where Jonathon and I usually nipped smartly onto the travellator and wove our way in and out of the dithering, still half asleep at six in the morning, tourists, I now just trudged on and stood there, wearily letting the moving walkway move me along with it towards the CIQ desks. At this point in the journey, we would usually greet the customs officials and hand baggage screeners with a happy *Sawadee Ka* from me, and *Sawadee Krub* from

Jonathon. Right now, I could barely muster up a hello in English, happy or otherwise. Well, definitely not happy. The *Land of Smiles* was probably the last place I should be right now.

From here, Jonathon and I would head for the little food court next to the tiny branch of Boots. One of us would bag a table overlooking the neatly manicured garden, while the other would go to Coffee Club and order delicious iced cappuccinos that came with a little jug of sugar syrup on the side. It had become our first day of the holiday early morning coffee ritual. All I wanted to do now was shut myself in a cubicle in the Ladies and have another silent cry, maybe not even silent. Between the crying and the alcohol it was a wonder my head wasn't thumping away with dehydration. Maybe it was and I was just too numb to notice. Small mercies – I supposed I should be thankful and all that.

Having changed my ticket at such short notice, I had been very lucky to get a standby seat as far as Bangkok – luckier than the poor person sitting next to me, who had probably wished they'd caught a different flight and not ended up with a silently weeping woman sitting next to them. The next few onward flights to Phuket were all full and I had three hours to wait. Even I couldn't hide out in the loo that long. Eventually I left my hidey hole, splashed my face with cold water and came out.

It seemed so strange, walking up to the Coffee Club counter and ordering only one drink. I probably should have gone somewhere else, but my feet just took me towards the familiar and, before I even realised it, I had ordered and paid. Then I tortured myself further by sitting in the very same area we usually sat in, watching travel tired but happy couples wandering about, choosing where to order whatever they were having, squabbling light-heartedly over little things that really didn't matter. That had been *us*.

Had he been in love with her while we'd been coming here? Had he been thinking of her when he'd been visiting my family with me? Had there been secret little text messages back and forth, each declaring how much they were missing each other?

I wondered how many of these men were thinking of other women, how many of these women were living in the same fools' paradise that I'd been in. And a fresh flow of tears began.

Chapter Sixty-Five

Jonathon

Bits and pieces were starting to come back to me ...

Cordelia warning me that Stella was getting cold feet about the wedding ...

Something about keeping my mum away from the wedding dress fittings because there was no dress ...

Trying to stop Stella getting that fake tan ...

Something about another man ...

Cordelia driving me to the library ...

The man by the door, stroking Stella's face. It was him she was in love with.

There hadn't been any stag do. I'd got drunk with Cordelia to try and blot out the pain. Stella didn't want to marry me. She was in love with this other man. This Craig she'd met at the library. It was him she wanted.

Cordelia said so.

Chapter Sixty-Six

Stella

The area outside arrivals felt and sounded even more chaotic than usual. They were still building the new international terminal – I'd forgotten about that.

It was three hours later than the time Jonathon and I would usually arrive, as that had been the earliest onward flight I could get a seat on, and without his hand in mine, I suddenly felt very small among the jostling throng. There were the usual passengers looking for their rides. Drivers and car hire people zoning in on possible customers. People waving cards with misspelled Western names on them. And touts of all kinds, eager to make some quick baht out of the gullible. They were all usually just part of the background colour and noise, but today they took on a nightmarish quality as the hot, humid air that normally wrapped itself round us like a welcoming cloak almost bowled me over in its ferocity. I searched the area for my parents. One of them usually met us by the ATM, a little to the left of the exit, where it was slightly less frantic, while the other stayed in the car in case it had to be moved. But everything had changed. I felt as if I'd come to a completely different place and I couldn't see either of them. Where were they?

With all the honking and hooting going on I didn't give the family on the motorbike pulling up in front of me a second glance, until one of them took off the helmet she was wearing and it turned out to be my mother. Getting down from the bike, she lifted up the toddler who'd been sandwiched between her and the young woman driving and slipped him back into what was presumably his mother's arms. She then handed back the helmet to the woman, who plopped it onto her own head, smiled and bowed her head first at mum and then at me and, clutching her child to her with one arm, drove off. It was the kind of thing I'd seen so many times in Thailand that I'd almost become used to it but, to my knowledge, none of my family members had ever been part of that dangerous equation before.

'Mum?' I croaked, half expecting her to turn out to be some mad tourist who just looked like her.

'Stella! I'm so sorry, darling,' my mother said, enveloping me in one of her magical hugs which, when I was a child, had always made everything feel better. I wished it could be as simple as that now.

'Mum?' I croaked again.

'Only in Thailand,' she exclaimed, letting go of me and shaking her head with the little exasperation of which she was capable. 'Some idiot lorry driver on the 402 careered across all the lanes and took a couple of taxis, an ice truck and a coconut truck with it. We couldn't move for sacks of ice and coconuts in the road. At any other time it would have been hilarious.' She looked at me. 'It's alright, nobody was hurt. And then these kind people stopped their bikes to see if anyone needed any help and a couple of them gave people lifts and that nice girl brought me here to the airport ...' As she said, only in Thailand.

In the taxi, which she got suspiciously quickly so I dread to think how much it cost, Mum chattered non-stop. After my sleepless night, my early morning start, and several gins, my mind kept tuning out and I failed to hear most of what she was saying, but that didn't matter. The comforting sound of her voice was just what I needed. Numbness had finally been achieved.

It was quite dark when I woke up. My head was thumping and my tongue was stuck to the roof of my mouth. The ceiling fan was gently ruffling the curtain edges, letting faint shafts of Mum's balcony citronella candle light filter through. As my eyes became accustomed, I realised I was in Mum and Dad's bed. Wondering what the time was, I started to turn over to wake Jonathon and a wall of grief hit me. He wasn't here. This wasn't our honeymoon. This wasn't even a holiday. This was me, running away to my parents because the man I loved, the man I'd been about to spend the rest of my life with had wanted the very woman I'd been afraid he'd rather be with than me, all along.

I sat up, pushing the image of Cordelia and her

legs, in his shirt, as far to the back of my mind as it would go. Swinging my own merely mortal legs onto the floor, my whole body felt like lead, as if I were going down with a bout of flu and it had all finally caught up with me.

He hadn't even been the one to tell me. What kind of coward lets his wedding day get as close as ours had without telling the truth? How late had he been going to leave it to tell me I wasn't the one he really wanted? Was he just going to not turn up at the church? Was I going to be jilted at the altar? Was that how he was going to let me know? Or had he been going to marry me and carry on seeing her? I couldn't imagine Cordelia putting up with that – but then, I couldn't imagine Cordelia playing the other woman for as long as it seemed she had, anyway. She must really love him to have stood back and watched us approach our wedding day. She must have really hated me. But not as much as I hated her.

I'd never been someone who hated. Mum and Dad had brought me up to always look for the good in people. But I'd never felt pain like the one that was tunnelling through me, burying itself deeper and deeper, turning my insides into what felt like an open wound being sluiced with salt water. I could understand animals turning vicious and lashing out when they were hurt. But the person I wanted to lash out at wasn't here. I screwed my eyes tight shut as I tried very hard to block out the image of her, of where she might be right now. And of who she'd be with, now they didn't have to hide and pretend any more. My eyeballs hurt when I finally opened them, but what were two more drops of pain, in the seething mess of all the rest?

The door gently opened an inch or two, spreading a hazy little line of light across the floor, before swinging wider and spreading out the light like an opening fan. I imagined I could smell Heinz tomato soup wafting in from the other side.

'I thought I heard you moving,' Mum said, placing one of her sunshine yellow mugs on the bedside table and sitting down on the bed next to me. 'We were wondering whether to wake you or let you sleep. Your dad's heating up some soup for you ...' Just like he used to do when I was a little girl and I'd been teased by the other kids at school for the weird things in my packed lunches, or had fallen over and scraped my knee. I was just wondering about the toast when I smelt it. Would he cut it into chunky soldiers as he had back then?

My parents' kindness brought the tears back to my eyes but I blinked them away as hard as I could – Mum and Dad were worried about me enough already. They were so full of love for me. But it was going to take a lot more than Heinz tomato soup and soldiers to make this better.

Chapter Sixty-Seven

Stella

I couldn't bring myself to leave the apartment the next day. Couldn't face the world outside. Just alternated between crying and sleeping, crying and feeling numb, crying and feeling too much.

The following day Mum made me go for a walk on the beach. It was the day before what would have been my wedding and she didn't want me to spend it lying on the bed crying. She tried to come with me but I wanted to be alone. I didn't want to talk or think about my wedding.

I looked along the beach for something to focus on. It was a lot emptier than I remembered it from our previous trips, even for low season. Mum had said something about the government cracking down on people hiring out sun beds, umbrellas and those uncomfortable triangular back rests that have always seemed so strangely popular, but I'd forgotten. I kicked off my flip flops, scorched the soles of my feet and immediately hooked my toes back into them again, half hopping, half stumbling to the water's edge. It was amazing the stupid things your brain forgot when your heart was broken – like sand on a sizzling sunny beach being scalding hot.

The last time I'd been here on this beach, Jonathon had given me a piggy back to the water's edge. He'd done that a lot – in spite of his mother worrying out loud that he'd do his back an injury if he persisted in picking up something as heavy as me. He'd play-acted dumping me in one of the approaching waves and I'd clung onto his neck, shrieking with laughter as he waded in and we tumbled together into the refreshing Andaman Sea, splashing about like teenagers. But I wasn't going to think about that. Gentle waves of that same water dribbled over my feet now, trickling backwards when they'd reached as far as they could be bothered. They seemed as sad as I felt. Here. Alone.

A jumble of voices made its way along the sand behind me. They sounded French, or Belgian – their accents standing out against the more usual Russians – a crowd of sun kissed, messy haired, good looking teenagers lugging cool boxes and backpacks, and goodness knows what else, ready for a day of fun and games on the sand. Jonathon and I always smiled a greeting to others on the beach, even if they didn't bother to smile one back, but today I just kept facing out to sea. Nobody needed my cloudy face spoiling their sunny outlook.

I couldn't help wondering what spin Joyce was busy putting on my running out on the wedding, to her golf club, and her very many helpful ladies. Had her joy at my finally being replaced by the daughter-in-law of her dreams outweighed her annoyance with me for all the last minute inconvenience? Had she made a start on returning all the thoughtful wedding gifts we had been given? I found that I couldn't imagine Jonathon doing any of it. I couldn't stop my mind's eye seeing him and Cordelia, hiding out at her place, probably wrapped up in her silky, five million thread count sheets, doing all kinds of things to each other that I'd been too dull, unimaginative and overweight to do. The thought of them together brought back, even stronger than ever, that feeling of my insides being like one great big open wound washed over by a giant salty wave. Would the intensity of that feeling ever lessen? Would that rawness be with me forever? I couldn't imagine a moment, even in the future, where I could think of him with her and not feel as if I were being turned inside out. I didn't want to think about them.

Had he taken her to our special place? Had it been their special place, too? Or had they had another place. In another thicket? Or had her stables been their perfect place? I tortured myself with the image of all those bales of sweet smelling straw. Maybe they'd had their own picnic blanket there. Maybe there'd been one in each stable, just in case …

Out of the corner of my eye I could see Nelson trotting, a lot less lopsidedly than you would expect from a three legged dog, along the sand towards me. Normally I would have been hunkered down, slapping my thighs and shouting "Here boy! Come on!" Jonathon would have been, too. We were a soppy pair for any un-Crufts-worthy dog – or rather we used to be. Cordelia would only have perfect Kennel Club dogs with the right nose to tail ratio or whatever it was, and all their limbs not only present and correct, but brushed and shiny and smelling of upmarket doggy shampoo. She would have no time at all for this scruffy mutt. He'd be as unwelcome and unwanted in her home as I, without even realising it, must have been. Except that last morning. She'd been more than happy to have me there then.

The memory of her, at my Sunday lunch just a few short weeks ago, dipping her piece of chicken in Jonathon's gravy, flashed across my mind. In my own kitchen, too. Had she been rubbing her feet up and down his legs under the table? Or had he been doing that to her? What had they got up to while Alli and I had been busy clearing up? Had they left Harry and Rupert playing X Box games, while they sneaked into the bathroom for a kiss and a cuddle? Or worse? An image of Jonathon sitting on the side of the bath while she straddled him, her skirt hitched up round her waist, her teeny tiny silky knickers – if she'd even been wearing any – tossed to the floor, one leg wrapped round his waist, made me want to throw up.

That stupid song, *It Wasn't Me*, or whatever it was called, started up, like a film soundtrack, in my head. Shaggy, or whatever the singer's name was, had a lot to answer for. If the inspiration for that song had come from a real life experience, then I wished him all sorts of nasty things needing several trips to the clinic hidden round the back of the hospital. And a lot of antibiotics – a whole truck load of them – preferably the sort that had to be injected in the bum with a big fat needle, and by a clumsy trainee nurse with a hangover and a bad case of the shakes.

Nelson shoved his soft, damp snout in my crotch by way of greeting, before hopping backwards, bowing down over his one front paw, bouncing up again and giving me a very pleased woof.

'If you're expecting me to reciprocate, you've got another think coming.' I rubbed the top of his head and fondled one of his floppy ears. He barked at me again, as if to say yes actually, that was exactly what he expected, but that I could carry on with the ear fondling thing while I did it, and then, when I'd finished with that ear, could I have a go with the other one.

'Sorry, dog,' I said, over his head, looking out to sea again and trying my best to ignore the prickling behind my eyes. 'If you're hoping for someone to scamper around and have fun on the beach with today, then you're going to find me a bit disappointing.'

Almost as if he understood, he gave a doggy snort, turned and started his three legged dash back towards the restaurant. Jonathon and I had had some lovely meals there. Tasanee and Thaksin had always gone out of their way to make things romantic for us, with special cocktails, special dishes that weren't even on the menu and petals all over the table. My eyes blurred with the tears that kept creeping up behind them and spilling over. How could I ever have imagined that the last meal we ate here, really would be the last meal we would ever eat here? The last Thai prawn and crab cakes. The last Thai yellow curry with steamed mussels and more fresh crab on the side. The last sticky mango and coconut rice. What delicious dishes would they have welcomed us with, in a few days' time, the first day of our honeymoon? The lump growing in my throat made me feel as if I'd never want to eat again. Not even Dad's Heinz tomato soup and soldiers.

'You've just had a phone call.' Dad appeared out of nowhere at my side, as if my thinking of him had conjured him up.

I wouldn't have thought it was possible for someone's stomach to leap up into their throat and plummet down to the soles of their feet at the same time, but that's exactly what it felt as if mine had done.

'I don't want to talk to him,' were the words that came out of my mouth. They surprised me. If I had ever pictured myself in a situation like this, I would have expected myself to run as fast as I could, to snatch at the phone and hear his voice, to hear him tell me how it was all a terrible mistake, that he had come to his senses and realised that it was me he loved after all. But that wasn't going to happen, was it. I'd seen the evidence for myself.

I had felt the pain of it and couldn't imagine a time when I wouldn't feel it. There was nothing he could say that could take any of that away, and I didn't want to hear any excuses, explanations or apologies. They would just be sour, mouldy cherries, staining the hard, cracked, yellowing icing on the big, fat, heavy cake of Jonathon's betrayal.

'It wasn't Jonathon, Stella love. It was Joyce.'

'Joyce?' That woman had never called Jonathon or myself whenever we'd been here. She didn't make international calls unless someone was dying. What did she want now? To crow? To stick the boot in? To let me know how happy she was that Jonathon had come to his senses and finally picked the right girl? As tactless as she was, I couldn't imagine her actually going to the expense of paying for a phone call here to do that. Maybe there were some gifts she was having trouble returning because they were from one of my family or friends and she needed their address. She really did want to get rid of all traces of me and the wedding that didn't happen as soon as she possibly could, didn't she?

'She wanted to know if we'd heard from you.'

'Why?'

'I don't know. I was in half a mind to say no we hadn't, when your mother walked into the room and asked me if I thought you'd like to go and have a massage to help you relax. You know how your mother's voice carries,' he grimaced. 'Joyce heard her and asked to speak

291

to you.'

'What did you tell her?' I sighed. The last thing I needed was to have to hear that voice. Wasn't it enough that my fiancé loved someone else? Wasn't it enough that he'd been unfaithful to me with her, and that my wedding was off? My ex future mother-in-law's voice was the last thing I needed in my head.

'It's alright, love,' Dad pulled me to his side and rested his head, lightly, on top of mine. His neck smelled of Imperial Leather soap, another comforting reminder of my childhood. 'I told her that you were too upset to speak to anyone and that you'd gone for a very long walk and we didn't know when to expect you back. I told her that there was really no point in her calling here again. Then I hung up and unplugged the phone. That was the right thing to do, wasn't it?'

'Yes it was, Dad.' I snuggled closer to him whilst keeping my eyes out to sea so he wouldn't have to see my fresh flow of tears. 'That was the right thing.'

Chapter Sixty-Eight

Stella

Dad had heated me up a tin of my second childhood favourite, mushroom soup for lunch, reminding me again of what he had always told me as a child, that my favourite tomato soup lost its magical powers if you had it too many times, too close together. He had, of course, made me a couple of rounds of hot, buttery soldiers to go with it. Apparently you could have as many of them as you wanted without them losing their efficiency. Tasanee had also sent up for me one of her wonderful chicken and coconut soups, choc-full of fresh, local herbs. It had long been a favourite of mine, although I usually ordered it when Mum wasn't eating with us so she didn't have to pretend not to disapprove of my participation in the murder of a poor, defenceless chicken.

Mum seemed to be the only one who understood that I really couldn't face the thought of food. Without a word, she got herself a spoon and started dipping in to share Dad's soup with me, surreptitiously eating most of it. Dad must have thought it was Christmas, Easter and his birthday all rolled into one as he tucked in to Tasanee's soup, allowed by my mother on the basis that it would be a shame to waste it, and rude to Tasanee after her kindness in making it in the first place.

As soon as I could, to escape more kindness and looks of concern, I took myself off back down to the beach.

'*Sawadee Ka*!' Tasanee called out to me from the terrace of her little restaurant as I walked past. 'How you feeling today, *Ka*?' She gave me that smile, the one where the person doing the smiling puts her head slightly to one side and turns the corners of her mouth down just enough to indicate how sorry they feel for you. I knew I was going to have to get used to seeing a lot of that smile – mostly when I got back to UK where I would be surrounded by people who had been invited to the wedding – and I was not looking forward to it.

I shrugged my shoulders and pulled the same turned down mouth little smile back at her, before remembering my manners. '*Kop Kuhn Ka* for the soup, Tasanee. Thank you. It was delicious.' It wasn't really a lie, as the look on Dad's face while he was so obviously savouring every mouthful could not have been clearer.

'Only best for Astrid daughter,' she nodded back at me with a smilier smile before her attention was called back by a customer wanting his bill.

Nelson had caught up with me by then and lolloped along after me for quite a while. He seemed determined to cheer up the sad human who, for some inexplicable reason, didn't want to play catch or throw or chase with him. Every now and then he would bound ahead, skid and spin around in front of me and perform some daft doggy trick in the obvious hope of eliciting a response. I did my best.

'Yes, Nelson. You're a very clever dog,' I told him, after he'd managed to skid to a halt on two of his three legs, just centimetres in front of a group of small kids building what looked like a fort out of sandcastles.

My best was clearly, sadly lacking. Especially compared to their shrieks of laughter, which must have felt like a much better reward for his theatrics. Without a further glance in my direction he stayed put and entertained his adoring new audience, leaving me to walk on alone. That was another male I'd managed to bore away, then.

About a dozen or so Russians were having a rowdy game of volleyball, the boys playing against the girls. It sounded like there was a lot of good natured cheating going on from the playful arguments that seemed to erupt from almost every volley. A bit further along, an elderly, Mediterranean looking man with very obviously dyed hair – he could have been a Berlusconi lookalike – was doing some kind of exercises under the shade of one of the coconut trees. His skin was nut brown and wrinkled like an old leather shoe and his Speedos left almost nothing to the imagination. It was like looking at a car crash and knowing that you should turn away. This was a sight which would have had Jonathon and I chuckling about people who don't own full length mirrors and who really,

really should. I could remember him, the first time we saw a similar sight on the beach here – and unfortunately it's a common one as people really do think that anything goes in Thailand – telling me that if I ever caught him even looking at a pair of Speedos in a shop, I should wallop him round the head with the nearest heavy object, and I should do it quickly.

Further along, one of the guys from the Reggae Bar waved and shouted '*Sawadee Krub*,' as I wandered past. Jonathon and I had loved that bar. I just couldn't face it today. I didn't know if I would ever be able to face going into any of our favourite bars and restaurants here again, not if I was going to have to see that sad, sympathetic smile when any of the guys who recognised me asked where Jonathon was. They all knew that we were expected back here sometime now for our honeymoon. They would probably all think I was mad for coming here alone.

I was almost at the Laguna. Without realising it, I had reached as far as where the water from the lagoon made a channel through the sand towards the sea. At certain times of the day you couldn't cross it unless you were wearing a swimming costume, or clothes you didn't mind getting wet. I couldn't remember what those times were, but it looked shallow enough to me so I started to paddle through. It only reached up to my knees so I kept going, my wet calves acting like magnets to the sand kicking up behind me as I walked, caking the backs of my legs, as well as my feet and ankles.

There seemed to be quite a lot of staff milling about in the garden area of one of the bigger, Laguna hotels that bordered the beach. There was probably going to be some kind of function going on later. I carried on, as I wanted to walk as far as I physically could before a combination of sea and rocks made further walking impossible. It was the quietest stretch of the beach, and Jonathon and I had often walked the whole length of that little bit of coast to get to it, so we could swim out, past the rocks to a rugged little outcrop. It was a lovely, if slightly hard to get to, spot and we'd never understood why we had always been the only people there.

Just like I couldn't understand why I was torturing myself by going there right now. Was it a need to be somewhere I had only ever been with Jonathon and where he had only ever been with me? Did my subconscious think that being there would somehow make me feel closer to him? As if some kind of telepathic communication would open up and he would sense my being there? Or did I have a need to be there without him? To stick two metaphorical fingers up at him and silently shout, 'Look! Here I am, without you! I don't need you!' Or maybe it was just a case of my feet knowing that my brain was on shutdown, and so they were just following a familiar path in an effort to be helpful.

Obviously I hadn't thought about where I was walking to when I set out after lunch. I wasn't dressed for swimming, but I splashed out into the sea anyway, until the water was half way up my thighs and lapping at the ends of my shorts. I wasn't really going to swim across in my t shirt and shorts. And the water would be waist high so I wasn't even going to wade across. Until I found myself knotting my t shirt up under my bust and doing just that. I supposed that was my feet trying to be helpful again and my hands deciding to join in.

My shorts sopping wet, I made for the tree with the dip in its biggest branch. This was where Jonathon and I would always sit when we swam over. It was the perfect fit for the two of us, almost as if it had been crafted especially for us. Now the dip felt too big with just me in it – much bigger than the space for just two people. I couldn't get comfortable in the middle, I couldn't get comfortable on the side where I usually sat. I felt a bit like Goldilocks, so I sat on the side where Jonathon had always sat and just let the tears flow, while I wondered where he would be right now, and what he would be doing. And whether he would be doing it with her.

The misery that washed over me obliterated all sense of time. I could have been there a few minutes. I could have been there a couple of hours. All I was aware of was the grief of my loss and the pain of Jonathon's betrayal. And the questions which were starting to eat away at me inside – how had I not known? What could I have done differently? Would he still have married me if I hadn't gone to Cordelia's and seen for myself what was going on?

It was the ants that eventually got to me. A vague tickling on my thighs had turned into a full on irritating slapping things away from me situation before I realised that my legs, stomach and arms were covered in them. And from the desire to slap the skin under my shorts and t shirt, I suddenly realised that the ants were crawling under my clothes, too. I jumped down from the branch and straight into the water, splashing about to rid myself of even the clingiest of them. Could this day get any worse?

As I trudged like the proverbial drowned rat, my clothes dripping sea water down my arms and legs, along the sand back towards the Laguna, I could see more activity going on in that hotel garden and on the stretch of beach in front of it. Was that a baby elephant wearing a sash that someone was walking around with? Well, there often was a much bigger elephant on the beach, giving rides to the tourists like our Blackpool donkeys, but I had never seen a baby one there before. Maybe it was there for a children's party. I could actually see a lot of balloons now I was paying a bit more attention. And lots of flowers – it looked like it was going to be a posh do.

Getting closer I could see staff in smart hotel uniforms, smiling and holding out trays of drinks. There were small glasses of red and white wine, tall glasses of various fruit juices and flutes of champagne. The guests, who must just be arriving, were being welcomed. They were a mixed looking bunch, some were dressed casually, some were dressed as if they were going to a …

Oh … Stupid me. How slowly must my brain have been working? The white balloons, the white silky canopy they must have been putting up when I walked past earlier, lots of white flowers. Even the sight of the baby elephant with its white sash tied across it, being led around the now gathering crowd hadn't set the cogs in motion. It wasn't until the short, buxom looking girl in the puffy white meringue stepped out from behind the baby elephant, a radiant smile lighting up her face as she gazed up into the eyes of what was obviously her new husband, that the reality of what I was witnessing slapped me sharply across the face.

Chapter Sixty-Nine

Stella

It took me ages to get to sleep that night. I was bone tired until I lay down, and then my mind would start whirring away, looking for clues about Cordelia, reading things into every aspect of my relationship with Jonathon. Had there been double meanings in any of the things he'd said? Anything she'd said to me? And what about all that business with the spray tan? Why had she taken me there? To make a fool of me? Had that all been deliberate? Surely she couldn't be that spiteful? Jonathon wouldn't have had anything to do with that – he'd have been furious with her if she'd done that on purpose – at least, the Jonathon I thought I knew would have.

Eventually I tried reading one of Mum's soppy self-help books, but my eyes kept wandering around the page or reading the same lines over and over and none of the words made any sort of sense. Logging on to Dad's laptop didn't help. The last thing I needed was to read my emails and see how sorry everyone felt for me. Enough humiliation had been heaped on me for now – the rest could wait until I was feeling a bit stronger, and a lot less raw. I couldn't even bear to read the well-meaning ones from Alli, much as my finger would be drawn to click on hers. My best friend would be full of indignation on my behalf, but she didn't know how this felt – and I'd never want her to – but this pain wouldn't be halved by sharing it with her.

I started a game of Patience, but couldn't concentrate and decided to go and make myself a drink. At home and happy, or what I'd thought of as happy, I'd have made myself some hot milk and honey, but I wasn't home and I wasn't happy. I wanted a nice chilled glass of Pinot Grigio – hell, I wanted a bottle of it and I didn't particularly care if it was nice, or chilled – in fact any old plonk would have done, but wine was ridiculously expensive here and so there wasn't any. Mum had a selection of Breezers in the fridge, but I didn't think their alcohol content was up to the job, not unless I drank all of them. Dad had a half bottle of Thai whisky tucked away in the cupboard where he kept his favourite spicy Thai snacks – the ones with enough chilli in them to make your eyes steam, rather than just water. The whisky was rough enough to strip several layers of paint with, but if it did the trick I could always get some medicine later for the holes in my tongue and stomach lining. Or not.

Pulling it down and grabbing a glass, I went back to the fridge for something to mix with it. There were no cans of ginger ale, Diet Coke – and for some reason Diet Pepsi just didn't exist here – or anything like that, so I grabbed the first couple of Breezers that came to hand – one strawberry and one watermelon flavour – well, it could hardly make the whisky taste any worse. I opened them and took all three bottles and the glass and let myself out, down the steps and outside, on to the beach.

It was hot, humid and fairly quiet, although random bursts of lively music could be heard from the direction of The Reggae Bar, further up the beach. There were sporadic roars of hastily shushed laughter, too. They must have been having a private party. Either that or the boss was away and the staff and their friends were letting off steam at the end of another long day. I could have gone along there for a drink, they were very friendly and even more laid back than my mother. They probably wouldn't even mind me turning up with my own booze, but I didn't want to be the sad, lonely girl getting drunk by herself in the corner, so I plonked myself down on the sand and poured my own cocktail. The mixture I ended up with didn't look too bad. I decided not to sniff it before trying it, just in case the smell of it put me off.

I watched a couple of tiny crabs scuttle across the sand, stop, and scuttle back the way they'd come, the first one always slightly ahead of the other as if they were rehearsing a quick step and the second one wasn't very good. Swatting at a mosquito that was buzzing round my ear, it occurred to me that some *Deet,* or *Stop,* or whatever animal friendly, non-fatal insect repellent my mother currently favoured might have been a good idea, but frankly, right then, I just didn't give a damn. 'Down the hatch,' I told myself, and poured half the glass down my throat, then coughed and wheezed while my eyes streamed and my throat burned. I emptied the rest of the first Breezer into it, to tone it down a bit, and swatted away another mosquito – or the same one – they've never been known for their ability to take a hint, have they.

I wondered what Jonathon was doing right now. It was the middle of the evening back home. The evening before our wedding. Would he and Cordelia be having dinner at his mum and dad's? No, of course they wouldn't. That was the sort of boring thing we had done as a couple. They'd probably be rolling around in her billion thread count sheets, congratulating themselves between multiple orgasms for getting rid of me before the big day. *Tomorrow*. How the hell was I going to cope with tomorrow? Was there any chance I could get drunk enough to pass out and stay out of it for the whole day?

Flapping my hand at the mosquito and his friend who'd now joined him, I took a more cautious glug, coughed a bit less and topped up what was left with more Breezer. I should have brought more of them out, I didn't think two of them were going to be enough to help me down all the whisky that was left. I'd go and get some more in a minute.

Another crab scuttled past my foot and disappeared down a hole before coming straight back up again and scurrying off again. Maybe he was late for rehearsals. Now my eyes were more accustomed to the darkness, I could see quite a few of them darting about this way and that, doing their little crab dances. It was like watching the group dance in a crustacean version of *Strictly Come Dancing*.

A quick blast of *No Woman, No Cry* came from along the beach. Beyond the chorus I didn't know the lyrics, but Jonathon had had two women on the go and he certainly hadn't been crying. That had become my department. *No Man, Plenty Cry*.

The thought of what should be happening tomorrow brought fresh tears to my eyes. Mostly, I'd managed to force the details from my mind, over the last couple of days. I'd refused to think of my much altered, beautiful dress, zipped up in its special cover, waiting for a bride who would never get to wear it. I'd forbidden myself to picture the flowers I wouldn't be carrying, the aisle I wouldn't be walking down, the rings we'd selected together, nestling, no longer needed, in their little box. I'd concentrated on torturing myself, imagining what must have been happening over the last days, weeks, months. And what was probably happening right now, at any given moment. Picturing them together. Forcing down one kind of pain by covering it with another. But now it was so close it overwhelmed me, as if someone had thrown a heavy blanket over my head.

I swallowed down some more of my drink, coughing a bit less again that time, swatted at that pesky mosquito party that had started up at my ears, while I watched a bit more of the crab cabaret and sloshed more

Breezer into the glass. I was a slow drinker usually, savouring a glass of wine, more often than not over food, or at least nibbles, and never on my own. The way this stuff tasted though, it needed to bypass all taste buds as quickly as possible. And that was just fine by me.

Alli and the rest of my girlfriends and I should be all dressed up now, having drinks at Nettles. Girly drinks with little pink umbrellas in them, or possibly little plastic naked men if Alli had anything to do with it – she'd known me long enough to know that a male stripper was a complete no no – accompanied by tasteful little canapés. That was what I should be doing tonight. Not sitting on a Thai beach in my pyjamas, with a chorus line of cavorting crabs for company, pouring gut rot down my throat in the dark and listening to other people enjoying themselves. I downed what was left in my glass, barely coughed at all, and this time topped it up from the whisky bottle. Strangely enough, the taste was actually starting to grow on me. And it seemed the mosquitoes had got bored and were leaving me alone now, so at least some teeny tiny little thing in my life wasn't complete crap.

'Cheers!' I shouted, waving my glass skywards.

A patch of light flickered across the sand as if someone had opened a curtain. Then everything went black.

Chapter Seventy

Stella

Someone drilling a hole in the top of my head woke me up. 'Oh God!' I heard a voice from somewhere in another part of my head croak. 'What the hell's going on?'

I opened my eyes. They felt like someone was trying to skewer them on kebab sticks from the inside. Everything was dark, pitch dark. Where was I? I started to turn my head to see where I was but even that much movement made my head spin and something disgusting rise up in the back of my throat. So I closed my eyes again. It felt like a pair of garage doors slamming down, sending a jolt through my already suffering head.

The next time I woke up it was because I needed to go to the toilet. I slowly opened my eyes. The pain was still agonising. How much had I had to drink last night? How had Alli let me get into such a state? Had she put me to bed? Was I at her place? My memory slowly crunched back to life. No. I wasn't at Alli's. I was in Phuket.

My last memory – if it was a memory and not part of a nightmare I felt sure I must have been having – was sitting on the beach, drinking something disgusting. I couldn't remember anything after that. How had I got back up here?

Gingerly, I pushed back the duvet and tried to get up, but was smacked in the face by a wave of nausea. I sat very still, swallowing down hard, waiting for the feeling to go away. Eventually the need for the bathroom overcame any concern I had about being sick on the way to it. I put my feet down on the floor and started to stand up.

In spite of kicking over the bucket that someone had thought was a good idea to leave on my bedroom floor, I just made it in time and sat there, slumped forward, resting my aching forehead on the cool porcelain of the little sink. I had no idea how long I stayed there, before there was a tap on the door and my mother, never one to be bothered by silly little things like privacy, came in with a mug of tea, the smell of the milk in it turning my stomach over.

'Stella!' Her voice reverberated through me as if my head were a gong that had just been banged with a very heavy hand.

'It's alright, Mum' I mumbled. 'Box of Panadol, bottle of Lucozade, I'll be fine.' Well, that's what Alli always swore by – I hadn't been on the receiving end of enough bad hangovers to be an expert. I'd always laughed at that description of a mouth like the bottom of a bird cage. Now, I realised, I was experiencing it, only the bird in this case had clearly eaten something that hadn't agreed with it.

'No, Stella! Look at you!'

'Can you just get me some painkillers, Mum?' My mother had never given me a hard time about anything in my entire life. Why was she choosing today of all days to start?

'You're going to need more than a few paracetamol, Stella.' She moved the toothbrush glass and put the mug down in its place.' Francis?' She yelled through the door, setting my teeth rattling.

'Mum,' I groaned, edging my head gently along the sink to find a fresh bit of cool porcelain for my forehead to rest on. 'No shouting. Please.'

'I'm not shouting,' she said, just as loudly, as my father's flip flops came flipping and flopping along the little corridor. It sounded like somebody being rhythmically slapped in the face, hard. And it felt like it was me.

'Mum,' I groaned a bit louder, setting flashing lights off behind my eyes, while I did my best to tug my pyjama top down to cover my dignity. 'I'm on the loo.'

'Oh, don't be silly, Stella. Look at her Francis,' she turned to my poor father, who was probably as uncomfortable about his joining us in the bathroom as I was, just not in so much pain. 'Why didn't you notice last night?'

'Notice what?' Dad's voice came from the door. 'Good God!'

'What?' I whimpered, wishing they'd just bring me some painkillers and something to wash them down with instead of treating me like some kind of freak show. I reached slowly round the back of my neck to scratch something that was starting to itch.

'Don't!' they yelled in unison, making me flinch.

'Francis, where's the eucalyptus balm?'

'It's going to take more than a jar and a half of even that stuff to sort her out.' My dad came in and squatted on his haunches next to me. 'Stella' he said to me. It was clear from his tone of voice that he wasn't just humouring Mum. I felt a prickle of apprehension, which turned into a full-on itch when he said, 'Whatever you do, Stella, don't scratch anything.'

'What do you mean?' Now he'd said that, the back of my neck started screaming out for me to scratch it. My right ankle was starting to tingle, too. And the sole of my left foot.

'Why don't we give you a moment to … er … sort yourself out? Just don't scratch anything.' He stood up, took Mum by the elbow and led her out.

As soon as he shut the door, I reached for the loo roll. That was when I saw my arm. I gazed at it in fascination for a moment before looking at the other one. Moments later, I'd seen the state of both my ankles and they felt like they were on fire. As did my elbows. And my ears. I never usually got bitten much by mosquitoes, but if I did, those were the places one of them would get me. How many of them had got me last night?

My arms and the lower halves of my legs looked as

if they'd been covered in old polka dot fabric, with very big, very red dots on slightly rusty coloured cloth. And, of course, now I knew they were there, and my body was starting to wake up from its Thai whisky, and strawberry and watermelon Breezer anaesthesia, they were starting to itch like hell. And as for the way the sole of my left foot was throbbing – I didn't even dare try to look at that. How had I not noticed I was being bitten to death?

Washing my hands, I caught sight of my face in the mirror and flinched, a noise like a cat with its tail caught in a door bursting from my throat. I looked like something out of a sci-fi film about an experiment that had gone hideously wrong. Could what was supposed to be the happiest day of my life get any worse?

Chapter Seventy-One

Stella

Mum had used up her jar and a half of eucalyptus balm on me, plus the entire contents of a new jar Tasanee had brought up as soon as she heard what had happened, and sent Dad out to get another couple. Or, more likely, the entire stock of every pharmacy, *Family Mart* and *Seven Eleven* in the village. I lay there in my underwear, bits of me covered in splotches of dark green goo, and all of me smelling like I'd rolled around in the most pungent vapour rub ever known to man. If we'd been in Australia, koala bears would have been kicking the door down and climbing over each other to get at me.

I was under strict instructions not to scratch, not to even move until he got back with more smelly green stuff for Mum to rub over my skin. She'd looked at the sole of my left foot and declared it to be just another bite, the same as all the rest, but the look on her face and the extra care she took as she plastered it with balm told a different story. Half of me wanted to look and see how bad it was and half was glad of my instructions not to move, so I couldn't.

She told me to imagine myself in my Happy Place to help me ignore my tingling, itching and burning skin.

Unfortunately my Happy Place was a hidden space in a little thicket of trees, with ferns at my head, a stream trickling past at my feet, and Jonathon playing the starring role, and that really wasn't going to help me right now. I tried to concentrate on something mundane and ended up wondering how long it would take Dad to go to every pharmacy in the village. Not that he'd need to. Just about every shop in Thailand sold that stinky green stuff. It was probably their biggest industry apart from silk, curry paste and anything to do with coconuts.

I'd been surprised, the first time I came out here, just how many little businesses they managed to cram into these villages. There were, of course, more restaurants, bars, massage parlours, money changing booths, car and bike rental shops, and places to book trips and tours than you could shake a stick at. There were also so many mini markets, pharmacies, fish foot spas, laundries and tailors, that you wondered how there were enough customers to go round so they could all make a living. Of course, they weren't all open all year round, and quite often some were closed down in the quiet months. Now I was just glad that we were surrounded by places selling more than enough of the gunky, green goo to stop me tearing my skin off.

Of course, the way my luck was going at the moment, there could have been a sudden run on it and every shop on the island could have sold out. I really, desperately hoped not.

Chapter Seventy-Two

Stella

I could have sworn I heard Jonathon's voice. Opening one eye for a moment, I hazily took in the view from my bed before sinking straight back into the slumber Mum had promised me as she'd handed me a couple of her herbal antihistamine tablets. At the time, a part of my brain had attempted to protest that antihistamine can't surely be herbal can it? But the rest of my brain told it to shut up, swallow and pray they worked.

It was some time later – it could have been five minutes, it could have been five hours – when I woke up again. My left foot was throbbing away as if a cartoon cat was hitting it rhythmically with a sledgehammer while a little mouse kept ducking out of the way. Almost as if it had suddenly reminded them, all my other bites then started to come back to life. I looked on the bedside table for one of the little green jars Dad had come back with a carrier bag full of, but couldn't see any of them.

'Mum!' I called, feeling pathetic and thinking I should probably care about that, but not bothering to make myself.

'Are you alright, darling?' She tip toed in to the room. 'I thought you'd sleep longer than that. Would you like a cup of tea?'

'Yes please,' I whimpered, pathetically, suddenly feeling thirsty now she'd mentioned tea. 'But first, can you put some more of that stuff on me? I'm in agony, especially the bottom of my foot. It's killing me.'

'Of course, darling,' she stroked my hair from my face, just as she'd done whenever I'd had a bad dream as a child. 'I'll just get it.' She looked like she was about to say something else, but must have decided against it.

While she was out of the room, I tried to recall what I'd been dreaming about. I'd dreamt I'd heard Jonathon's voice but that was about all I could remember. What time had it been? Had I dreamt or imagined hearing his voice at the time that I should have been arriving at the church for our wedding? Or would it have been at the time we should have been exchanging our vows? Or at the time we should have been pronounced husband and wife?

'Here we are.' Mum breezed back into the room with the washing up bowl, a towel, a face cloth and a couple of jars of balm. 'Your dad's making the tea.'

The cold water was so soothing against the burning itchiness as, with the old face cloth, she gently wiped the residue of the last application of balm from my left leg and foot. Then she lightly dried the limb with what was probably the softest towel she had and tenderly applied a large blob of the green stuff to the bottom of my foot.

'Could you rub that in a bit more?' I asked, desperate but unable to scratch the itch myself. If she could just rub a bit harder ...

'And start off the itch-scratch cycle?' Mum looked at me knowingly. 'Do I need to send your father down to Tasanee for some oven gloves? Or shall I run you a nice cold bath?'

I groaned, thinking back to the time I'd had chicken pox as a child and hadn't been able to stop myself scratching the spots. Mum had taped her bright red cockerel oven glove to my right hand while Dad was dispatched to the nearest shop to buy a second one for my left. I'd then spent the rest of my convalescence waiting for them to leave me alone for more than a couple of seconds at a time so I could rub at the spots as hard as I could with my padded-gloved hands. The momentary deliciousness of succumbing to those itches had soon been overcome by the increased craving to do it again, only harder, until Mum threatened to make me sit in a bath tub of cold water all day.

Dad came in with a mug of tea while Mum was anointing my newly cleansed left arm and shoulder. They exchanged the sort of look they used to when one of them – more often than not Dad – thought they should tell me something and one of them – more often than not Mum – had decided that they shouldn't. I wondered if my left foot was going septic and Mum was trying out some hippy cure on it.

'How's the patient then?' He put the mug down on the bedside table and gave me an over-bright smile. Now I knew something was wrong.

'You tell me?' I looked from one to the other of them. 'There's something badly wrong with my foot, isn't there?'

'Your foot?' Dad looked puzzled and glanced from me to Mum and back again.

'It's just a couple of big bites really close together so the itchy areas are overlapping each other, that's all, Stella.' Mum looked at me. 'It feels a lot worse than it really is and bites always itch much worse on the soles of your feet anyway, trust me.' She took the face cloth out of the bowl, squeezed the excess water out of it and made a start on my right arm and shoulder. 'How about I put my dressing gown on you after I've finished doing this? You know, the flowery, cotton one. It's old so it won't matter if this balm gets all over it.' She nodded to Dad who left, presumably to go and fetch it. She couldn't mean the dressing gown I thought she meant, as that wasn't old, it was actually really pretty and one of her favourites.

'It's ok, Mum, I'm probably better just in my undies,' I looked down at the oldest of my bras and knickers – the ones I was least bothered about getting green gunk on – that I was wearing. 'Don't mess up your dressing gown.'

As if on cue, Dad came back in with Mum's beach kaftan over one arm and the dressing gown over the other. 'I wasn't sure ...'

'Honestly, Francis!' Mum shook her head with a

smile. 'I'll help Stella into this ...' And then she shooed him out of the room with an unusual amount of respect for my privacy, especially considering I'd been lying there in my bra and knickers for the whole conversation.

After I'd leaned forward so she could see to the bites on the back of my neck, she slipped the sleeves of the dressing gown ever so gently over my arms. I didn't want to wear it, but I didn't want to hurt her feelings, particularly as she was ruining a perfectly good garment for my benefit. So I co-operated as best I could, feeling like a dress up doll, until she'd finished lightly wrapping the front across me and loosely tying up the belt.

'Now lie still and drink your tea,' she advised as she gathered up the washing up bowl, face cloth and towel and carried them out leaving one of the jars, which looked like it still had some balm in it, on the bedside table next to the mug. She gently pulled the door to behind her.

The second she was gone I sat up and started to undo the belt. It was way too warm to be wearing this and I wanted to get it off me before it became completely covered in splodges of green. I managed to lift it off my front and shoulders without transferring too much on to it. Then I manoeuvred my legs so that I could stand on my right foot and shrug it off my back. Once free of it I hopped, as quietly as I could, over to the chair and draped it over the back of it. That was when I caught sight of myself in the mirror. I'd gone from being red polka dotted to being green polka dotted. I looked like a green and rust coloured Dalmatian. Cruella De Vil certainly wouldn't want any of this.

Holding on to Mum's words about it feeling worse than it was, whilst dreading what I was going to see, I steadied myself on the arm of the chair and raised my left foot towards the mirror. Then gazed in horror and fascination. Was that *really* my foot? It looked like something that should be hacked off and exhibited at the science museum. Or one of those old circus freak shows. I could probably ring up whoever made the *Alien* films and tell them I'd got a terrific prop for them if they wanted to make another. Or *The Elephant Man*. Except my version would have to be called *The Elephant Foot*. That hideous mound couldn't be the result of just two bites. How could the skin stretch that much without breaking?

Tears started to form in the corners of my eyes at the unfairness of it all. Wasn't it enough that this should have been my wedding day? Wasn't it enough that I had to imagine my ex fiancé spending this day with *her* – captivating Cordelia and her magical, never-ending, smooth as silk, catwalk model perfect legs? Did this also have to be the day that I turned into some sort of green, red and pink monster covered in lumps and bumps, that could only hop along dragging its revoltingly deformed foot behind it? Maybe I should go and find a cathedral bell tower to hide myself away in.

The only teeny tiny crumb of comfort I could find in all of this was that Jonathon wasn't here to see the state

I'd managed to get myself into. This was one image of me he'd never have to put up with flitting across his mind while he was gazing in awe at Cordelia's perfect body and wondering what it was he'd ever seen in me.

I wiped a fresh tear away from my eye, realising my mistake a micro second too late – I'd managed to get some of the balm on my hand when I was taking the dressing gown off. My eye stinging and streaming, I fumbled along the top of the little dressing table for the box of tissues. Grabbing one, I wiped at it but it was no good, I needed to wash it out, and quickly.

One eye squeezed shut, nose now running in sympathy, I hopped towards the bedroom door, yanked it open and turned into the little corridor. I'd almost made it to the bathroom door when I heard footsteps behind me.

'Mum,' I started to say, hoping she wasn't offended about the dressing gown but really needing to get some water on my eye. 'I just need ...' Then my words dried up. It wasn't my mother standing there looking at me, squinty one eyed, runny nosed, hopping along the corridor in my least attractive bra and knickers and covered in pungent smelling green blobs. It was Jonathon.

320

Chapter Seventy-Three

Stella

If this wasn't a nightmare then I wanted to go to sleep and have one, because whatever nightmare it turned out to be, it couldn't be any worse than the one I was living right now. Rather like a one-eyed rabbit in the headlights, I couldn't move, couldn't breathe, just stood there frozen, staring at him.

'Stella?' The voice of the man who, today, should have become my husband, seemed to come both from a very long way away, and from very near. 'Oh Stella, you poor thing!' He started walking towards me but stopped as I hopped through the bathroom door. I couldn't see what he did next as I was running the cold tap and sloshing water into my stinging eye.

'Jonathon? Oh Stella, no!' Mum's voice now came from behind me too. She must have taken one look at me, bent over the sink like a demented stork that had rolled in something leaked from a nuclear power station, and dived into my room, coming back out in double quick time with her dressing gown. She tried to wrap me up in it again while I tried to dry my eye on the first towel that came to hand. It had to have been like trying to stuff a wet and sticky shop dummy's arms into a display garment. But at least her actions were saving me the trouble of trying to think of something more original to say to him than "What are you doing here?"

'Astrid, I just ...' he started to say.

'Jonathon, go back to the kitchen. You were supposed to wait until I told you she was ready.' She spoke to him in the voice she saved especially for jobsworths who wouldn't listen, or men with chainsaws waiting to cut down trees that she was part of a battle to try and save. I'd never heard her use it on him before. 'And after I'd gone to all that trouble to cover you up,' she turned back to me with the same voice, as he obediently made himself scarce. 'I knew you wouldn't want him to see you looking like that,' she added a little more quietly, although not as much as I'd have liked. 'The dressing gown covered up the worst. I can't believe you took it off as soon as my back was turned.'

And I couldn't believe, now that I was starting to come back to my senses, that she was wittering on about a dressing gown when surely the only topic up for discussion should be what my ex fiancé was doing here. Had his mother demanded that he use the flight rather than waste the money for the ticket? Although the tickets we'd booked wouldn't have got him here today. What was going on? Was Cordelia ensconced in a luxury suite or poolside villa further down the beach at one of the posh Laguna hotels, waiting for him? Had he come to ask for the engagement ring back so he could sell it and use the money for a deposit on another one, something more suitable for his new love? Well he could have it and good riddance!

'Mum?' I sounded like a stroppy teenager which, under the last forty eight hours worth of circumstances, I reckoned was pretty restrained.

'Look, Stella, he turned up a couple of hours ago.' That must have been when I thought I'd dreamed of hearing his voice then. 'You were finally sleeping and we didn't want to wake you, your foot was so painful,' she stroked my hair back from my face. 'We thought we'd wait until you woke naturally, then I'd tidy you up a bit and ... well, I hadn't allowed for you hopping out to the bathroom ...'

'Why didn't you just tell me he was here? Why is he here, anyway?'

'What would you have said if I'd told you he was here straight away, Stella? After the awful few days you've just had? You'd just woken up, you were in pain and itching all over. It just seemed best to make you more comfortable and let the new application of balm start working on your bites and then tell you.'

'Is *she* here?'

'God no! And there is no *she*, anyway ...'

'What do you mean?'

'Look, just come and sit in the living room. You can put your foot up on the sofa and get comfortable.

Your dad and I, we'll go for a walk and leave the two of you to talk ...'

'But what do you mean, there's no *she*?' I hopped along while my mother gently steered me towards the little living area. 'I saw her! She was wearing his shirt ... and absolutely nothing else ...' I could feel my blood pressure start to rise as that most unwanted image slipped into my head.

'Let Jonathon tell you all about it,' she soothed, manoeuvring me onto the milk chocolate brown sofa bed she kept covered with a variety of Thai silk throws. The current one was orange, which I thought would clash nicely with my green splodges. 'I'll bring your tea back through for you,' she said, disappearing back towards my bedroom.

As Nelson lifted his head and thumped his tail at me from his fleece-lined bed in the corner of the room, Dad and Jonathon poked their heads round the kitchen door. 'Is it safe to come out yet?' Dad half whispered. He'd probably got it in the neck for letting Jonathon come and find me in the hallway and wasn't risking getting it a second time.

'You're going for a walk apparently,' I told him, 'while Jonathon and I talk.' My stomach did an involuntary flip as I said those words. Was it really possible that he'd come here to sort things out? Had he realised that she wasn't really the right girl for him? But did he expect me to just forgive him and for things to go back to the way they were? My stomach reviewed the situation and curled up in anger.

'Yes,' Mum swooped in with my mug, setting it down on the nearest corner of the little coffee table so I could reach it. 'Come on, Francis! Nelson!' Both Dad and the dog leapt to attention and followed her out the door.

Chapter Seventy-Four

Stella

'So ...' I started, looking Jonathon straight in the eye. There was no reason I should make any of this comfortable for him.

'Stella,' he started, holding my gaze, looking like he wanted to come and sit on the sofa bed with me, but diffidently opting for the safety of the arm chair instead. 'I know what it must have looked like, when you turned up at Cordelia's that morning, and I can only imagine how hurt you must have been to think that I would do something like that to you ...'

'Do you, Jonathon? Do you really?' I practically harrumphed.

'I was furious with her when I realised what she'd done ...'

'I'm sure you were. It must have been a nice little ego boost having two women at your beck and call. How inconvenient for you though, for the one who thought she was the *only* one to find out about the other ...'

'That's not what happened at all, Stella. I got drunk. I have no recollection at all of how I got to Cordelia's. The first thing I knew was when I woke up there the following morning ...'

'In her bed?' I snapped, not wanting to hear the answer but unable to stop myself asking.

'Well ... yes,' he shuffled in his seat, 'but nothing happened!'

'Yes, well you would say that, wouldn't you,' I sneered. 'So what's gone wrong then? Did she turn out to be just a bit too high maintenance for you, so you decided to come and find good old Stella and see if you can give her another go? Is that why you're here now?'

'No! Stella, I'm here now to explain to you that there was nothing going on between Cordelia and myself. Not that night, not ever. Stella, I would never have believed this of her, but it turns out Cordelia's been trying to split us up for ages. She told me you were seeing someone else ...'

'She what?'

'She told me you were getting friendly with some man you'd met at the library. She's been hinting to me for ages that you were starting to get cold feet about the wedding. I told her she was imagining it. Then she told me she'd seen you with this man, Craig. 'I didn't believe her, of course I didn't ...'

'Craig? He's just a new customer. A temporary customer from London ...'

'Yes, she said he was from London. She said that after I left you there you spent the day with him ...'

'What? I was on what was probably the train after the one you got on. Ask Alli ...'

327

'I know you were now. Alli told me ...'

'Oh, so you don't believe me but you believe Alli ...'

'That's not what I said, Stella. Look, I'm explaining this all wrong ...'

'No kidding!'

'She kept saying that you didn't really want to marry me but that you didn't know how to break it off. That was why I overreacted when I saw the spray tan. Knowing that you know how I feel about things like that, it seemed to be something you would only do if she was right about you trying to get me to call it off ...'

'That's insane!'

'Then she drove me to the library on Monday afternoon. We parked across the green and there you were, with this Craig, by the door. He was stroking your face. The two of you looked so ...'

'So what? How did we look? Like two clumsy idiots who'd just bumped heads while they were picking some dropped leaflets up off the floor? And one of them was concerned he might have hurt the other? Is that how we looked?' I was getting louder and louder but I didn't seem to be able to stop myself shouting.

'I'm sorry. She was there, twisting everything we were seeing and making it look like you were seeing this guy behind my back. After the spray tan and all her little hints that you weren't happy with me ... I told her to drive me home but she drove to a pub out in the forest. She said

I needed a drink to calm me down before I went home. But one drink turned into ... I don't know how many ... and then, it seems she drove me back to her place rather than home. She undressed me and put me to bed ... yes, in her bed and yes ... it seems she did get in and sleep in it with me, but I was passed out. I couldn't have done anything with her even if I had wanted to. Which obviously I wouldn't have.'

'No. Of course not. What with her being so hideously ugly ...'

'Stella. I promise you,' he started to lean forward as if to try and hold my hands, but clearly thought better of it. 'The first thing I knew was when I woke up in the morning and didn't have a clue where I was, as I obviously hadn't ever been in her bedroom before. She came into the room wearing nothing but my shirt ...'

'The new shirt I'd just bought you ...'

'Yes,' he shuffled in his seat again. 'But I didn't give it to her to wear. She must have helped herself to it after she undressed me and put me to bed ...'

'Do you really expect me to believe any of this?'

'Well, she managed to get you drunk and spray-tanned, so it isn't exactly like she doesn't have form for it, is it? And why would I come here and tell you all this if I wanted to be with Cordelia and not you?'

'Maybe you've realised the grass isn't greener after all and these are just a load of excuses to justify sleeping with her!' I yelled.

329

'I didn't sleep with her.' He was shouting now. 'Not in the sense that you mean.'

'And why should I believe you, when you found it so easy to believe the worst of me?'

'I'm so sorry, Stella. I know I should never have listened to her. I know you wouldn't do anything like that ...'

'Oh, so you know that now, do you?' I heard myself snarling. 'Well, it's a pity you didn't know it a few days ago. Just think of all the heartache you could have saved me. Do you actually have any idea just how much you've hurt me?'

'Stella ... I ...'

'Just go, Jonathon. Get out ...'

'But Stella ...'

'If you could believe all that of me so easily, then maybe you're not the man I thought you were ...'

'Stella ...'

'Go!'

I couldn't look at him as he got up and walked towards the door, I heard him stop by it as if waiting for me to change my mind, but I kept my head turned away from him and eventually he got the message and left.

Chapter Seventy-Five

Jonathon

Well, that didn't go at all how I'd hoped. It had never even occurred to me that Stella wouldn't believe me. She's known me for years. We were a couple of days away from getting married. How could she suddenly be so sure that I'd cheat on her? But then I'd believed it of her, hadn't I? And I didn't even manage to tell her that Cordelia had set that thing with Craig up, did I? That he was an old friend of hers and that she'd persuaded him – I could only guess how – to help her out with this ridiculous charade.

Cordelia had a lot to answer for and then some, going to open the door to Stella wearing nothing but my shirt. I'd known her all my life and had no idea she could be so cruel. I could see how it must have looked but surely Stella knew me better than that.

I'd never seen Stella so angry, so cold, never known her unwilling to listen to the other side of an argument. She was almost a different person. How could somebody change that quickly? But then, that must have been what she'd thought about me.

Maybe if I'd got here sooner – she must have spent the last couple of days and the entire journey the day before, reliving that scene in her head and, without anything to contradict it, she must have suffered. If I'd got here then, talked to her then, I could have got through to her. But now … How was I supposed to convince her that I was still the man she fell in love with, the man she was going to marry?

Bloody Cordelia! I could swing for her. I'd had no idea she felt like that about me – if I had I would have put her straight. And I would never have listened to any of that rubbish about Stella.

I didn't know what I'd had to drink that night – I couldn't remember. But I've never been much of a drinker so it wouldn't have been much. I was starting to wonder if Cordelia had slipped something into my drink to knock me out enough for her to get me up the stairs – running a stables for a living she probably has access to all sorts of horse tranquilisers – and I don't know how she managed to get me up there. I wouldn't have thought she was strong enough to carry me, so maybe she dragged me? It can't have been easy to undress an unconscious man and put him to bed. And then came the creepy bit – I was sure there were dozens, hundreds even, of men out there who would think that they'd died and gone to heaven to have a naked Cordelia in bed next to them, but I'm not one of them. It was like finding out I'd shared a bed drunk with my naked sister. I didn't even want to think about her cuddling up to me. It was all just too … well, Stella would know a good word for it. Let's face it, she'd looked like she was ready to fling a few good ones at me when I had tried to talk to her.

Stella's parents had said I could stay on their sofa bed while we sorted ourselves out, but that was before I spoke to her. While Stella was so angry with me, that wouldn't really be practical, so I was going to book myself into a room at one of the nearby condotels. Tasanee and Thaksin knew all the staff and so, of course, Francis and Astrid had made friends with most of them. And it was only a couple of minutes' walk away.

The last thing I needed was to walk slap bang into somebody else's argument, as I approached the reception desk. But there were half a dozen very angry Westerners shouting at a couple of young looking locals, and a couple of receptionists – one Thai and one Russian sounding – trying valiantly to calm everyone down and all but failing, although mainly because they couldn't be heard over all the shouting. I was just about to turn round and go and find another place to stay – the village and the surrounding area certainly weren't short of accommodation – when the Russian sounding girl noticed me and gave me a harassed but warm smile. Feeling cornered but not wanting to appear rude, I went up to her.

'Good afternoon. How can I help you?' she asked loudly in heavily accented English.

'I came about a room ...' I started to say, just as loudly.

'You came from Tasanee?' she shouted, as a couple of the men started yelling something about phoning the police. I was beginning to wonder if this was really a place I wanted to stay in. It seemed strange that the only people I knew here had recommended it so highly. It looked lovely, but a battle zone was the last place I wanted to be.

I nodded, and watched her take a key card from a drawer beneath the desk, programme a room number into it and come out from behind the desk. Her Thai counterpart gave her a smile with her lips and a glare with her eyes that probably said thanks for leaving me to cope with this lot on my own.

'Don't worry,' she told me as she walked me away from the fracas, up a flight of steps, along an outdoor corridor towards the last door. 'The angry people are owners. The two guys work for company they use for rentals. The company don't pay people all the money that take. Now they don't answer their phones. Everybody is very angry.'

***

Francis had mentioned something about an ongoing dispute to do with some foreign owners of local apartments and rooms but I hadn't associated it with this place. I supposed I hadn't really been paying attention, after all I had been a bit preoccupied with my own problems. Maybe though, while I waited for Stella to calm down – and who knew how long that was going to take because I had never seen her this angry before – maybe I could find out if there was anything I could do to help. I didn't know what differences there were between the rules for renting out other people's property here, and back home, but I was pretty sure it wouldn't take me long to find out and then I might be able to offer some kind of solution, or even just give some advice. A little voice at the back of my mind said that if I could do something to help these people it might help to remind Stella of the man that I really was and not the cheating rat that she'd now decided I was. Obviously that wasn't the reason I wanted to try and help these people, but if it helped in some way to get our relationship back to where it was supposed to be, then that would be a great added bonus.

Chapter Seventy-Six

Stella

I managed to keep still while he was in the room, but the moment the door closed behind him my whole body started to shake. I'd never been so angry in my life.

He'd listened to her over me. He'd believed her lies about me, above his own experience of what I was like. How could he have done that? Did our relationship mean that little to him that he could throw it away on somebody else's whim? Did I mean that little to him?

The tears started to course down my face again. They knew the way well enough by now after the last few days. What was I supposed to do now? How was I supposed to get past this?

Jonathon had been my future. But how could I have a future with somebody who didn't even know his own mind where I was concerned? And I knew that that worked both ways. I had believed what I'd seen – what Cordelia had wanted me to see – above my own experience of what Jonathon was like. We'd both been taken in by someone else's manipulations. But surely if we'd been strong enough as a couple we wouldn't have allowed that to happen?

I didn't even hear Mum and Dad come back. It was

only Nelson sticking his great wet snout in my ear that brought me back to the real world.

'I take it that didn't go as well as we hoped,' Dad said gently, sitting down on the arm of the sofa.

I shook my head, not trusting myself to speak. I couldn't trust myself with anything at the moment.

Chapter Seventy-Seven

Stella

'They told us there was hardly any business at the moment, only the odd weekend, but they were letting it out continually and keeping all the rental income for themselves!' One very red faced man standing up in the second row was shouting, when I hobbled in to the back of this Monday lunchtime meeting. I was surprised how many owners were there at such short notice, but Jonathon had spent the whole of Sunday talking to those already here and contacting those abroad to set this meeting up. Feelings were running high, and the chance to meet face to face with someone who might help would have made a lot of last minute flights to the island seem like a very good idea. He looked very calm and business like, Dad only slightly less so, sitting at their table at the front of the horseshoe of rows of chairs, making new notes as they went along and referring to the ones they'd brought with them.

'They did that to us too,' a woman further back, in a black, yellow and green Bob Marley t shirt joined in. 'We only found out because one of the cleaners mentioned something when we came to stay here ourselves. She thought we knew about it ...'

'That's right!' Red Faced Man shouted his

338

agreement. 'That's how we found out, too. She said it was nice we'd managed to find a slot where we could come and use the apartment ourselves ...'

'She told us it was nice to have some quiet people staying in ours for a change,' Bob Marley T Shirt Woman jumped in. 'It sounds as if ours has been let to a lot of lager louts ...'

'Ours looks as if it has been, too,' a man with his hair in a man bun spoke up. 'One lot of "guests" broke the glass top of the balcony table. Someone at reception told me these crooks had kept their security deposit to repair it and then just hid it and put the little coffee table out on the balcony instead. It wasn't made for outdoor use, so what with the rain, the sun and the humidity the wood's absolutely fu ...'

'Thank you!' Dad banged his spoon on the side of his coffee cup. 'If I could just remind everyone that there are families here, and ask that however angry everyone is and however justified that anger, can we all please refrain from using profanities?'

'They charged us an absolute fortune for items we didn't want or need ...' A thin, pale woman with an equally pale ponytail grabbed her opportunity to speak.

'Yes, and you just know that they paid a fraction of what they charged you for those items,' Red Faced Man interrupted her. 'They did exactly the same thing to us. I demanded receipts but they just kept saying "Yes, yes, we'll find them for you", and of course they never did ...'

'Half of what they charged us for we haven't even set eyes on,' Pale Ponytail Woman added. 'It certainly isn't in the apartment now. And when you ask them they just say something about a natural amount of breakages. I don't think they even bothered buying half the things in the first place. They just took our money and kept it!'

'How are they still in business?' An American accent piped up from somewhere, I couldn't see where he was sitting. 'We've only just signed up with them as we bought our unit recently from someone who must have just been fed up with not making any money out of it. I wish they'd warned us not to sign up with these guys.'

How they were still in business was the question Jonathon and Dad had been asking themselves. If this had been the UK, Jonathon said, they'd have been shut down long ago. He'd done plenty of research on the company since his arrival here and had been amazed that the Belgian couple, Yvette and Bruin, had managed to stay in business for four years when their business practices were so shoddy. He and Dad had spent a lot of time shaking their heads, tutting and saying "For God's sake!" and "How the Hell?" and "You just wouldn't credit it!" while they'd been finding out what, if anything, could be done about the pair of so-called letting agents. If this had actually been our honeymoon I think I might have been a bit fed up about the timing of Jonathon's interest in this dispute. As things were though, I was glad he was here and, it seemed, so were a lot of very disgruntled apartment owners.

The moment the meeting broke up for half an hour for refreshments and anyone needing the loo, he and Dad were both swamped by hopeful people. These were the less forthright ones, the ones who hadn't had a chance to speak up yet and possibly didn't think they would, making their own particular tales of woe known to the two men who might – or might not – know what to do about it, before the more confident speakers took over once the meeting started up again.

I watched Jonathon and Dad try to take down as many notes as possible. They clearly weren't going to get a break and if I could have got a cold drink over to them without spilling most of it, I would have, but my foot was causing me to walk like Quasi Modo, so carrying liquids was a bit of a no no. Luckily that nice Russian receptionist seemed to be taking care of them and had a couple of cold Singha beers on a tray. Mind you, she seemed to be taking a hell of a long time giving Jonathon his. Was it really necessary for her to stand quite so close to him? Or for him to laugh quite so loudly at whatever she'd said to him? What was it about my fiancé that had all these women throwing themselves at him? *My fiancé* – that gave me pause for thought. I hadn't allowed myself to think of him as that since I came here. Or even since he turned up here. But it seemed I didn't like other women assuming he was single. My emotions were all over the place. But he was still here. That had to mean he hadn't given up on us, didn't it? Unless ... I hadn't seen him at all yesterday. He'd been here talking to the owners. And she'd probably been here too. And she was very attractive. Was he staying here hoping to sort things out with me? Or, in light of my telling him to get lost, was he enjoying being flirted with by a pretty girl who was obviously interested in him? Had I pushed him away?

Chapter Seventy-Eight

Stella

Mum had done a late morning Thai cooking class with Tasanee, which was why she hadn't been at the meeting and now she was doing an afternoon one. I could have done with talking to her, or Dad, running by either one of them what was running through my head about Jonathon, in the hope of getting some perspective. Dad was around somewhere, helping Thaksin make or mend something. I had a feeling that Dad was hoping to persuade Thaksin to start up a little rental agency between them. They'd clean up, just from the disgruntled owners in that one condotel alone. And if they got themselves a good reputation for being honest and reliable, they could do really well out of it. They worked well together and I thought it was a good idea. Mum wasn't so sure, but I think that was just because, although she loved it here, she didn't want to be a tied to one place and if they had a business here then she would feel as if she was. It hadn't occurred to her that taking in Nelson had already done that.

I didn't know where Jonathon was. He and Dad had disappeared into the office with the Russian girl after the meeting. I'd seen Dad since, but not Jonathon.

There was a horrible feeling in the pit of my

stomach, telling me that I'd been given another chance with Jonathon and that just because I was angry and proud, I'd tossed it away. And what if I didn't get another chance?

Chapter Seventy-Nine

Stella

'Why don't you go on down ahead of us, as it takes you longer to get down the stairs,' Mum suggested, later that evening. 'Your dad and I'll catch you up at the table.'

We were having dinner at Tasanee's restaurant. Just the three of us. Not that I really felt like any food. I didn't know where Jonathon was eating; nobody had seen him all afternoon. That knowledge just added to the sickly feeling worrying away at my stomach. I really had pushed him away, hadn't I?

Mum had suggested I wear a lovely purple long sleeved cotton tunic that she'd bought from one of the stalls on the beach. It was pretty so I put it on, although I didn't see what all the fuss was about – I must have eaten there dozens of times and they must have eaten there hundreds. But I didn't want to look ungrateful, so I grabbed my little bag with my mosquito spray and my eucalyptus balm in it and hobbled down the stairs ahead of them.

I went to sit at the nearest table to the bottom of the stairs, but Tasanee came bustling over, 'No, *Kuhn* Stella, table outside on veranda, *Ka*.' I stifled a grumble about the extra hobbling distance – she just wanted to give us a nice table overlooking the sea – and followed her onto the veranda. She indicated a table to the left and I turned and stopped in my tracks. There was now only one table on the veranda and it was set for two, with candles and petals and a bottle of Pinot Grigio in an ice bucket. And Jonathon was sitting in one of the chairs. He was wearing a cream linen shirt, his hair was just damp from the shower and he looked gorgeous. My stomach did a wobbly thing inside and I found I didn't know what to say.

He stood up and came to help me over. As soon as I was sitting down, he whisked the bottle out with a flourish, showing me the label, 'A glass of Pinot for madam?'

'Thank you,' I smiled tentatively, resisting the urge to say actually it's still mademoiselle in case it sounded snippy. I was suddenly glad Mum had suggested this top.

'You look lovely,' he smiled at me, pouring the wine. 'That colour really suits you.'

'Thank you, you look very handsome too. New shirt?' I wished I hadn't said that as soon as the words left my mouth – he might think I was sniping about his last new shirt.

'Yes. I packed quickly and didn't bring a suitable one with me ...'

'A suitable one for what?'

'For ...'

'Pssst!' A voice came from behind me. I turned

346

round as Jonathon stood up. It was the pretty Russian girl. Well that was lovely. Should I just go now and leave them to it?

'I won't be a moment,' Jonathon squeezed my hand quickly and strode over to where she was half hidden in the doorway. Maybe I wouldn't have to go and leave them to it. Maybe they were going to go and leave me to it. He disappeared into the restaurant with her.

Sighing, I turned back to face the table and picked up my glass. If this was going to be painful I needed alcohol. I took a good glug and played with some of the petals on the table, wondering how long I should give him before I just hobbled back up the stairs with the rest of the bottle to drown any sorrows that had somehow managed to keep swimming. I was just picking up my glass for a second glug when he reappeared and sat down again. He had an envelope in his hand.

'You ready for the starter, *Kuhn* Jonathon?' Tasanee materialised by my elbow with a platter of all our favourite appetisers.

'That looks lovely, Tasanee. *Kop Kuhn Krub*,' he said, as she placed it on the table.

'Enjoy, *Ka*!' she said and disappeared back inside.

'Well, you heard what the lady said,' he told me, handing me the serving fork.

I helped myself to a Thai prawn and crab cake and a deep fried tiger prawn wrapped in vermicelli, while he topped up my glass. I still hadn't said a word since he

347

came back to the table. I still didn't know what to say. And my stomach was still in knots.

He picked up his glass and held it out to mine. 'Cheers!'

'Cheers!' Our fingers brushed as we clinked glasses. My mouth went dry at his touch. I took a mouthful of wine. What was the matter with me? A week or so ago, this man was like another part of me. I couldn't have been more comfortable around him. And now? Now just the touch of his fingers against mine and I was going hot and cold all over and my stomach thought it was on a rollercoaster. What was happening?

'Stella,' he put his fork down, clearly as unable to eat as I was. 'I know that our wedding hasn't happened, but ... the events of the last week or so have shown me that I don't want to be without you. You make me happier than I've ever been before in my life, and this time we've spent apart has made me miserable. I can't fathom what made Cordelia think it was alright to do what she did to us, but I believe our love is strong enough to get over it. I also believe it would be a terrible waste of that love to let her actions ruin it for us.' He put his hand in his pocket and pulled something out. 'I know you stopped wearing this but, Stella Moon, will you please put this ring back on and reschedule our wedding?'

'You ... you still want to marry me?' I could barely get the words out.

'Of course I do, you daft bat. I love you!' He

jumped up and came round the table and took me in his arms. Fireworks started to fizz through me. I had my Jonathon back. It was me he was staying here for. Not whatever her name was. Not anyone else. Me! 'You are going to put the ring back on and say yes, aren't you?' he teased.

'Of course I am. Yes!' I cried, as he slid my engagement ring back on my finger where it belonged. My hand felt right with it there. It had felt too light, as if a part of it were missing without it. 'I love you Jonathon Hazard.'

'I love you too, Stella Moon, soon to be Hazard.'

'Do you want to hear something silly?'

'Always!'

'I thought you were going to run off with that pretty Russian girl ...'

'What, Olga?' he laughed.

'You seemed to be spending a lot of time together ...'

'That's because she was helping me with something,' he said mysteriously. 'I was going to give it to you at the end of the meal ...'

'What?'

'Well, originally I was going to give it to you on our wedding day, but ... well ... And then I didn't bring it with me, so Olga and her printer came to my rescue and ... Do you want it now?'

'Well yes!' I exclaimed. 'How could I not after that

build up!'

He sat back down again, picked up the envelope and passed it to me. 'That's obviously not the envelope it was meant to be in ...'

I looked at the envelope. It bore the condotel logo. I slid my finger into the flap, opened it and took out a couple of sheets of printed A4 paper. It took me a moment to realise they were hotel reservations.

'Burgh Island?' I looked from the sheet of paper in my hand to Jonathon and back to the paper again. 'You've booked us a murder mystery weekend at Burgh Island?' I squealed.

'It isn't until next year ...'

'You've booked us into the *Agatha Christie* room,' I squealed even louder.

'That's why it isn't until next year. That one gets booked up the furthest in advance.'

I jumped up from my seat, hopped round the table and threw my arms around him.

'I take it you like it then,' he said into my ear.

'It's perfect. You couldn't have found anything more perfect,' I said into his neck.

'Is it safe to come out now?' Mum's voice came from behind me.

'Come out, come out,' Jonathon beamed at them. 'She said yes, by the way.'

'As if there was ever any doubt,' Mum said, hugging Jonathon while Dad hugged me and surveyed the uneaten seafood on the table.

Jonathon caught my eye and I nodded. 'I'm sure Tasanee would heat up the things that can be reheated for you, Francis, if Astrid looks the other way, as it is a special occasion. And there's sticky mango and coconut rice for afters.'

Dad had the platter off the table and half way back to the kitchen before Jonathon had even finished saying it.

'You two not hungry then?' Mum asked, knowing very well what the answer was.

'Oh, my fiancé and I'll grab something later.' Jonathon winked at me. And with that, he swooped me up over his shoulder, just like he used to do by the water's edge and carried me away. Only this time he headed straight for the stairs. And I must have lost more weight than I thought, because his feet just flew up them.

Epilogue.

I gasped at the sight of the restaurant, the veranda, and the beach in front – Tasanee, Thaksin, Jonathon, Mum and Dad must have worked like cart horses to get it all decorated in the time we'd been gone. It looked like they'd begged, bought or borrowed every fairy light and citronella candle in the whole village – the ones indoors were already lit. The bright, golden yellow ratchaphruek blossom, the multicoloured marigolds and the purples and pinks of the orchids should have clashed hideously, but they just looked and smelt so vibrant and joyous. Which was pretty much how I felt. Jonathon too, if the big soppy grin on his face all week was anything to go by.

'What do you think?' Alli threw her free arm round me, chuckling, as we got back from picking up Joyce, James, Harry, and more luggage than I was expecting, from the airport. 'Up to the standard of Joyce's flower ladies?'

'Don't!' I groaned. That had been a long drive. Now I knew how wrong I'd been about Ma Hazard – which was something I was going to have to stop calling her – I felt so guilty. Even though she didn't know all the things I'd suspected her of, some of which had been Cordelia's doing and some just genuine mistakes – on both our parts – I felt as if I had a lot to make up for. Mind you, she seemed to be struggling with a similar dilemma regarding myself and Cordelia – who'd apparently left staff in charge of the stables and disappeared to London with someone who looked like a young Hugh Grant.

'You like it though?' She gently nudged me.

'It's stunning!' I exclaimed. 'Absolutely stunning!'

'Good! Now go and get in the shower. You're far too sweaty for a bride ...'

'Charming!' I snorted, 'You're not exactly bridesmaid fresh yourself!'

'I just have a little job to do and I'll be heading up to get ready myself.'

'What little job?' I attempted to get a look at the bag she'd been trying to shield from my sight. It looked like one of Joyce's.

'Just go!'

It had taken us almost a week in Bangkok to sort out the paperwork – the nights, a pre-wedding honeymoon. Mum and Dad had organised everything else, along with Alli who'd flown over as soon as she could – with my finally finished dress – to help.

Their week had been busy with something else too – Dad and Thaksin were indeed going into the holiday letting business together – they already had the one condotel's owners signed up and word was starting to spread. So Nelson's home was safe – as if it had ever been in doubt.

'You look so beautiful, darling,' Mum gave me a hug. 'Jonathon's a very lucky man.

'I'll make sure he doesn't forget that,' I hugged her back.

'I don't think he'd make that mistake again. You're both going to be so happy!' She kissed my cheek and left me to finish getting ready.

As I reached the bottom of the stairs and turned to take Dad's arm, my eye was drawn to the table in the corner. It had been empty earlier. Now it held a simple, but beautiful, two tiered cake, topped with miniature versions of the orchids and marigolds. Someone had worked very hard and very quickly making those decorations, and interspersing them with showers of little golden yellow dots to symbolise the ratchaphruek. It brought a tear to my eye.

'Alright, my lovely girl?' Dad beamed at me, though there was a tell-tale moistness to his eyes too.

I couldn't actually speak so I smiled and nodded and turned to Alli for my bouquet. Harry started the music, a recording of Alli playing an amazing piece she'd composed years ago for her degree, and the three of us floated out to the veranda, down those last few steps and on to the beach.

And there was Jonathon, in the cream linen shirt he'd worn to re-propose to me. My heart did a little flip as he turned to smile at me.

'Did you see the cake?' he whispered as he stepped closer to lift the little veil from my face.

'It's gorgeous,' I whispered back.

'Mum spent a whole week practicing those flowers ...' He moved the gauzy fabric backwards on my head.

'Your mum made it?'

'She insisted,' he winked. Then we both jumped as the registrar coughed. Our tiny congregation smiled, and we turned to face the person who was about to make us husband and wife. 'She knows how much you love her carrot cake.'

Acknowledgements

Hazard at The Nineteenth started life as a one page competition entry at Emirates Lit Fest's inaugural Literary Idol contest. To my surprise it won. So my first thanks must go to Judy Finnigan, and Francesca Main of Picador Books, the judges who picked it. And of course, as always, my heartfelt gratitude to the organisers and everyone behind the scenes at Emirates Literature Foundation – ELF. These hard working elves have worked their magic on many a writing career.

Equally magical is the Romantic Novelists' Association – a fabulous organisation to be part of. I'll never stop thanking Allie Spencer and Adrienne Dines for advising me to join.

My sparkly friends and fellow RNA members, the Tonbridge Diamonds – Sue Mackender, Denise Barnes, Terri Fleming and Tessa Shapcott, and my Dubai sparklers, Sharmila Mohan and Jane Northcote – you all keep me sane ... well, as much as possible anyway! Thank you for all your love and support. Enormous thanks too, to my wonderful blog Fairy Godmother, Morgen Bailey – a very patient lady without whom my blog wouldn't exist.

I have a new editor for this book, the brilliant Caroline (Caz) Kirkpatrick – I'd like her to be my editor forever! Thank you, Caz, for your insights, advice and

357

lovely comments. And thanks too to Kate Ellis, the Go To lady at Accent – how she has enough hours in her day to do everything she does I don't know!

My family have been there with me through every twist and turn, full of loving support and encouragement, and ever ready with lifts, spare rooms and sustenance. I can't thank them enough for all they've done for me.

And last but not least, my husband, Andrew, whom I've forgiven for breaking my pasta machine – luckily he cooks a great steak and jacket potato!